D0595429

PRAISE FOR
The Language of Cherries

"…a brilliant and unique take on the timeless YA themes of communication, empathy, and first love—and all of their attendant and perennial obstacles. Evie and Oskar's relationship is spun in gorgeous, unexpected lyricism; even the setting (friendless and freezing and diametrically opposed to Evie's Miami home) infuses the novel with a surreal and mythic quality: every detail weighs on her discovery of Oskar's secret. THE LANGUAGE OF CHERRIES is impossible to forget; for me, it reads like the classic it deserves to be."

—Daniel Ehrenhaft, *Ten Things To Do Before I Die* **(Delacorte) & the Edgar Award-winning** *Trust Falls* **(HarperCollins)**

"…a lush, heady, magical book, much like first love itself. Evie and Oskar are unforgettable characters with passions and desires who, despite their initial language barrier, deeply understand and support each other. The vibrant writing and unique Icelandic setting, combined with an inventive structure, make this book a YA standout reminiscent of Anna-Marie McLemore and Sarah Addison Allen."

—Rachel Lynn Solomon, *You'll Miss Me When I'm Gone* **(S&S) &** *Our Year of Maybe* **(S&S)**

"...unlike anything I've ever read. I immediately fell in love with the premise, the characters, and the world. Richly textured with a mixture of crisp prose and poignant verse, it's the kind of book you read in one sitting, and then you read it again to savor. A brilliant gem of a book about how the heart needs no translator. I adore this book!"

—**Elly Blake,** *New York Times* **bestselling author of the Frostblood Saga (Little, Brown)**

"Come to THE LANGUAGE OF CHERRIES for the irresistible premise of a girl believing the boy she's falling for doesn't speak her language, and stay for the lyrical, magical tale of two people daring to reach for their dreams. Hawkins' memorable coming-of-age romance is infused with the same wit, charm, and originality as Joanne Harris' *Chocolat*, and likewise will leave readers deliciously satisfied."

—**Kes Trester,** *A Dangerous Year* **(Curiosity Quills)**

THE LANGUAGE OF CHERRIES

Jen Marie Hawkins

Owl Hollow Press

Owl Hollow Press, Springville, UT 84663

This book is a work of fiction. Names, characters, places, and incidents are products of the author's imagination. Any resemblance to actual people, living or dead, or to businesses, companies, events, institutions, or locales is completely coincidental.

The Language of Cherries
Copyright © 2020 by Jen Marie Hawkins

All rights reserved. No part of this publication may be reproduced, distributed or transmitted in any form or by any means, without prior written permission.

Library of Congress Cataloging-in-Publication Data
The Language of Cherries / J.M. Hawkins. — First edition.

Summary:
When Evie Perez visits the cherry orchard behind her guesthouse, she paints a boy she's never met. Oskar is startled to see himself on her canvas. As Evie returns day after day, their connection deepens, and Oskar must decide how long to maintain his silence.

ISBN 978-1-945654-45-9 (paperback)
ISBN 978-1-945654-46-6 (e-book)
LCCN 2019955950

OWL HOLLOW PRESS

R045700202013

For Jeremy...
Te amo.
A chuisle mo chroí.
þú ert mér allt.
I love you in every language,
even the ones with no words.

"Words are a pretext. It is the inner bond that draws one person to another, not words."

-Rumi

ONE

Evie

*E*velyn Perez's summer began with a peace offering: cherry pie at midnight.

Solstice sunshine pinched a squint around her father's eyes as he watched her dig a fork through the crumbling, flaky crust. She pushed it around, not eating it, painting a crimson ribbon with the filling across a bone china plate. Pie wasn't the same as her abuela's cherry pastelitos, the very epitome of summer. The wrongness of having a cherry confection *here*, of all places, trickled sadness through her bones.

"*Lo siento*, Evie," her father said again. He'd promised to be back for a late dinner, but at ten she gave up and ate without him. Words like *late* and *early* were terms relative to nothing in this strange, foreign land. They may as well have been synonyms. Or tap-dancing chupacabras.

"It's fine, Papá."

It wasn't fine, though. Not even a little bit. She was being robbed of a real summer. And sleep, courtesy of the midnight sun.

She rubbed her eyes with her thumb and forefinger and slumped in the rigid ladder-back seat, trying to avoid the sun's inescapable glare. For a week, she'd been alone in the Icelandic countryside of Elska, behind four cottage walls, while her papá dug through the earth's crust for the US Geological Survey, researching ways to harness geothermal power—or some kind of boring scientist crap like that.

"*Un regalo*. Besides the pie." He grinned as he reached into the brown paper sack on the floor. A package bulged from the top, wrapped in shiny carmine paper. She trained her dark glare elsewhere. *Don't you dare look.* He lifted it and placed it between their pie plates on the wobbly table.

She glanced at it, and then fixed her gaze on the uneaten pie. The shimmering foil taunted her peripheral vision. By its shape, it was likely a package of pre-stretched canvases. Probably Belgian linen.

He pulled out another wrapped package, also the color of a beating heart, and set it down. Winsor & Newton acrylics, if she had to guess. When they'd landed in Iceland, he'd given her a new set of Kolinsky sable brushes imported from Russia, stainless steel palette knives, and a leather messenger bag to carry it all in.

Dr. Alberto Perez wasn't skimping on art supply quality, as if bribery atoned for forcing his sixteen-year-old daughter to forfeit her social life. Away from hard-earned friends in Florida, a lifeguarding job at the best Miami water park, and Ben Benson— the first cute guy at Saint Bart's who'd ever shown interest in her. Not to mention Abuela, her favorite person on the planet.

"Go ahead," Papá said, proud-of-himself grin twitching at the corners of his mustache. "Open it."

Tensing her jaw, she dropped her fork on the plate. The clatter made a sharp statement she wasn't bold enough to make herself. Presents wouldn't make up for yanking her out of what could've been the best summer of her life. Her Catholic politeness kept her from saying so. For now.

She tore the paper from the smaller of the two. Twelve tubes of rich colors peeked at her through a stream of dusty sunlight. She risked a glance at her papá's excited expression, and she manufactured a smile of her own—one as artificial as her mother's had become before she left.

As she ripped the wrapping paper off the corner of the large square, a linen canvas poked out. Her papá traced the grooves in the table edge with a hairy-knuckled index finger, waiting expectantly for her gratitude. If he paid attention, he'd know she only painted in winter.

She wasn't even sure she wanted to study art in college in the first place. That C she'd received on her self-portrait last semester still niggled at her confidence. Anyway, her senior year of high school loomed ahead. She didn't have to decide right this minute.

"*Gracias*." She dragged reluctant thumbs over the soft ripples of canvas. "Where'd you find these, anyway?"

He crossed his arms over a proud, puffed chest. "The general store up the road. Grimmurson's. Same place I got the pie. Agnes helped me special order them."

"Oh." She squinted at him. "Agnes?"

"The owner."

He must've spent a pretty penny on expedited shipping to the Arctic Circle. Still. She wasn't going to jump for joy, no matter how much he wanted her to. "I could've painted at home, too, you know. Abuela loves painting with me, and—"

"Evie," he interrupted, impending lecture bleeding through his tone. "We've been through this. Abuela can't take care of you in an assisted living facility. It's beautiful here. Don't miss this opportunity to explore. You're only here for the summer."

Only. Oh, the terrific irony of that word. She whispered a sigh.

"You chose Iceland over New York because of the opportunities to paint," he reminded her.

As it turned out, she gave exactly zero shits about painting in Iceland. She just said whatever she had to in a pinch, choosing here over New York because any city where her mother resided would always be too small for them both. Besides, Evie refused to leave her father alone like her mother had. She just wished he'd reciprocate a little. Loyalty was worth a lot more when it was a two-way transaction.

"Think of all those landscapes out there waiting for you." He wadded the foil paper into a ball and pitched it across the box-cluttered room toward the recycling bin. It thunked into a half-empty cardboard box instead. *Another miss.*

The landscapes Evie painted were from her favorite songs, not depressing gray horizons. During Florida winters, she measured her breaths in notes and brushstrokes. Short days were spent baking with Abuela. Long, chilly nights were spent listening to music and painting—buttery paint smudging her fingers and dotting her nightclothes. She barely stayed awake in school the day after those art benders. But that was a brand of sleep deprivation she could tolerate.

A rendering of *Three Little Birds* hung in Abuela's yellow breakfast nook back home, serving as a reminder that *every little thing's gonna be all right*, because summer was always just around the corner in Miami. Summer—that glorious time of year when temperatures hovered near Hades, the sharp scent of chlorine clung to her impossibly thick hair, and her sun-kissed skin tingled under the air conditioning vent while she fell asleep.

Which was much easier to do in Florida, since it actually got dark there at night.

But summer would pass her by this year. And even the finest Siberian paintbrushes couldn't paint pretty over that melancholy. She scooped a bite of pie and shoveled it in her mouth, mostly so she wouldn't have to explain all of that to her clueless papá.

Her teeth sliced through crust and punctured plump cherry flesh. Juices sweet and tart spilled across sleeping taste buds. Her eyes fluttered closed and the room fell silent, as though all other senses had to shut down to make room for the taste. For a moment, she could almost pretend she was home, having cherry pastelitos on Abuela's front porch as summertime fireworks exploded from the streets of Little Havana.

"Sorry there's no ice cream." His voice shattered her daydream. *Night dream, whatever.* It was so good it didn't even need ice cream. But she'd never say as much and give him the thrill of thinking his bribery was working.

"Pretty fresh for imported pie," she mumbled around a second eager bite. Fresh was an understatement. These cherries had a soul.

"It isn't imported. There's an orchard behind Agnes's store. The pie is homemade."

Evie quirked a brow. Seemed improbable for cherries to grow this far north, but the moment he said it, her imagination painted a picture: trees sloped on a hillside, exploding with sanguine bubbles of fleshy fruit, waxy green leaves shimmying with the wind. According to her mother, she was short on a lot of things, but at least she had her imagination going for her.

"In a greenhouse or something?" She gobbled another bite.

"Nuh-uh." He shook his head, digging into his own slice. "Outside. Just over the hill beyond the sheep pasture. I wouldn't have believed it if I hadn't seen it myself. *Increíble.* You should go see it."

Evie cast a dubious glance out the window at the hill, mossy edges glowing gold beneath a gray sky. It somehow managed to be sunny and cloudy at the same time. Condensation haloed around the panes, evidence of the summer's frosty breath.

The two of them finished their dessert in quiet. Soft chewing, satisfied grunts, and the space heater's tiresome buzz saturated their small cottage. Evie scraped the last bite from her plate, sad to see it go.

"Where's your necklace?" An unspoken accusation seeped around his words. Evie touched her bare neck, fully aware she wasn't wearing the gold chain and crucifix he'd given her for Christmas. Under the sleeve on her wrist, she wore the silver

Saint Christopher charm bracelet Abuela had given her instead. *Patron saint of travelers*, Abuela had reminded her before she left. She hadn't taken it off since. The necklace clashed with it.

"Didn't put it back on after showering."

He nodded, lines in his face suddenly deeper. Disappointment always carved itself in his forehead, so everyone was sure not to miss it.

"One more thing." He pulled a black silk eye mask from his jacket pocket and set it on the table. "Try to get some sleep tonight. This might help. The Internet will still be there *mañana*."

The Internet barely worked when nobody was awake to use it, much less during the day when everyone in the string of mossy-roofed guesthouses on the property tried to tap into the Wi-Fi. At least if she stayed up to chat with her friends, she sometimes got a solid ten minutes of communication before the bandwidth petered out again. Five hours ahead of Miami, she had to make it to midnight, minimum, if she wanted to catch Loretta and Ben after their shifts at Wild Waves.

"Okay." Her chair clunked across the knots in the floor as she slid backward and stood, gathering empty pie plates.

Her papá raised his hand to stop her.

"I'll get those. Get to bed, *mija*. Maybe we can do some exploring this weekend. It's supposed to warm up to the sixties tomorrow."

"The sixties?" A sarcastic laugh elbowed its way out of her chest as she fastened the sleep mask around the top of her head. "*Caliente*," she deadpanned, and then loaded up with the new art supplies she had no intentions of using. On principle, of course.

"I have to go into the city for a bit in the morning, but I'll be back before you wake up," he said, ignoring her tone. *Sure he would*. And she would grow a third ear by morning. An extra, so she'd have a place to store all his empty promises.

Meandering through their unpacked life, Evie pushed open the creaky door to her summer cell. "Goodnight, Papá." She gently kicked the door closed behind her, not waiting for his reply. After dumping the canvases and paint on a tattered wing chair covered by her winter clothes, she sank onto the thin mattress of the single bed. The patchwork quilt Abuela made for her glowed toasty-warm through her pajamas from a spray of sunshine. After yanking the shade closed, she wiggled a finger over her open laptop's track pad and held her breath as her messenger app came to life.

Ben Benson – active two minutes ago.

The cursor blinked back at her. She wished she could freeze-frame the way he'd looked standing in the parking lot outside Wild Waves that night the week before she left. Tousled hair hung over his eyes and his body stretched downward into his lifeguard trunks. Those trunks weren't the only reason red was her favorite color, but they definitely boosted its case.

He'd tilted his head and leaned forward, and anticipation had lit her on fire. But then he'd spoken, and the magic of the moment evaporated like sea mist. When she tasted his sour tongue, his hand tasted the inside of her swimsuit top. Before he could get it untied, she pushed him away.

Whether or not that was a mistake still remained to be seen. Loretta seemed to think she was being a baby. *Make him beg for it*, she'd said. *But don't shut him down or he'll find it somewhere else. You'll be gone all summer.* It's not that Evie wasn't risk-the-fiery-pits-of-hell curious. She was—she wanted to feel, to experience something real. But only under the right circumstances. She liked Ben, but when he groped her like that and let clumsy, stupid words fall out of his mouth, she felt *nothing*. All that penned-up emotion vanished, leaving her wondering if it'd ever been there to begin with.

He's a Zip-It, Loretta had joked. *Stand there and look hot, but please shut the eff up.* A lot of guys her age were Zip-Its. Until that moment in the parking lot, though, Evie thought the dipshit persona might've been an act. Nobody ever saw her for her real self, either. She still had hope. With trembling fingers, she typed *Hi.*

She stared a hole through his status—waiting. Her eyelids grew heavy, despite the sun's invasion through the linen shade. She stretched out next to the screen, pulling her sleep mask down. *I'll just rest my eyes for a minute.*

TWO
Oskar's Journal

There is nothing more infuriating
than someone telling me
what I should or should not do
with something that belongs to me.
Cut your hair.
Stop wasting your talent.
Don't harvest the cherries from the *Aisling* tree.
My hair will stay unkempt.
I'll play when I feel like it.
And do what I want.
My hair. My music. My tree.

Fat, icy raindrops
pelt the top of my head
as I move through the orchard
toward the warm shelter of the store.
They slide over my scalp, running through the maze of hair
until they gather at the base of my neck.
I pause under the overhang
outside the door
and shake myself off like a mongrel.
I'll finish this tomorrow

or when the sky stops weeping.
Whichever comes first.
There are days when I wish my family
had never planted this orchard.
Sometimes I think we'd be better off,
Agnes and me,
if we didn't have to tend
the abandoned dreams of loved ones lost.
But my aunt is a typical pushy Scot
about the property my parents left in her care.
I figure I take more after
the Icelandic side
of my family.
But Agnes is all the family I have now.
Get ye to gatherin', Oskar!
Agnes's Scottish brogue
booms off the wood-paneled walls in the shop
the minute I step back inside.
We can't waste 'em.
They're ripenin' faster than I can fill the jars!
She drops her ladle into a tall, steaming pot
and wipes her hands on the front of her apron,
smearing warm cherry preserves
across starched white cotton.
I point to the window with a grimace
rather than replying
to avoid my inevitable stutter.
But—Bs are the worst.
They glue my lips together like bark gum.
Rain slicks the glass, pooling in the sills.
So what? Agnes says. *It's rainin'!*
You can sit on yer dry arse this winter,
when we have plenty to get us through the cold.
She pushes a hefty bucket across the counter.

The metal screeches to a stop as it hits me in the stomach.
I narrow my eyes and grab it.
Shove that snarl back inside yer head, boy.
Tuck it under that mop of hair.
She thunders back over to her pot on the stove,
watching from the corner of her eye as I about-face.
I breeze through a narrow aisle of homemade jams and pies
and push the side door open with a whoosh.
The wind snatches it and slams it against the barn-red exterior.
The overabundance is my fault.
Because I've been lazy.
I've been gathering cherries
from the base of the *Aisling* tree.
The one tree we aren't supposed to harvest.
Never mind the fact it's *my* tree.
It's easy pickings,
because the fruit gathers right on the ground.
When I don't have to use a ladder,
I can scoop them by handfuls.
The faster I'm done,
the faster
I'm free.

THREE

Evie

*E*vie pirouetted through the bleary in-between bordering asleep and awake.

Tingly edges of a dream tugged at her. It whispered gauzy coils into her head, asking permission to materialize, but the remnants were strange, hard to mold with concrete things like words. A nearby animal grunt nudged her, once and for all, away from her slumber. She opened her eyes to complete darkness.

What the...

Then she remembered the eye mask.

Snatching it upwards, her matted lashes met splotches of light. She crawled on her hands and knees across the disheveled bed and opened the shade. The blazing glow made her recoil. Focusing through a painful squint, she found the source of the noise. A puffy white sheep toed at the dirt outside her window. It turned and made eye contact with her and spewed the most godawful noise she'd ever heard through its flat yellow teeth.

She shrieked, flailing her arms. If the window had been open, she could've reached out and shoved it. It chewed a sloppy mouthful of something and looked away, bored.

In her suburban Florida bedroom, Evie often woke to the sounds of lawn mowers and laughter. But never had bleating sheep interrupted her slumber at—she glanced at the antique cat clock on the wall—*noon.* Mother Mary, she'd slept until noon!

The sheep whined again and she yanked the shade closed, rubbing her face and collapsing backward onto the squeaky mattress. Out of habit, she reached over and touched her laptop to life, still open where she'd left it.

Ben Benson – active 9 hours ago.

Another gasp sucker-punched her lungs. He'd responded, and of-freaking-course she'd missed it.

Ben Benson – Wanna grab some grub after work tomorrow? (9 hours ago)

Huh? Her brows cinched. She'd been gone a week. Surely he hadn't forgotten already. She blinked a few times and clicked refresh. After a ten-second delay, another message populated the thread.

Ben Benson – My bad. That was meant for Loretta. You doing ok? Hope your having fun in Greenland. (8 hours ago)

She stuck a mental thumbtack in the grammar blunder and concentrated on the other thing he said. Greenland? And even worse—Meant. For. Loretta.

She let it settle in.

Loretta was her best friend. Supposedly. Loretta didn't read or paint or even listen to the same kind of music as Evie. But Loretta knew people, and she'd taken Evie under her wing at school junior year—even convincing her to start going by her full name. *Evie is a little girl name,* Loretta had said, flicking a wisp of blond hair behind her thin shoulders, *but Evelyn is sophisticated. Old-school names are in again, you know. Distinguishes you from all the Emmas and Brittanys.*

Everyone had always called her Evie. But she went along with Loretta's identity overhaul, which included trading her flip-flops for heels, painting her nails, and going on a diet.

Before all of that, Evie was a nobody, by their impossible standards, until Loretta scooped her into the fold. Maybe it made her a grade-A sellout, but reinventing herself had been the ticket to a real seat in the lunchroom and a coveted job at Wild Waves, since Loretta's dad was part-owner.

Loretta had been distracted lately, though. She barely managed to respond in complete sentences to Evie's instant messages. Ben Benson might have something to do with that. Evie fisted a handful of comforter, letting the jealousy clamp like a vice around the muscles in her neck. Maybe calling dibs on a guy became void when you left the country.

And Ben! He wasn't exactly innocent either. She could forgive the fact that he regularly mixed up *your* and *you're*, but he couldn't be bothered to even remember which country she was in? She'd told him no less than three dozen times.

She slapped the laptop screen shut and flung herself on a pillow. Loneliness would just have to be her new BFF here in *Greenland*—land of nothingness and sheep.

As she hid behind her lids, trying to forget the full tank of anger with no place to go, her dream tried to surface again, like a ghost tapping her on the shoulder.

She was in a cherry orchard—she knew that much for sure—and it was exactly as she'd first seen it in her imagination. A boy had stared through the leaves of a low branch at her. Probably Ben, since she'd fallen asleep thinking about him. But the details, like the boy's face, evaded her, turning into a swirl of color that got blurrier by the minute.

Like a painting left in the rain.

On Christmas Eve last winter, she'd started a painting outside. It was meant to be a gift for Abuela. Tired eyes had halted her progress, so she went to bed and left it on the porch to dry. During the night, a winter rainstorm blew in and soaked the canvas. The paint drizzled into a river of blended hues. Though she knew what she had painted when she found it the next morning, if she stared at the blob too long, she could forget what had been underneath.

A similar sadness plagued her as the retreating dream smeared colors through her subconscious. She was forgetting what Ben looked like. Already. What a flake she was. Maybe that's why it seemed like he had forgotten her, too.

She turned her head away from the glare of daylight, searching for clarity, but instead found the heap of pricy art supplies on the wingback next to the bed. Her fingers fluttered against her will.

Maybe she could translate that dream to canvas.

She reminded herself she wasn't going to paint. Her papá wanted her to, and he had enough control over the decisions affecting her future. She hung her feet off the end of the mattress and bounced them in a nervous rhythm, staring at the canvases. Maybe a little sketch wouldn't hurt.

She reached under the pile of clothes, toppling sweaters and scarves and art supplies to the floor, searching with her fingers. Once she found her bent-corner sketchbook and grabbed a pencil from her desk, she flipped open to an empty page and began to transcribe.

Within a few minutes, the gentle swish of charcoal had rendered a black-and-white version of her dream. Evie propped the pencil against her lip, not quite satisfied. There was too much missing, too much still hiding in her brain.

It needed color.

She glanced at the acrylics, now lying on the floor with the clothes. Who was she really punishing if she didn't paint? Evie didn't like the answer.

Anyway, it was past noon and based on the lack of response to her yell at the sheep, Papá wasn't home early like he promised. There was nothing comforting about knowing nobody could hear her scream in this tiny, moss-covered hobbit hole. Refusing to paint wouldn't change any of that.

She forced herself off the bed, pulled the red crocheted beret Abuela had made over her bedhead hair, and slid her feet into flip-flops. *Icelandic weather be damned.* Her jaw tightened as she shoved all of her supplies into her leather cross-body satchel and tucked a canvas under her arm. Screw it. She'd barely left this room since they arrived. If an orchard really grew in Iceland, she wanted to see it for herself.

She was through the cottage and out the door in moments, gaining elevation through wet grass with every slippery step. The chilly wind breathed down her neck as she dodged sheep pellets littering her way. Maybe her shoe choice was ill conceived after all.

When she crested the hill, the most sensational feeling of déjà vu silenced the swishing of her silk pajama pants and she froze mid-stride. The horizon opened onto a show-stopping panorama.

Holy shit.

There really was an orchard in Iceland—an exact replica of the one from her sketchbook and her dream. Little details swam to the surface in her mind, bit by bit, as she made her feet move again, toes pointing and planting down in the spongy earth.

Dozens of cherry trees danced in the lukewarm breeze. Their sloping rows couldn't have been more symmetrical if they were drawn on lined paper. They clung to the hillside as though determined, at some perfect moment, to slide into the glassy water below.

Rays of sunlight glittered a magnificent sheen on waxy leaves and decadent red globes. Something enchanting shimmered in the leftover raindrops clinging to them. And just beyond the orchard on the edge of the water, a barn-like building loomed, painted cherry red to match. A few cars sat in the parking area out front. Across the distance of the water, a white lighthouse trimmed in deepest crimson jutted from the horizon, standing bastion at the edge of the sea.

Evie had intended to set up and paint on the hill, but sweet-smelling breezes beckoned her forward and the landscape drew her into its essence. One moment she stood on the hill, taking in the scenery—the next, she stood at the fence in the back of the orchard, staring at the largest tree among them, so dazed she didn't remember the walk itself.

There was something different about this tree, and not just because it was the first one she came to after climbing through the bars of the white fence . It tugged at her heartstrings, a vague sense that it anchored everything below it. She set her supplies against a paint-chipped post. The soil under her feet gripped her flip-flop treads as she walked, making a sucking slurp when she stepped in the wettest spots. When she reached the shelter of the shade, she stilled, feeling oddly at ease. Welcomed, even.

A cluster of cherries hung from a branch at eye-level, as if the tree reached out to hand them to her. The delicate ruby bulbs glistened as they touched her fingertips. She plucked a few and took them back to her spot by the fencepost, rolling one between her thumb and forefinger. The fragrance squeezed moisture into her mouth.

She plopped one past her lips as she sank to the earth and set her tabletop easel on the ground. Silky flesh separated under her teeth, and the pulpy middle melted on her tongue, perfectly ripe and alive with possibility. She discarded the pit on the ground next to her. As she chewed the next two and propped her sketch-book against the fencepost, her dream's details materialized in fragments.

But was it a dream? It felt familiar, somehow—like a song she'd once heard but had forgotten the words to. She hurriedly set up her paints, determined not to lose her grip on it. The wet ground seeped through the thin silky pajamas and brought her back to reality, if only briefly, making her wish she'd brought a blanket to sit on. But a wet butt was a minor inconvenience in the urgency of the moment. She had to paint the scene tickling her cerebellum while it was fresh, emerging in bright flashes of light. It was just like all the times a song made her grab a canvas and rush to relay the scene, sometimes without a sketch.

This time, there was no song to reference, no pause button to press, only a glimpse pinging around in her brain. She trembled as she mixed colors with sticky fingertips, hurrying to smear the paint and then wipe the excess on her knees.

The first layer transpired into a barely coherent clump of color. Blues and grays and whites washed the sky; swaths of green bathed the ground. A second layer added depth and distance. Tree trunks of umber reached toward the sky with bony fingers. Rings of sunlight rimmed feathery white clouds.

By the time she'd painted the third layer, her hand moved of its own volition. Like the minute hand of a clock, it knew exactly where to go without having to be told, and for just the right amount of time.

Cherries thudded to the ground intermittently around her like an irregular heartbeat. The breeze exhaled a gasp that stole her crocheted hat and tossed it on the ground. She barely noticed as her hair whipped around her face and brushed her collarbone.

Once she'd swept verdant leaves onto climbing branches and speckled them with cherries, she focused on the alabaster blob in the foreground. It was the only thing in her painting she didn't have the advantage of glancing up to reference, because it huddled only within the confines of her subconscious—an abstract place she could only reach with a paintbrush.

Slow and patient, stroke by stroke, it became a boy.

The sinewy lines threading his torso and arms came to life beneath her smudged hands. She stared at the rendering, biting her quivering bottom lip. He had a farm boy's body, scratched and dotted with dirt. A tattoo engraved his right bicep, a black symbol she'd never seen before. Three lowercase i's leaned into one another—they looked like lit candles converging—and were surrounded by a circle. She painted the symbol without even glancing at her sketchbook for comparison, as though she'd invented the intricacies herself.

As she added final touches—golden highlights in his messy blond hair, dimples twinkling against a stern jaw (left one deeper than the right), distressed denim clinging to his long legs, and a silver bucket overflowing cherries at his feet—her heart sped to a satisfied staccato.

Decidedly *not* Ben Benson. If this boy were real, he'd know the difference between Iceland and Greenland. She'd bet on that.

A dreamy haze swam laps around her as she studied her work. It was easily the most beautiful thing she'd ever painted. Completely ridiculous, but she was crushing on a boy she made up, falling in love with a song she'd never even heard.

FOUR
Oskar's Journal

After unloading
my third haul of cherries,
I head to the back of the orchard.
My clothes stick to me, damp from the morning rain.
The sun stretches its muscles, growing warmer by the minute
so I peel off my shirt and tuck it in my back pocket.
I've waited months for winter to get out of my face,
so I could feel sunlight on my skin.
But most importantly,
so I could get back to work on the lighthouse.
It is the only remaining place
I feel their presence
rather than their absence.
Today makes five years since the accident.
It still pounds my ears
like the torturous
drum beat
of memory.
And if I think hard enough,
glass shatters through a dizzy spiral
of crumpling metal.
But I sneak around the thoughts,

sly as a thief.
My broken strings echo
louder
and louder
and louder
when
I
sink
into a pit of painful recollection.
Not that I really talk to anyone besides Agnes,
and she pretends not to notice
when I trip over syllables
and fall flat on my face.
But lately, she notices other things.
She peeks out the window, shamelessly spying on me.
I wonder if she knows
I've been bringing her cherries
from the *Aisling* tree.
I prop the ladder up and climb it,
one rung at a time,
in case she's watching.
I get to the top, set my bucket down and stop.
Someone hums.
A feminine melody
braids itself into the breeze.
There's a splotch of red on the ground, bunched in a pile.
A crimson hat points in her direction.
My hands grip the ladder a little harder when I see her.
She crouches beneath my tree,
twirling a long-handled brush
between paint-dappled fingers.
The hint of a smile
tugs at the periphery
of her humming mouth

as she stares forward at a canvas.
Her complexion absorbs the sunlight,
and long dark hair
cascades
down
her back.
She's like rainforest royalty,
displaced on top of the world.
A series of rapid blinks
won't reduce her
to something imagined.
Splatters of color freckle her clothes
as if to announce
she's here to impress
nobody at all.
The light touches her angular face,
accents the bottom lip
she chews without apology.
I lean forward to feed my curiosity
and knock the bucket
off the top of the ladder,
spilling a tidal wave of cherries on the ground.

FIVE
Evie

*C*langing metal startled Evie from her daze.

Her feet launched into autopilot, catapulting her vertical. Brown paint splashed across her naked toes and she dropped her brushes next to a pile of pilfered cherries. Trespassing was probably a crime in Iceland too, and an artist's hunger always made a terrible defense. Glancing down at her disheveled pajamas—*Por Dios, she was wearing her pajamas*—she gulped a panicked breath.

Chilly wind squeezed water into her eyes as she spun, searching for the source of the sound. She scanned the beautiful emptiness until, all at once, the void dissipated. Through rivulets of sunbeams, a tall boy stood beneath the knobby knuckles of a low-hanging branch. Four steps and a golden glare separated them.

Making a tentative move forward, Evie shielded her eyes from the sun.

Loco shirtless natives think this is warm weather, she thought in the split second it took her to recognize the lines in his stomach—ones she'd painted with painstaking precision only moments ago. Like a road map, she followed those lines north. Well-used arms hung at his sides, one with a familiar tattoo. His damp hair stuck to his face, like he'd come straight from the shower. Or a rainstorm. Or a humid borough of lumberjack heaven. Because *damn.*

He wore water-splattered jeans and a curious smile, one exaggerated dimple pitting his left cheek. She opened her mouth to speak, but his thundercloud eyes rendered her mute as Mozart—*or was that Beethoven?*—despite the symphony playing in her head.

Maybe she was still asleep. She squeezed her lashes shut, slowly peeking through them after a few moments. Still there. His blond brows pushed a wrinkle of skin together on his forehead.

"Is it okay if I work here?" Evie finally managed to croak, throat scratchy as sand. "My name is Evelyn. I'll leave if it's a problem. I'm just painting."

He didn't respond but kept chomping on the piece of gum in his mouth, dimples flickering as he chewed. He narrowed his eyes as he studied her with a trace of something—irritation?

She'd read online that Icelanders were shy and reserved, and here she was, face-to-face with one, not only imposing, but looking her absolute worst. She hadn't even brushed her teeth this morning. She hoped he couldn't smell her breath. *Oh, don't mind me, the pajama-rama color monster creeping your orchard.* She crossed her arms, trying and failing to hide all the skid marks of paint.

"I'm staying at *Fryst Paradis* for the summer." She nodded over her shoulder toward the hill separating the guesthouses from the orchard, hoping he'd look at anything but her. "It's really pretty over here. I just came to try and capture the beauty."

She watched in horror as his gaze traveled to the painting behind her, propped against the fencepost in a pool of sunlight. Like a spotlight of humiliation.

Capture the beauty might've been a poor choice of words, she realized, as he gawked at the painting. His mouth dropped into fly-catcher mode for a split second before he snapped it shut again, a glimpse of green gum frozen on the center of his tongue. Though she could've done a leaping swan dive and landed on top of the painting, it was way too late for such acrobatics. He'd seen it, and judging by his startled expression, he wasn't at all impressed with her stage-five clinger vibe.

"I can explain..."

He took a slow step backward, cocking his head to the side the way someone facing a wild animal might.

"Wait." She held her hands up. "It's not what it looks like." Maybe he couldn't tell the boy in the painting resembled him a scary lot. She took a peripheral glance at it, then back to him. *Crap.* Of course the one time it would've suited her to paint something all wrong, it didn't happen. The exactness of the tattoo made it impossible to dismiss as coincidence.

"Okay, maybe it is what it looks like, but I definitely wasn't like, stalking you. I can explain." But could she, really? She wore her awkwardness like a feather boa and tried to imagine his face if she told him she got her inspiration from a dream. That would only level-up her freak status.

He glanced at the pile of cherry pits on the ground next to her palette. *Double crap.* Now she was a stalker *and* a thief. "I'm sorry," she pleaded. "My papá bought some incredible cherry pie from the store yesterday. It made me want to see this place. Can you just tell the owner that I'll buy something? I have money. I didn't mean to cause trouble."

He still didn't speak. Could he even understand English? He flexed his jaw, almost as if his uncertainty had graduated to anger. His eyes flickered from her eyes to her lips, sending a shudder right through all the molecules that made her a girl. Then he peered over her shoulder to the painting.

"I know it's—" But before she could utter another breath, he turned his back and stormed down the hill through the trees, fists coiled at his sides.

"Hey! I said I'm sorry. Do you speak English?" she called behind him, but he didn't seem to notice. She shook her head, watching him leave. He could've said *something*. Google told her almost all Icelanders spoke a bit of English.

"Rude," she muttered before making a beeline to grab her things and scram.

SIX
Oskar's Journal

Things never go
the way I imagine they might.
My brain overrules the southern command
the minute she opens her mouth.
It's not even the painting
that turns me off most.
Which says a lot
considering how long
she must have been sneaking around.
Never mind that it's a very *good* painting,
accurate to every minuscule flaw.
It's the American mentality
that triggers my upchuck reflex:
Take what you want—
when there's a problem,
throw money at it.
How convenient it must be
to have that option.
I wouldn't know.
The orchard's paid off now,
thanks to money tossed to us by the guilty American
who caused the accident.

But we have very little else besides cherries.
And she was taking those, too.
Did the fence not tip her off
that the area's private property?
My boots stomp through the sludge.
The burn of the morning's scratches
make me wince as I clench my fists.
I zigzag through the trees,
avoiding her gaze
like a spray of shrapnel.
Stupid, selfish Americans.
Of course I can speak English,
But I'll never speak it to her.
As much as I'd like to tell her
how wrong she is,
how self-centered and presumptuous,
she would only hear broken strings,
the stammering of missed notes.
And then she would feel sorry for me.
Because there are some things
even money cannot fix.
She is just as bad
as the assholes responsible
for making me
an
orphan.

SEVEN

Evie

"What'd you do today?" Papá asked Evie over dinner without looking at her.

He strolled into the *Fryst Paradis* café to meet her at eight. She was trying not to complain. It was better than midnight, at least.

She shrugged as she pushed a clump of unidentified meat around in her soup—something chunky and brown that looked like it'd already been digested once. Aromas of onion and thyme floated in the steam, eliciting a skeptical growl from her empty— save for the cherries—stomach.

Happy chatter hummed over the honeycomb windows of the lively little café. The tourists around them were from all over the globe, based on the lilt of their accents. They crowded the mismatched tables and chairs, conversing happily. Though the languages were different, the tones of voices hit a similar note: they were the victorious travelers on the trip of a lifetime.

Evie envied them. She envied their choices.

"Mmm, *sabroso*," Papá mumbled around a mouthful of the poop soup.

She'd spent the day re-reading *One Hundred Years of Solitude* and refreshing her messenger app with the kind of desperation that made it hard to look in a mirror. Maybe she was just as destined to repeat history as the Macandos were. After all, Abuela had been torn from her home and dropped in a foreign land when she was a teenager, too.

When three video chat calls from her mother had come through, half an hour apart each time, she ignored them. She had no desire to repeat that history. But Evie had no plans to tell her papá any of that.

"I went and saw the orchard."

His eyes widened and he looked at her for the first time since he'd sat down.

"Well?" He dropped his spoon in the bowl and suspended his oil black eyebrows in perma-surprise. "Did you paint?"

Evie's nostrils flared. Could mystery boy have tattled to the store owner, which resulted in a phone call to Papá? Saying yes would invite him to ask to see the painting, though, and she'd already met her quota for embarrassment today. She shook her head, risking the lie, and made a note to start keeping a written tally of things to bring up in her next confessional. Not that she was always 100% honest with the priest, but her sins were beginning to pile up.

"It'd be a beautiful scene, I think." He wiped dripping soup from his mouth. "Why aren't you eating?"

"The food's weird here, Papá." Evie rolled her eyes. "Everything is weird here."

The way his face fell, wrinkles in the corners of his eyes pointing down instead of up, mouth settling in a drooping arch, sent a jolt of guilt all the way to the tip of her empty soup spoon. Sometimes she forgot he was still grieving her mother's absence, blaming himself for not making her happy. Not that anyone could ever make her mother happy.

"I liked the cherry pie, though." Evie did her best to say it in a hopeful tone.

He nodded. "They serve lunch over there too, and they have homemade salsas and jams. I think I'll stop tomorrow on my way back and get some."

"I'll get it," she blurted, then lowered her voice and peered around to see if anyone noticed her alarm. They hadn't. "I mean, it was nice to get out of the house today. I don't mind going." No way could she let him find out she'd already made an enemy on her very first excursion. "Anyway, where do you have to go tomorrow? Aren't we going to Mass?"

A sigh deflated him. "I'm sorry, *mija*. Research is weather dependent, and the forecast changed. Chance of rain is slim to none." He offered an apologetic shrug.

Abuela had raised Papá to attend Mass religiously, pun intended. It was one of those obligatory things Evie just accepted with a resigned sense of dread. So it made very little sense how much it bummed her out that she'd miss it for the second week in a row.

EIGHT
Oskar's Journal

Within these pages lives my solace.
It's the only place I can share my thoughts
without having to avoid sounds
that seize in my throat
or get caught on repeat.
From the time I learned to talk
my brain has moved faster than my mouth.
Words get clogged up
as they press against the back of my teeth.
I'm an alien
flying under the radar
on a fluent planet,
but everyone knows it when I speak.
Music is my only refuge,
because when I sing,
my strings aren't broken.
When I was little,
the speech therapist told Mamma
to encourage me to sing
for this reason.
So I write my words here
between these pages

where they hang, ripe for the plucking,
and only sing them
when I want to be heard.

NINE
Evie

*A*lone in her room the next day, Evie cast sidelong glances at her painting.

Humiliation aside, it was an impressive depiction, if she did say so herself. Maybe she'd seen the boy at some point since she got to Iceland but hadn't noticed. Like when she had first arrived. Or when she rode to town with Papá for groceries. The only reason he even seemed interesting is because she'd cooked up this idea that she saw him in her mind before she met him.

Because it wasn't like that was something that could actually happen. She wasn't Miss Izzy from the El Rey strip mall in Little Havana. She didn't peer into a clear plastic bowl full of dollar store marbles and see the future. Then again, neither did Miss Izzy, if she was being technical about it. Miss Izzy told Evie a few days before she left Miami that she'd meet a kind and handsome boy and that she'd never stray far from home. What a crock of lies that had been.

Maybe Miss Izzy should've splurged for the more expensive marbles at the flea market, since her vision only got one detail right. She threw on a pair of jeans and a hoodie and dug her fingers through her hair, like she could scrub the thought of him away. Maybe he was nice looking in that brawny, could-lift-a-Volkswagen sort of way, but his personality left a ton to be desired. Kind of like Ben. Were all boys such insufferable ass-holes? She'd have to get Abuela's input on that.

He'd claimed enough of her curiosity for one day, so she pulled up iTunes and clicked a playlist of reggae tunes. A happy Bob Marley beat flooded the guesthouse silence. His music always made her think of Abuela. It was the one musical compromise they had no trouble making. Abuela felt a kinship with him because she'd read in the papers that he too had fled to Miami as a refugee. She'd seen him live once at Jai-Alai Fronton in the 1970s, and she never tired of telling that story. Her dark eyes got three shades lighter each time.

Alberto was but a niñito, Evie, but I carried him on my hip through the concert crowd. I was empty from your abuelo's departure back to Cuba. But when the music began, the notes filled all that vacant space in my heart. There was a spiritual healing in his message and the way he moved as the words rolled through him. It was a positive vibration, indeed, nieta.

Keeping her hands busy, Evie unpacked clothes—something she'd been putting off to delay the reality of this summer sentence in the cold. She hung sweaters, folded pajamas, and shoved bras in the small white armoire with a too-short leg. It rocked and thumped on the floor each time she opened a drawer. As she searched for something to stick under it, the messenger screen dinged on her laptop.

She stumbled and nearly ate hardwood trying to get to little desk next to the bed. Pressing pause on the music, she opened the messenger screen.

Ben Benson: Sup girl? Hows the North Pole?

Wrong location again. But God, at least he was talking to her. That's more than she could say for any of the other people she'd encountered lately. She sank into a chair and glanced at the painting again.

Evelyn Perez: Spectacular! I met some locals yesterday. Thinking of hiking the rim of a volcano this weekend.

And by hiking the rim of a volcano, she meant going to buy cherry jam. She refused to let him know how lame her day—scratch that, entire trip—had been.

Ben Benson: Right on.

She grumbled and stared at the blinking cursor, trying to think of something interesting to say to keep the conversation going. The blank grew in her head like spilled white paint.

A purple notification box popped up on the screen.

Loretta Devereaux is now online.

Panic shoved her into typing another message. She had to get his attention back.

Evelyn Perez: I've been thinking about that night.

There. She smiled to herself. She'd put that in his mind. Maybe it'd be a convenient segue into a clarification conversation: Are you my boyfriend? She wasn't sure if she'd be able to ask him like that, outright. But she wanted to. She needed to know where they stood, and she hated that she hadn't cleared it up before she left. They'd been on a few dates—mostly group excursions after work. Were those even dates? They were before the kiss, so she wasn't sure. Now that she thought about it, her doubts doubled down.

She waited. And waited. And waited some more. Finally, she gave up and clicked on Loretta's name, promising herself she'd resist the urge to ask about her *grub-grab* with Ben.

Evelyn Perez: Hey stranger.

The response was instant.

Loretta Devereaux: Hey girl! How are you?! Do you love it there?

She thought for a moment. What would impress Loretta? She chose her words carefully.

Evelyn Perez: It's amazing! Wish you were here, though. Going to hike a volcano tomorrow.

She'd keep her lies consistent. Maybe Loretta and Ben would even discuss the adventures of Evelyn and be jealous of her world travels.

Loretta Deveraux: Right on.

Evie frowned. So Loretta was adopting Ben's dismissal phrases now. This did not bode well for the hypothetical are-you-my-boyfriend conversation.

Evelyn Perez: It's pretty dangerous, but I'm going with a local guide. I'll try to take pics.

Loretta Devereaux: You probably look adorable all bundled up like an Eskimo. I bet you miss swimming, though! Speaking of, I bought the hottest bikini today. Bright blue. Looks good with my eyes. Gonna wear it to the July 4th celebration at WW.

Evie deflated under her bulky hoodie. She could swim here, but the natural geothermal water in the guesthouse pool smelled like farts. As it turned out, the earth was a gassy beast and Iceland didn't keep the secret.

She didn't want to hear about Loretta's bikini or the weather that allowed her to wear it. Not to mention the awesomeness of the 4th of July bash she'd miss. Loretta's dad had secured FloRida as the musical act. *FloFreakingRida.* Resentment burned at her fingertips. Screw it, she was asking her.

Evelyn Perez: How's Ben? I heard you guys had dinner.

After ten minutes of the cat clock on the wall tick, tick, ticking the seconds away, Evie accepted that Loretta wasn't going to answer.

She clicked back over to Ben's IM window for one last-ditch effort.

Evelyn Perez: Wanna video chat?

After the message was marked read, a notification popped up on screen.

Ben Benson is now offline.

Maybe they weren't getting her messages. Maybe it was the shitty Wi-Fi. Evie shut her laptop and swallowed a gallon of unshed tears. All of this time away was going to cause her to lose them both. Maybe that meant she never had them in the first place.

TEN
Oskar's Journal

The chord progression
makes the hair on my forearms stand.
The notes are sure of themselves.
Right at home.
There's nothing better
than translating feeling to art.
I lounge backward on my bed and readjust Pabbi's old
    guitar.
Dragging my pick across the strings,
I play the familiar melody again.
A minor, F major, C major,
G major.
And again.
Notes reverberate
through my loft bedroom
upward through the morning sunlight
echoing in the rafters above.
I haven't wanted to play lately.
But for two days,
this song has refused
to leave me
alone.

It wars for space in my head
with the spoiled American girl,
who invites herself into my thoughts
the same way she invited herself
into my orchard.
I take it from the top.
Before my fingers slide to G,
her annoying accent
creeps into my ears.
Muffled words.
I didn't mean to cause trouble.
But trouble is exactly what she caused.
Trouble squared.
As I strum again,
her voice comes from the air vent
in the wall below me.
Talking to Agnes about *that boy in the orchard.*
I drop my guitar on the ground.
The reverberating *bonnnng*
is quieter than my panic.
She's here.

ELEVEN
Evie

*E*vie was on sensory overload from the minute the bell clanged against the shop door.

Grimmurson's smelled like home. The scent of warm pastries and cherries inundated the cozy, wood-walled space. It gave her the urge to both stay and leave as quickly as possible. Because as much as the fragrance of baked goods and homemade preserves reminded her of Abuela's kitchen, it just made her miss her even more.

The carefully curated souvenirs lining the shop shelves brought back memories of the roadside mom-and-pop places she'd seen in the southern Appalachians when her Papá had taken her and Abuela to the mountains of Tennessee one fall—the year her mother left.

Evie was surprised to find a Scottish woman running the place. Agnes was a tall, robust woman with long red hair pinned to the back of her head, a hospitable smile radiating from her rosy face. She wasn't at all how Evie had pictured her. But she seemed nice enough, so Evie took a leap and told her about the ordeal in the orchard. And then she told her about the grumpy boy she'd met there—hoping to clear herself of any wrongdoing.

"Oh, ye mean Oskar? Aye, the boy's a strange one." Agnes grumbled in that strangely affectionate way adults often complained about young people they cared about.

Above them, the faint strumming of guitar chords came to an abrupt halt. Agnes's bright green gaze followed the absence of sound to the rafters. Evie turned and looked above and behind her to a dark loft area.

The boy stood there, hands on the railing, looking down at them. Evie whirled back toward the counter, swallowing the nerves lurching up her throat. Agnes punched keys on the cash register, tallying the order.

"Does he speak English?" Evie asked, barely above a whisper.

Agnes glanced up again, and it took everything Evie had not to look back at him, too.

"Nay," she said as she bagged the sandwiches and jam. "How will ye be paying?"

"Oh." Evie fumbled with her wallet. "Do you take cards?"

"Surely do." Agnes gave her a polite nod as she took the Visa. Evie gave in to temptation and peeked up and over her shoulder again while Agnes swiped her card. He was gone.

Evie had lots of questions for Agnes, but the nervous energy made her mind go blank. "So are you sure you don't mind if I paint in the orchard?" *Stall. Think.*

Agnes glanced down at Evie's card as she handed it back. "I said it was fine, didn't I, Miss Perez? Customers are welcome back anytime." An exasperated grin pulled her wrinkles away from her starched collar.

"Oh, good. It's just that your orchard is an artist's dream. I don't think I've ever been so inspired," Evie babbled. "After I had the pie, I knew I had to see this place. The cherries are really delicious, too." Evie searched every corner of the shop, taking it all in, wondering where he went.

"Yes, dear. Matter o' fact, here are some fresh cherries to take with ye. On the house. We have lots of them." Agnes reached under the counter, hands coming out with a small plastic bag full of cherries.

"Oh, wow. Thanks. That's very kind of you." Evie took the bag. As she turned to go, the floorboards above creaked, someplace just beyond her line of sight.

"Come back and see us, lass," Agnes called.

Evie nodded. *Oh, don't worry*, she thought. *I definitely will.*

TWELVE
Oskar's Journal

The wall fits coolly against my back.
Agnes's voice nags at me the moment the door closes.
Care to come out of hiding and tell me what that was about?
I step to the catwalk again and look down.
Not r-r-really.
Crossing my arms, I prop my elbows on the railing.
People decide who you are whether you tell them or not.
I don't plan to give her ammunition
to feel sorry for me.
Bonny lass. Surely ye noticed.
I won't dignify rhetoricals with an answer.
Where's the fearless boy Maggie always spoke of?
Don't plan on talkin' to her?
She asked about ye.
I resent the third degree
and the way she brings up my mamma
when she's trying to manipulate me.
Tha-tha-tha-thanks for not telling her.
I'm grateful for that, at least.
Isn't mine to tell, lad.
Agnes pins me in place with her trademark grimace.
She'll be back, you know.

Which is her fault.
Maybe if Agnes knew
what had been in that painting,
she'd be less inclined to hand out open invitations
to the entitled American girl.
I don't want company while I work.
I leave the conversation
and head back to my room.
When the embarrassment passes, the cherries await ye.
My neck tingles with heat,
either from leftover anger,
or the way her *rassin*[1] looked
in those jeans.
Channel it into the song, I tell myself.
So I pick up the guitar
open up my veins
and bleed music
over the strings.

---

[1] rassin (**ras-sin**): [Icelandic] *ass*

THIRTEEN
Evie

*E*vie waited a couple of days before she dug in to the goodies from Grimmurson's.

She'd wanted to prolong the reward. And part of her wanted to wait to enjoy them with Papá. No such luck there. She'd kept herself busy inhaling books and taking walks around the guesthouse property, not wanting to stray too far in case her papá came back and wanted to spend time with her. But she'd barely seen him for more than five minutes each day, and she fell asleep each night thinking *quizás mañana*.

Tomorrow was here again, and she had nothing but the food to keep her company. Everything she bought from the store had same ingredient: pure culinary magic. Roasted ham with cherry glaze on open-faced bread made her taste buds squeal with delight. She gobbled it up with a quickness that made her regret not savoring it.

So she ate half of the one she bought for Papá, too.

It wasn't like he'd be home any time soon. Besides, she waited three whole days on him. He came and went while she was sleeping most days. And she'd barely eaten anything since they arrived in Iceland. The cherries were addictive. The leftover pie sat in the fridge—and she spent the afternoon fighting the urge to cut a slice and eat it, too. If she didn't watch it, she'd be a

Sea World sideshow by the time she got back to Florida. Her mother's voice taunted her still.

Eat more carrots, less chips. Move your ass, Evie. Jog.

You aren't wearing that, are you? It looks like a tent.

I guess you got all the Cuban genes.

Thank God for that last one. The more she could separate herself from Rhona, the better.

Despite all her distraction techniques—Netflix binges being first and foremost when the Wi-Fi was cooperating—Evie couldn't stop thinking about being in the orchard. She had become mildly obsessed with running into the boy again, now that she knew he wasn't being rude. He simply hadn't understood her. Maybe now that her expectations were different, she could get some kind of reading on him. Find out how old he was, what he liked, and if he was kind, like Miss Izzy predicted.

Oskar. She liked the way his name sissed past her lips. Like a little sizzle.

She packed up her supplies and made the haul over the hills, through the fence, and into the orchard, breaking a sweat from the weight of her supplies. A briny sea breeze brushed her skin as she weaved a path through dappled sunlight, looking for the perfect spot to set up her canvas. She searched beneath the branches for a few minutes before she invariably found her way back up to the far side of the orchard, to the sense of kinship she felt in the shade of that single tree.

As she lounged against the fencepost and set up her easel, another inexplicable image burned itself into the recesses of her mind.

Her process sometimes began with a song. She'd see a picture the lyrics painted, sketch it, and then she'd listen to the music on repeat until the painting was done. But something different was happening now, something she couldn't pin down or explain. The image was already in her mind somehow. Loud and ever-present through the silence, it was like a borrowed memory, stored in a drawer of her brain. Instead of controlling the scene, the scene controlled her.

Time escaped her as she did a quick sketch and then translated it to canvas.

Beneath her paintbrush, a young boy with golden-blond hair huddled in the shadow of a cherry tree, much smaller than the ones surrounding her. His legs were crossed, his elbows propped on his knees, and his chin rested between dirty palms. He was waiting for something. What, she had no idea.

FOURTEEN

Oskar's Journal

I was stupid to think
she wouldn't have the guts to come back
just because several days have passed.
As I swing my arm, the empty metal bucket smacks against
    my leg.
I tell myself it's something I always do.
Which is completely untrue.
I just want her to hear me.
I glimpse a red blob between branches.
The side of a slouchy red beret.
I take a tentative step.
Her bottom lip lies trapped between her teeth,
dark eyes pinch ever so slightly,
as if she's staring at a glare
from the shade.
She sits
poised as a statue,
her wrist the only movable joint.
Come here to harass me some more?
she asks without looking up,
scrunching her nose.
I jump

at the sound of her voice.
So irritating
I almost laugh.
I bite the inside of my cheek instead.
The song plays so loud in my head now
my lips itch to put words with it.
Maybe I could sing her a song,
    start this whole thing over.

FIFTEEN
Evie

"The lady who owns the store said I was welcome here, in case you're wondering." Evie said it with way more confidence than she felt.

The words were still coming out wrong, though. Too defensive. He intimidated the hell out of her. His air of mystery left her filling in too many blanks. Broody Icelandic boy who worked for a Scottish woman and didn't speak English. Her pulse galloped in her throat, remembering the way Miss Izzy had said it. *A hahnd-some boy. Si. Muy guapo. Muy amable.*

Never mind that Miss Izzy was tweaking out on God-knew-what almost every time Evie stopped in to bring her a load of cookies or pastelitos. Abuela had been on a mission to bring the pseudo psychic to Jesus, so she sent her plates of baked goods regularly by way of Evie once she'd started having directional blunders and couldn't make the nine-block trek to and from Miss Izzy's place herself.

Oskar propped his ladder against a tree adjacent to her and hooked the bucket around his forearm, ignoring her as he climbed. She pretended she wasn't watching him from the corner of her eye. He reached through the fronds, plucking the ripest cherries in the bunch with a methodical cadence. Evie couldn't tell if he noticed her or even cared. The uncertainty crawled under her skin and burrowed there.

"Oh, so you hum but you don't talk? How charming," she said, shooting for flippancy. Maybe he wouldn't understand her words, but tone transcended languages. Evie put her brush down and stretched her back, placing her hands behind her on the damp ground.

Her fingers tripped over something cold and smooth. Turning, she found a rectangular rock, engraved with a somewhere-in-her-brain familiar symbol.

She felt the warmth of his gaze through the branches and it distracted her. She twisted her body around and stood, then walked to the base of the tree where he worked. Abuela would tell her to face her fear head-on. *Sé valiente.* It was time to confront this irrational intimidation factor.

Evie watched him as he filled the bucket more quickly, Adam's apple bobbing in his throat. She concentrated on the plunk of the cherries against galvanized steel and waited. He climbed down and hooked the ladder around his left shoulder, chewing furiously on a wad of gum.

"What is your deal?" she asked him. "Can you not understand me at all?" How did he communicate with Agnes?

He said nothing. There was no indication he could understand her, so she decided to be brave and test it.

"So, would you like to model for me or what? I can do a full nude this time." Evie giggled and heat painted cherries on her cheeks as she twirled her paintbrush between her fingers. It was so freeing to be able to say whatever she wanted. "Go ahead and strip down. I'll wait." She crossed her arms, heart beating in her throat.

Oskar froze, staring at the tree's bark, and she thought she detected a change in his breathing. It could've been her imagination, probably was. But when he turned to face her, his stormy eyes flashed with something mischievous.

He took a step forward, into her bubble of personal space, her comfort zone. She could've reached out and touched any part of him. The dimple in his left cheek twinkled. He studied her like a piece of art, starting with her feet and stopping only once he reached her face. His lips parted, and she breathed a whiff of spearmint.

Time left them there, locked in a gaze, as it moved on without them. Nobody had ever looked at her like that, much less for so long. She forgot what she'd even asked. Abuela told Evie once that body language was the most important language. *It will tell you all of the things a person isn't saying,* nieta. *If words are kind but the face isn't smiling, the person is being insincere.*

She tried to decide what his body language said in this moment, since there were no words to compare it to. His chest rose and fell under his dark t-shirt in even, calculated breaths. His feet planted firmly to the ground, shoulder-length apart. Hands clutched white-knuckled—*nervous?*—around the ladder and bucket, and his gaze sizzled against her retinas, unflinching. She remembered from a book she once read that more than ten seconds of direct eye contact meant the person either wanted to screw you or kill you.

She couldn't think straight enough to decide which one she wanted it to be.

SIXTEEN
Oskar's Journal

Never once has a girl so brazenly flirted with me.
But that's because all the girls I know
have heard me speak.
This is a different situation entirely.
Because I can be whoever she's already decided I am.
The intensity in her eyes worries me, though.
Like she's already too close to the truth.
When she looks at me like this,
it's like she can pick apart my life
with her inquisitive smile.
Like the universe
may tell her
whatever she wants to know
because it's just as brainwashed
by the way stolen cherries
stain her mouth
as I am.
And yet I'm drawn to it.
I try to recover
But even the strings inside my head
are broken now.
I retreat from her stare

and turn my attention to her painting.
It hits me then.
The past bombards me.
A little boy that looks just like Ivan
hunches at the foot of my tree
in her painting.
My lungs stop budging,
even under the pressing need for air.
The wild cowlick at the crown of his head
makes his cottony hair stand up.
His elbows are rusty
as an old spigot.
So real.
So alive.
So perfect.
I expect to hear
our mother yelling
from inside the painting
to come in, wash up for dinner.
On his feet are the little black boots
he was wearing the day of the accident.
Agnes and I found one of them
in the field next to the road
when we returned
to the crash site
weeks later.
I swallow
the ball of knives
wedged in my throat
and wonder
how
this girl knows
about my dead brother.

SEVENTEEN
Evie

*E*vie had seen a lot of weird things since she'd arrived in this foreign land: sheep wandering down paved roads, food with eyeballs intact, glaciers touching volcanoes.

And all of that was before she'd even left the airport. But what she saw now in the boy's expression took the prize for strangest.

His eyes resembled thick storm clouds, even more so with the moisture brimming in them. She made a mental note to learn how to say *What did I do now?* in Icelandic. Emotion darkened his face for a few moments as he looked back and forth between her painting and her face. Evie's chin quivered and she clamped her teeth shut, at a loss.

"What? Is it that bad?"

But he turned his back and retreated, climbing a tree further away. His boots stomped the rungs with more force than necessary.

He'd crept onto her canvas before she ever met him. Something irrational made her wonder if the young boy in the painting was him when he was little. Maybe she had some kind of weird, dreamy insight into his life and it made him uncomfortable. The resemblance was undeniable.

"Why are you stomping?" She mimicked his motions, hoping to establish some line of communication. Little flickers of chilly dirt sprayed the tops of her feet.

No response. The dribble of cherries got quieter as the bucket filled.

With a resigned sigh, she sank to the ground and returned to her painting. She touched up the foreground with a few of the cottony-looking dandelions she'd noticed growing near the water's edge, then brushed wisps of clouds in the sky.

Sadness trickled over her skin like a slow-starting rain.

Her paintings always conveyed the emotion of a scene, the way she felt when she heard a certain song. The ones she wanted to paint, anyway. The ones she painted as assignments all had the same flat, heartless void. Maybe that's why she'd never received anything better than mediocre marks on the art she was forced to create. She spent too much time comparing her work to others, trying to cover up her brushstrokes. That's what had happened with the self-portrait. She blended and blended until it didn't look like her at all. *Be honest about the flaws,* her art teacher had said, making an example of her in class. When she brought that assignment home, Papá had applauded it—because he thought it was a portrait of Abuela.

That's why she didn't want to go to art school, no matter how many times Papá had mentioned it. Only her original compositions, the ones made under the spell of music, were worthy of a second look. She had to want to create something in order to make it beautiful.

Things were different in this orchard, though. Staring at her work now, she didn't need the measures of a chorus to know that, if this scene had been based on a song, it would've been a sad one.

When Oskar moved to another tree, she'd had enough of the silent treatment. She stood up, gathered her things, and moved them to the base of his ladder. She waited until he met her gaze before she sat down again. Just because he didn't speak English didn't mean they couldn't communicate.

"Do you know something about my painting?" She pointed and gave him an exaggerated shrug.

His gray eyes narrowed and his jaw tensed. His lips tightened into a straight line as he returned to plucking. She waited, as though the spell would suddenly be broken and he'd talk back to her. The tattoo on his arm clenched and expanded under his t-shirt sleeve with the movement of his arm, like hieroglyphics in motion. Three lowercase i's leaned into one another, surrounded by a circle.

Evie blinked. "Your tattoo! It's the same symbol from the rock. That's where I've seen it before."

Nothing. Not even a grunt. He wasn't going to try.

Fine. Maybe she would do all the talking for a change.

EIGHTEEN
Oskar's Journal

I thrash around in the jaws of a trap.
Agnes must have sent her to pester me.
My aunt is always reminding me
of the things I should be doing.
Be more social and make some friends, Oskar.
Stop isolating yourself from the world, Oskar.
That's easy for her to say.
Since I can remember
I've made people uncomfortable.
When I lost my family, things got worse.
Their expressions say what their lips don't:
Poor, motherless boy.
Fatherless boy.
Brotherless boy.
Can't even string a sentence together.
My peers won't look me in the eye.
I've only ever had one friend,
and friend is a loose term.
It's more of a business arrangement.
Maybe I like that you don't talk to me,
she calls to my back.
Taunting.

Paranoia creeps up.
Does she know I'm faking?
The painful accuracy of her painting tugs at me.
I want to look at it again and see my perfectly rendered little
 brother,
as real on her canvas as the leaves beneath my fingers.
But there's no way she could know about Ivan
unless Agnes told her.
She talks as she paints,
refusing to take my hints to shut up.
Boys who talk never say the right thing, anyway.
Of course not, princess.
That's what I want to say,
in a smooth, devil-may-care way.
Impossible, of course.
This guy back home kissed me
before I left to come here.
And do you know what he said before he did it?
She shudders to herself.
I wanna taste you.
My hands tighten around the bucket handle.
Can you believe that?
Maybe I wanted to kiss him
until he opened his mouth,
but that killed it.
I try to picture her kissing someone
but stop the exercise immediately when I realize
I can only picture her kissing me.
Because seriously, where the hell did he get that?
A dollar store erotica novel?
She cuts her eyes up at me.
I've stopped picking cherries to listen.
I didn't let it go further.
Got in my car and drove off.

Pretty sure he's banging my best friend now.
So it's probably for the best.
She shrugs like she doesn't care.
But it's obvious that she does.
Hopefully he got to know her
before making her part of his daily calorie intake.
Zip-It and Bitchface, sitting in a tree.
I have no idea what she's talking about.
She drops her paintbrush in her water bottle
and wipes remnant reds and greens
on her jeans
as I descend the ladder.
I want to tell her not to ruin those jeans.
Those perfect jeans.
But maybe she has more.
Maybe all jeans hug her body
the way the stupid parts of me want to.
So I guess you're done now?
She eyes my bucket.
I glance down.
It's full.
About-facing,
I turn toward the barn.
Irritated with myself for lingering
and allowing her to notice.

NINETEEN
Evie

An email from her mother waited for Evie when she got back to the guesthouse.

Evie, I've been trying to reach you via video chat. We need to discuss plans for the school year. Ping me when you get this message.

Yeah, no thanks. She'd already told her she wasn't interested in going to the Magnet Arts Academy in New York City before she and Papá had ever left Florida. If Papá's travel schedule kept him out of the states by September and prevented her from returning to school at Saint Bart's, she'd just emancipate herself or something. No way in holy hell would she start over somewhere else her senior year.

And with her mother, of all people!

This was the woman who had different eyes and hair and nose from her. This white lady, who everyone always assumed had adopted Evie out of the goodness of her heart, when that was anything but the case. Evie never would've believed she'd come from her if her papá hadn't watched her emerge with his own eyes.

She'd lived to criticize her. She'd reminded Evie, on nearly a daily basis, of all the ways in which she was lacking. Her cruelty refueled itself on her daughter's silent pain. Despite all this,

Rhona had some kind of inescapable hold on her until the summer when Evie turned thirteen—when everything changed for good.

Since she'd finally wrestled free of her mother's resentful grasp, she had no reason to ever want to be near it again.

Evie lounged on her bed and ate the pilfered cherries she'd collected. Why not, right? She spent the day blathering to a strange foreign boy who couldn't care less about her company, she was hallucinating subjects for her paintings, and Papá wasn't back—as usual—so she figured she might as well eat her feelings.

Her feelings turned into another sketch, and then a painting as the evening stretched on, unending daylight streaming through her window. It materialized on the canvas, so potent with melancholy she could hardly remember she was the painter instead of the subject under her brush.

A woman kneeled, facing her. Long strands of penny-red hair blew around the woman's young, rosy face. Her green eyes twinkled, either from sadness or hope—those two things were always so hard for Evie to differentiate—and she reached toward something off canvas, something that'd sit right in Evie's spot. Rich, dark soil caked her fingernails and speckled her hands and forearms. Loamy piles of it clumped at her knees.

Evie thought maybe the woman was digging.

How could it be that she didn't know for sure? Once again, the scene had turned Evie into a marionette, painting its every command. She put the finishing touches in the background—rolling hills, a body of water, and a distant lighthouse behind her on the horizon. It was then she realized that it was background scenery from the orchard, except without the cherry trees.

But what was this woman digging? What do people dig when they're sad? A thought tugged at Evie.

A grave.

Chills spread over Evie's arms, all the way up to her ears. She didn't like thinking about graves or dying or death. It always led her back to the certainty that she'd outlive Abuela. Age was a cruel thing. Abuela was getting older now, within a decade of normal human life expectancy. Give or take. Evie tried to push the fear away, but in the silence of a room that wasn't even hers, she couldn't shut it out.

Thousands of miles away, Abuela was trapped in an assisted-living apartment. She saw nobody but the nurse who came to deliver her meds twice a day and occasionally her neighbor, who rolled an oxygen tank between hacking coughs. *Clunk clunk clunk* over the floorboards, the noise carried through the walls. Evie grimaced at the memory of that sound, of the lost freedom it represented.

Abuela no longer baked pastelitos for her Little Havana neighborhood. Evie wondered if the neighborhood kids still lounged around on the porch of her empty house, dripping the fillings of somebody else's kitchen creations on their shirts.

Abuela no longer played dominoes with the *hermanitas* from the Fifth Street parish. She no longer took walks to Miss Izzy's to hand-deliver baked goods. She no longer spent hours listening to Bob Marley, or cooking in the dingy little kitchen, or painting with her granddaughter. She'd been stripped of her identity and locked away, because nobody was home to look out for her.

The weekend before Evie left for Iceland, which was also the weekend before they'd moved Abuela into the retirement village, the two of them had sat on the porch painting pictures of the ocean, with "High Tide or Low Tide" playing on repeat—a rare warm weather session. Bugs swarmed around the porch light, and the two swatted at them when they'd perch on their skin, damp from the Miami heat that never let up, even after dark. *Look at me,* nieta, *I'm a regular Picasso!* Abuela exclaimed after a failed attempt at a seagull made her give up and fling a blob of paint on the canvas to cover the mistake. The two of them had melted into pools of sweat and giggles. Things were as fine as they'd ever been.

Evie vehemently disagreed with Papá's decision to put her in assisted living. It's not like the original incident had been that big a deal in the first place. Abuela had simply gone for a walk one day and got turned around, lost her way back home. It happened to people all the time. Abuela's sense of direction just wasn't what it once was. And the fact that it got dark that one particular time made it worse.

But then it happened a second time. And then a third.

They'd tried to convince her to stop taking walks alone, but Abuela was the independent type. She had to be. She'd been dropped in the country in 1960, barely a teenager, on Operation Pedro Pan. She didn't know a soul when her feet touched American soil, nor a single syllable of English. She'd found her way then. She always found her way.

Guilt tugged at Evie, though. They'd left her there, just like Abuela's parents did—and for reasons much less valid than escaping a communist regime. *Abuela forgets things*, Papá had said. But how could they expect her to remember anything, when all evidence suggested she herself had been forgotten?

Evie couldn't lose Abuela. The only times she really felt like she knew herself was on that porch swing, or in her faded yellow kitchen. It was the only time she was somewhat okay with the way her parents always had better things to do than spend time with her, even when she was just a little kid.

"Evie?"

She whirled around, breathing in the scent of the frigid evening air Papá brought with him. She had been so lost in her sadness she hadn't heard him open the door.

"Are you crying? What's wrong, *mija*?"

A moment later she was curled against the stiff cold clinging to his coat, face pressed hard into a button that would surely leave an imprint on her forehead. His hug almost wrung out all the borrowed sadness from her canvas.

"Evie, your paintings! *Espléndido!*" The exclamation was enough to slow her tears. Excitement blew his words wide open, stamping everything she'd done with his endorsement. "Look at the detail." He let her go and stepped closer to get a better look. "Which song is this from? Tell me so I can listen." His eyes flashed with investment.

Evie wiped her tears and cleared her throat. She hated how much she needed this approval. "It isn't from a song. I might've seen it somewhere before, I don't know."

"These are fantastic." His eyes played between the woman on her knees and the boy in the orchard. She'd had the good sense to put her first painting in the closet and cover it with a blanket. No way could she risk him seeing that one.

"I'm sorry you're sad, Evie. But this—*es temporal.*" He gripped her shoulders and forced her to face him. His tired eyes shimmered with relief. "This is good, though. I'm glad you're painting again."

Evie nodded, another tear slipping from between her lashes. "I miss Abuela."

"Listen, *mija,*" Papá said, voice brimming bright with optimism. "I know you miss her, but she'll be so excited to see these paintings when we go to visit her."

Visit implied she'd always be locked away. Under surveillance. Evie clamped her trembling lips together, pressing both hope and rebellion back down her throat. "When we get back home, you mean? When things go back to normal?"

All the times he'd tried to talk her into moving to New York with her mother gave her little reassurance that things would ever really go back to normal. He smoothed his expression and took an even, careful breath.

"This will all be behind us in a couple of months. Just remember that." When he nodded, his black-rimmed glasses slid down the bridge of his nose. "I'm so proud of you. Abuela will be too. Why don't we try to video chat with her this weekend? I'll call her nurse and get her to help set it up, okay?"

The thought of seeing Abuela and talking to her eased all of the worry and heartache in an instant. She couldn't just call her at will here—thanks to the time difference and the lack of an international phone—and maybe that was part of the problem. Evie nodded so hard it made her dizzy. "Yes, Papá. I'd really love that."

He was proud of her. And they were going to talk to Abuela. That was enough for now.

TWENTY
Oskar's Journal

Meddlesome adults
are a recurring theme in my life.
So it's no surprise when Agnes tells me
Edvin Jonsson came by to see me.
I was at Bjorn's playing music,
I tell her.
Which is partly true.
I don't tell her I went to Bjorn's
because I saw Edvin's truck parked out front.
School is no longer required for me since I turned seventeen.
And regardless of my old teacher's dreams for me,
I don't share his vision.
He wants me to go to a conservatory
in America or Europe or even Reykjavik.
But leaving this orchard
means forgetting what used to be here,
what's still here,
in the orchard and the lighthouse.
To change the subject,
I hurl the accusation at her
I've been sitting on for days.
I did no such thing!

Agnes's voice pounds the walls
like an angry fist.
The echoes careen across the surface
of the glass jars on the shelves,
causing a barely audible
high-pitched shriek.
Her adamant denial doesn't convince me.
In fact, it makes me even more certain
she's full of shit.
Let's be honest, though, Oskar.
Ye need motivation like the orchard needs rain.
Ever since the girl's been comin' 'round,
you've been playing again.
Of course that's what this is about.
She feels indebted to my mamma,
believes it's her responsibility to make me chase dreams
I don't even have anymore.
Look, if you don't want to talk to the girl,
don't talk to her!
She scowls, ripping her apron off the counter
and tying it on with furious fingers.
But don't be accusin' me of playing Cupid.
I've got more important things on me mind
than your love life.
Her assumptions just piss me off more.
I never said anything about a love life.
I want to ask her
how else the girl could know about Ivan.
Did she show her a picture?
I can't bring myself to ask.
Even holding my brother's name
on the tip of my tongue
conjures tears.
I can't lose it in front of Agnes.

She's never been the affectionate type.
She's nothing like my mamma was.
But the sight of a nearly grown man
crying over his dead family
might be enough
to make her clasp me
against her bosom and smother me
with an uncomfortable hug.
And, well,
that's a scene I'd care to avoid.
It wouldn't be the worst thing, Agnes says,
if you had a friend besides that hooligan Bjorn!
I don't tell her Bjorn isn't really my friend.
I just buy *gras*[2] from him.
Instead of yelling,
I shove another piece of gum past my teeth
to keep my mouth busy.
I want to tell her
to stop trying to manipulate me.
But the bell on the door
interrupts the words that won't come out.

---

[2] gras (**grass**): [Icelandic] *marijuana*

TWENTY-ONE

Evie

*E*vie's determined march into the storefront was met with sudden hushed silence.

Agnes jerked her head toward the intrusion, a red blush crawling out of her starched white collar and lighting her round face ablaze. She grabbed a rolling pin off the shelf behind her.

"Mornin' to ye," she barked.

"Hi," Evie said in a pipsqueak voice. Oskar's gaze met hers across shelves of homemade jams a nanosecond before he diverted his attention to the crate in front of him. He stacked glass jars, either pretending not to notice her or ignoring her entirely.

The tension in the air hung thicker than geyser steam.

Evie got the distinct impression she'd interrupted something important. Some Icelandic conversation they could've continued speaking in her presence, and she'd never have known the difference. She had no real reason to be here. But her curiosity had kept her on a leash lately. Questions had swarmed her brain for days. She'd barely slept.

The warm, tart aroma of a cherry dish swam through the air, and she inhaled it. Her mouth watered. She strolled the aisles, every footstep an amplified thud against the wood floor in the quiet space. As she pretended to browse, working up her courage to ask Agnes some questions, she lifted jars of jam and salsa, reading ingredients on the labels.

It was then that she noticed the logo on all the product labels—the same as the symbol on the rock beneath the tree, and the tattoo on Oskar's arm. She opened her mouth to say something, and then closed it again. Oskar must be more connected to this place than she'd originally thought, or else he really loved his job. Evie strolled along the side wall, until she noticed a framed poem hanging next to the orchard door. Again—the same familiar logo inscribed the top.

Bless this orchard
As we sow
Limbs and bark of
Ev'ry row.

From midsummer
To Samhain[3]
Gestate cherries
Red from green.

Take blood and sweat
For ripened fruit
Our sacrifice
And gratitude.

---

[3] Samhain (**saa-ween**): *a Gaelic festival marking the end of the harvest season and the beginning of the darker half of the year.*

Evie pulled her attention away from the framed poem and glanced back at Oskar. He worked diligently to unload products, seemingly oblivious to her presence.

"Looking for anything in particular?" Agnes eyed her as she dipped her hands in flour and rolled dough, a puff of white making a cloud above her workspace.

Answers. She wanted to know why she felt such a connection to this place. Why the woman she'd painted looked like a younger version of Agnes. Why the boy she'd painted in the orchard looked like a younger version of Oskar. Why she'd painted Oskar before ever meeting him. Why, after being in the orchard, she suddenly had no control over her muse.

She'd prayed to Saint Dymphna, patron saint of nut bags, hoping for a little mental clarity. But being a little less devout than Abuela left her with disappointing results. Before she dialed up Miss Izzy in Miami and tried to tap into her shaky Santeria, Evie had decided to do the most logical thing: Ask.

"Actually," she said, setting the jar back on the shelf, "I have a question about the orchard."

Agnes cocked a copper brow.

How was she supposed to word this without sounding like a complete lunatic? An idea blossomed as she glanced at the sign in front of the counter.

Fresh-picked cherries available, priced by the kilogram.

"I was wondering if I could maybe pick some of my own cherries," she ad-libbed. "My father took me to an apple orchard in Tennessee a few years ago, and we picked our own apples." She'd loved that trip and her connection to the place as she'd picked fresh fruit.

Agnes's forehead rumpled. She dropped the dough on a wooden board and slapped her hands across her apron, then bent down in a heave behind the counter. She came up with a silver metal bucket, like the one Oskar had been carrying. She outstretched the bucket to Evie, but it swung in the air between them.

"I'm not sure I'd know how to pick the ripest ones though. I mean, surely it's different than apples. Could you—"

"Pay attention to the color, lass. Darker means riper." Agnes cut her eyes at Oskar, then back to her. "Pick from any tree but the one next to the back fence at the top of the hill."

Evie opened her mouth to ask why not that tree, but shut it again. She didn't want to admit she'd already been picking those. "Maybe you could show me?" Evie batted her eyelashes, innocent as she could manage. If she could buy just a few minutes of Agnes's time, she would ask her some questions once they got in the orchard.

The bell on the door clanged and a group of young patrons poured in, clad in backpacks, laughing among themselves.

"Sorry, lass. I'm the captain of this vessel. Oskar can show ye, though." She looked over Evie's shoulder and clenched her jaw, then said something incoherent, heavy on ys and ks. Icelandic, Evie assumed.

Glancing behind her, Evie noticed Oskar's disgruntled expression before he could smooth his frown. He mumbled something, then shoved his empty crate into a corner and headed toward the orchard. His reaction sent ripples of panic through her. He made her nervous enough as it was. She didn't want to be reluctantly babysat by him.

"But I don't speak Icelandic," Evie blurted.

Agnes stuck one finger in the air, then retreated around the counter to a little section in the back of the shop with souvenirs and books and framed pictures. Plucking a small blue volume off the shelf, she marched over and handed Evie the book.

Icelandic-English/English-Icelandic Dictionary

The little blue hardback shivered in Evie's icy hands.

"Won't be perfect," Agnes said with a smirk, "but it should help ye understand each other. Go on now."

Agnes placed her heavy hands on Evie's shoulders and spun her toward the side door where Oskar waited, arms crossed against his broad chest, chomping the life out of his gum. You'd think she'd told him to potty train a puppy instead of escort a girl through an orchard. *Geesh. Pout much?*

She swallowed the lump in her throat. It left a bitter after-taste.

"Don't look so miserable," Evie grumbled as she breezed out the door past him, bucket in one hand, translation dictionary in the other. "I didn't come here to talk to you, anyway."

TWENTY-TWO
Oskar's Journal

But talk is exactly what she does.
Nonstop.
It's like nobody has ever listened to the girl
for as long as she's lived
and she's just discovered
I can hear her.
It's infuriating.
Agnes forced this little rendezvous
not five minutes
after denying she'd ever do it.
Deep down,
I know she means well.
All these years
she's been telling me I need to let them go.
She worries about me
and my coping skills
or lack thereof.
I get that.
But she's no shrink.
And I'm not her.
I deal with things in my own way.
So let's get to business,

Evelyn says.
The wind paints her golden face
light pink at her cheekbones.
My traitorous heart sputters
like a pönk[4]
as I hoist the ladder
from the side of the barn.
Feel free to take your shirt off, she says.
My feet stutter across the ground
and she lifts an eyebrow.
I force my face calm,
oblivious,
and hope it's working.
Do not react, I remind myself.
She is just a girl.
An entitled American girl.
Who cares?
She steps ahead of me,
hips tilting like a see-saw
as she moves.
Suddenly my zipper is tight.
Me.
I care.
When she blows a dark tendril of hair
out of her eyes
I catch a whiff of her shampoo
and have to hold my breath.
Which means meddlesome Agnes is winning.
Her flip-flops crunch the pebbles
on the dirt trail between the trees.
The girl has no real shoes.
I force my pupils down

---

[4] pönk (**punk**): [Icelandic] *punk*

down
down
to her heels
as I climb the hill behind her
(even though they keep trying to sneak back up).
She ducks under a low-hanging branch
next to the fence surrounding my tree.
The bucket slides down her fingers
as she drops it on the ground with a clang.
She chews her lip,
flipping through the translation dictionary.
I can't believe
the length at which
I've let this go on.
I should just tell her now.
Play for her on broken strings.
Watch her go.
Because that's all it would take
to foil Agnes's plan.
But every time
I part my lips and try,
I'm paralyzed with reluctance.
Because I don't want her to go, stupid as that is.
My brain knows this will never work,
but my body isn't getting the message.
I crave this confusion
I feel when I'm near her,
though there's nothing
I can do about it.
She stops on a page and narrows her eyes.
I look away and focus on a red-throated loon
preening in a nearby puddle,
more sure of itself
than I'll ever be around this girl.

Pro-ska-dur?
she tries to enunciate.
Ripe.
She tries twice more,
playing with the syllable stresses.
The words roll around in her mouth, at home
even though she's saying it wrong.
Þroskaður.
Can you tell me which ones are ripe?
Pro-ska-dur?
She points at the cherries dangling from the branch,
then to the words on the page.
I step closer to her
read the word over her shoulder
Silently.
The English word.
I play my game as she plays hers.
I know she knows how to find the ripe cherries.
Because she's already been plucking and eating them.
I give her a curt nod and prop my ladder against a tree,
returning a moment later with examples of each.
I trade her the cherries for the book.
Flip it over and search my brain
for the Icelandic words
for firm and soft,
dark and light.
I've spoken English
almost exclusively
since Agnes took over for my parents.
It was important to my father
that I know both languages.
My trouble talking
didn't change his expectations.
Speech has always been difficult for me.

But it got worse after the accident.
When I lost them, I stopped trying.
I ran out of things to say.
I point to the words when I find them.
She points at the ripe cherries.
These are ripe?
Faked innocence.
Impressive poker face.
She's so full of shit!
A grin sneaks across my lips
without my permission.
She smiles back.
I forget what we're doing.
We stand here
grinning at each other like stoned cartoons
while the moment
s   t   r   e   t   c   h   e   s
too far.
I grab my ladder and turn to go,
dropping the dictionary on the ground.
Wait. Oskar.
My name on her lips
sounds different.
Musical.
Like some new chord
yet to be invented.
Somewhere between
A-minor and D-d-d-damn.
My muscles restrict,
tighten and lock down
before I let myself turn to face her.
I have one more question.
Her dark hair cloaks her shoulders
as she bends to retrieve the book.

She flips pages while walking backward,
beckoning me to follow with a nod.
I have no choice but to obey.
Well.
I have a choice.
But the part of my brain
storing that information
is inaccessible
right now.
She stands next to my tree
and points at the rock.
The one Agnes placed there
the day we scattered their ashes.
What does it mean?
Her curiosity adds smoky depth
to eyes so beautiful
I want to change my favorite color to brown.
My ladder leans against the fence.
I've seen this symbol on your store labels, too.
And your tattoo.
It's the symbol for *awen.*
Describing its complexity is nearly impossible,
even if words came easily.
I take the book from her.
Tak-nid?
Symbol.
What's this taknid?
She points at the rock.
Then, reaching up, she touches my arm,
the matching tattoo.
I flinch,
not letting her linger.
She pulls her hand away slowly,
eyeing me for an answer.

Even if I could talk to her,
I wouldn't know how to explain it.
Silly superstition or not,
it meant something to my mother.
So I bit into a leather belt
while a miscreant tattoo artist
who smelled like motor oil and whisky
dragged the burning ink through my bicep.
Though the English word for rune
is the same as the Icelandic
I flip through the book
for a distraction.
Brain all scrambled
by the explosion of adrenalin
her fingertips left in their wake.
I point.
Rune?
She scrunches her nose.
Like a pagan thing?
The rune has always been a comfort to me.
But under her judgmental gaze,
I'm just a superstitious *hálfviti.*[5]
Her American religion must be superior.
Suddenly the life is sucked from everything between us.
Birds stop singing.
An eerie stillness falls over the trees.
We both look around,
notice the absence of sound
simultaneously.
Blink. Blink. Blink.
When the reality of what's coming sinks in,
it's too late to get back to the barn.

---

[5] hálfviti (**hal-vee-tee**): [Icelandic] *imbecile, half-wit.*

Blink.
The ladder vibrates and totters next to her.
She turns her startled gaze toward it.
Earth rumbles under our feet,
at first gentle
but half a blink later
a nauseating wave.
There are a number of things I could yell to warn her.
Duck, for example.
Or *Earthquake*!
Instead, I dive on top of her
shielding her from falling branches
and the heavy wooden ladder
that whacks the side of my face
with skull-splitting force.
Good to know that
in a pinch
I sprout Thor's *eistu*[6]
and save the day.

---

[6] eistu (**ace-too**): [Icelandic] *testicles.*

TWENTY-THREE

Evie

*E*verything shook.

The ground. The sky. Evie's crumpled limbs. Even the hulking body blanketing her from falling debris tremored, a bone-deep rattle that rubbed against her with enough heat to ignite her clothes. It was an unnerving sort of friction she would definitely appreciate under different circumstances.

The earth seemed capable of vicious things, like it might gulp them up without warning. Evie had never experienced an earthquake before. Florida's worst natural disasters were hurricanes, but at least they usually gave notice.

Seconds stretched into minutes, and minutes stretched into some other unquantifiable period of time. When it was over, it seemed to have lasted only a blip. Moments slipped away before she could grab them. Oskar remained completely motionless on top of her, his neck pressed against her chin. Neither of them breathed until something warm and wet and sticky hit the side of Evie's face. Rain? Bird poop? When it dripped down to her hand, she gasped.

Blood.

Oskar looked down and met her eyes for one heart-stopping moment. He was slow to move, and when he sat up and climbed to his knees, Evie freed herself and understood why. The ladder and a heap of fallen branches lay strewn across his back. It would've all been on top of her if it hadn't been for him. That's when she saw the wound. Above his left eyebrow, a two-inch gash drizzled liquid richer and darker than the ripest cherries.

"You're bleeding!" Evie's voice scraped a layer of flesh out of her throat.

Oskar shook his head, waving her off, and wiped his brow with his shoulder and arm, which smeared a grisly streak across his tattoo. Like it was nothing. Like the earth got angry and threw things at him all the time. She started to protest, but Agnes's voice filled the orchard.

"Oskar!"

His eyes grew three times their normal size and he grabbed Evie's hand.

Grabbed. Her. Hand.

She couldn't even process the warmth in her fingers before they were running for the shop's side door, toward Agnes.

"Aftershocks!" she said, calm but loud. It was a warning, a declaration—spoken as if from years of experience. Oskar yanked Evie's hand so hard that a wave of pain ripped into her shoulder. He didn't let her go even as they darted inside and crouched against an exterior wall, behind the sofa in the sitting area of the shop.

His fingertips were callused, and their sandpaper texture moved against her knuckles in a nervous rhythm as they hunkered down. She stared at their joined hands before her gaze crept up to meet his. He let go when they did, and an indescribable cold settled into her.

Agnes dropped down beside Evie. "Are ye hurt?"

Her lip quivered, but she said nothing, still too shocked to absorb the last few minutes. She shook her head as the building rumbled again. Glass jars jangled against the wooden shelves. Some hopped off into the floor in a burst of crackling glass. Evie curled into the fetal position, thinking of her papá working outside. She whispered prayers to Saint Emigdio that the arctic earth hadn't pulled him into its grumbling belly. Her teeth chattered as fear and worst-case scenarios played like a horror movie reel on a lonely screen in her brain.

Rumbles squeezed through the building in waves, rising and falling like a fleeing tide. Evie stayed there for what could have been days, hiding in a dark corner behind her lids.

"Get up now, it's safe," Agnes said gently, sometime after the shaking had stopped. "It's over now."

She opened her eyes to the two of them staring down at her. They seemed to know for sure it was done. The ground beneath Evie wobbled still. It was that same sensation of sustained motion she always had after crawling off the big roller coaster at Busch Gardens with what was left of her sanity.

Oskar stood over her, holding an ice pack to his brow. He looked away as she stumbled to her feet. Mason jars lay ruined all over the floor. A bookshelf hunched on its side. Drawers behind the counter hung ajar. The only thing unmoved was the framed poem hanging behind her on the wall. Somehow, the building itself remained intact in the most un-compromised way.

"How do you know it's over?" She couldn't suppress her teeth chattering, even now.

Agnes sighed and nodded to Oskar, some unspoken conversation taking place before he took the stairs to the overhead loft. She wondered what lingered past the edge of darkness up there.

"We don't, lass. But we're used to them. The first one was a beastie, maybe close to a five, but the others weren't so bad." Agnes surveyed the damage in her shop. "Could've been worse. Come on, sit here." She led Evie around to the sofa with a firm grasp on her elbow. Evie's legs gave out just before she sank into the plush leather cushions.

Oskar appeared in the stairwell with a red blanket bunched over his arms. Agnes took it from him and draped it around Evie's shoulders. It smelled like something vaguely familiar. A

tangy scent she remembered smelling at odd times back home—
on country roads when they'd driven up to Tampa. In the girls'
locker room at Saint Bart's, when their fitness instructor had
sworn there was a skunk loose in the building. *Weed?* No matter—it was warm and she was shivering.

Agnes crouched, bright eyes shimmering with a maternal instinct that reminded Evie of Abuela. "Everything is fine, lass.
Stay as long as you like. I need to tend the mess."

She nodded, curling against the couch with the skunky blanket. She toured the rubbled shop with her eyes. In the back of the
store behind the couch, in the souvenir section, several small
paintings sat askew on their easels. Others littered the floor. All
of them were landscapes of the Icelandic countryside, each la-
beled with a location name she couldn't pronounce even if she
wanted to.

Agnes and Oskar cleaned up the aftermath, dancing around
cherry puddles full of glass. Evie stood and gathered the paintings from the floor, placing them on what looked like their
respective displays, glancing down at the artist's signature in the
bottom right corner. She replaced books and postcards, keeping
her hands busy as she tried to will her breathing to slow down.

Her distraction stopped working when the rain began pounding the glass doors of the shop. Evie returned to the fear of her
papá's whereabouts. If an earthquake hadn't interrupted his
work, the rain definitely would. She turned her head, focusing on
the books she placed back on the shelves. They were a mix of
Icelandic guides and volumes of Nordic and Celtic mythology,
with a few saga retelling novels tossed in. Once she was finished,
she stepped behind the counter with the cash register and began
tidying up all the cookbooks and supplies that had fallen.

When the bulk of the chaos in the shop had been tidied, Agnes commanded Oskar to the sink. He winced as she wiped his
brow with a wet cloth, cleaning dried blood out of his eyebrow

and hair. Evie peeked at them from the corner of her eye, not missing the tenderness in the way Agnes took care of his injury.

Why had he jumped on top of her like that?

She tried to remember that moment exactly, when she'd looked up at him. The sunlight made a halo around him—an Oskar-shaped eclipse towering over her—before he climbed to his knees and they both stood.

Oskar must have felt her watching him, because his gaze met hers with sudden determination.

"Hold still, ye difficult boy!" Agnes grumbled.

Evie risked another glance at him. The moment she did, he looked away.

Agnes smoothed a second butterfly bandage over his brow and grumbled something indecipherable.

As Evie replaced a cookbook with a leather cover, the yellowed pages started slipping out the bottom, and a piece of partially-folded parchment with blackened edges hit her knee. She set the cookbook down and picked up the page.

That same symbol was inscribed at the top.

Both symbol and words were a deep, dark red. As if they'd been written with ink made from the cherries themselves. She finished unfolding it and read the words, some of which she couldn't even pronounce.

O mór[7] *Alban Hefín*[8]

---

[7] Mór (**morrr**): [Gaelic] *great*
[8] Alban Hefín (***al*-bin *hef*-fin**): *druid specific word for summer solstice*

Lend us your draíocht[9]
with powers of awen[10]
engraved upon rock.

I scatter these ashes
on mourning tree roots
infuse here an essence:
their spirits through fruits.

May love here still flourish
And comfort our loss
By the otherworld's link
With harvest and blás.[11]

When sea winds blow gently
Through midsummer's veil
Preserve here the stories
While cherries tell tales.

May only the purest
Inspired eyes see
The memories kept here
By the Aisling tree.

Evie stared at the page, dumbfounded. *While cherries tell tales...* She read it again, trying to make sense of it. Was it a poem? The more she studied it, the closer she got to making out the word pronunciations with the rhyme scheme.

---

[9] draíocht (***dree*-oct**): [Gaelic] *druid magic*
[10] awen (***ah*-ooo-win**): [Gaelic] *druid symbol meaning poetic inspiration. Is used as a symbol for the order of druids.*
[11] blás (**bloss**): [Gaelic] *beauty through taste*

Before she could read it one more time, the page evaporated from her hand in one swift jerk. Evie startled and fell backwards on her butt. Agnes looked down at her briefly before folding the page and slipping it beneath the cash register. Evie wanted to ask her what it meant, but based on Agnes's mood shift, she felt like she should be apologizing instead of asking questions.

"Didn't mean to startle ye, lass. I've been looking for that." She brushed off her apron and fidgeted, not meeting Evie's eyes. "Oskar's going to take you back to your place—"

Evie got her balance. "Oh no." She stood, stretching herself shy of Agnes's height. "Really. I can walk myself back. I'm fine." The lie trembled on her lips. If it happened again, and she was alone... What if the earth started moving the moment she stepped into the orchard again? The fears upended her equilibrium. Some part of her hoped she could just huddle in the safety of the store until Papá showed up to get her.

"No arguing," Agnes insisted. "He'll drive you. It's become a *dreich* day. Terribly nasty out."

With a reluctant sigh, Evie walked behind Oskar out the glass shop doors, bell clanging behind her. He didn't so much as glance back at her, which made her feel silly for following. Maybe he didn't know he was supposed to be driving her back. She could just turn right and head down the road on foot instead. The rain pelted her skin with pinprick stings, and she realized how badly that walk would suck.

He opened the passenger door and looked up at her then, holding her gaze only a moment before looking away. He walked around and got in on the driver's side of the gray SUV.

Okay.

So he did know.

Evie climbed in, and the worn vinyl passenger seat chilled her backside. The vehicle was an older model of some Icelandic brand she'd never heard of. Spearmint gum wrappers polluted the cupholders, and the carpet reeked. Maybe the blanket had been in his car at some point, because it smelled just like it.

"Did you run over a skunk or something?" Evie asked, trying to lighten the mood, even if she was just talking to herself. Anything to call attention away from her rogue nerves. "Do you even have skunks in Iceland? Or are you a stoner?" She giggled nervously, but he ignored her. Being alone with him in an enclosed space was different than standing in the shop or the orchard, especially after The Earth Moving Incident.

Oskar put the car in gear. Little bits of dried blood flaked in the blond hair on his arm, across the tattoo peeking from under his tee shirt sleeve. Over the hum of the engine and the wet prickle of raindrops on the windshield, she listened to the gentle whoosh of his breathing. She tried to imagine what color his breath would be if she painted it. Green, maybe. Like his spearmint gum. She wished she could place her ear against his chest, so she could hear his heart too. She wanted to know if it was beating as fast as hers.

Stop thinking things like that, Evie.

The ride was much quicker than the walk over the hills separating the orchard from *Fryst Paradis.* "I'm all the way in the back." Evie pointed down the road into the dreary muck, relieved that her voice didn't shake. He seemed to understand the gesture. When his car slowed outside the little turf house that huddled in the side of the mossy hill, he nodded to it, eyebrows raised in question.

Evie gave him a weak smile and pointed. "That's it."

Her stomach sank with heavy disappointment as the car came to a stop. As she gripped the cold metal door handle, she gave herself permission to look at him. *Really* look at him. Something burned in his stormy eyes—some unrecognizable emotion just beneath the surface. It un-jarred a swarm of fireflies inside her, fluttering down her arms and legs.

"What you did today—" she paused for a sigh—"that's the swooniest thing a guy has ever done for me. Better than words. Better than a kiss, even. I know you don't know what I'm saying, but I just wanted to say thank you." She stressed the last two words, searching his face for any level of understanding. Surely he at least knew *thank you*.

"You're kind," she said. Fact. Unkind people didn't turn themselves into human shields for strangers. Miss Izzy was now two for three.

His cheeks deepened in color, but that could've been her imagination. Or the cold. He stared at her with the same disarming intensity for another moment before directing his gaze to the windshield. So much eye contact, but he always looked away first. The reflection of the windshield wipers moved in his pupils.

A dismissal?

"Anyway…" She tensed, squeezing the door handle and opening the door. She didn't look back as she slammed the door and ran to the front overhang. Stupid, senseless tears prickled her eyes as she shoved her key in the doorknob and stepped into an empty guesthouse. She peeked over her shoulder. Oskar's brake lights turned into tiny red streaks in the distance.

TWENTY-FOUR
Oskar's Journal

I leave Fryst Paradis and head home.
But when I see the white oversized truck
parked in front of the store again
I pass the barn and keep driving.
He must've come by to check on us,
make sure we are okay after the quake.
Though Edvin Jonsson is the only teacher
who ever tried to understand me,
the truth of it is,
my goals aren't the same as his.
I'm not sure I even have goals anymore.
Or if I want them.
I always make plans
when it's too late to execute them.
If I had just dove over the middle seat
on top of Ivan that day
the way I dove on top of the girl,
he'd probably still be here.
Sometimes I remember little things
I wish I could take back.
Like that doll he used to carry around—
the one he found in the bathroom

at the National Museum.
It had ice blue eyes and long blond hair,
and wore a red and green Christmas dress.
He named her Annika.
I made fun of him.
Told him boys don't carry dolls around.
She's my friend, he argued.
But she wasn't.
She was a doll.
I was his friend,
but I didn't act like it.
He only wanted that stupid, fucking doll
so he wouldn't feel alone.
Rain hammers my car.
An unending blur of gray
swirls beyond the headlights.
Regret precipitates in my gut
until I can't separate it
from the weather.
My tires hug the curves of the road
up the hills and back down
into a stone tunnel
and through a gust of steam.
I turn next to a row
of brightly colored postboxes
and follow a winding road that dips
into the bowel of the valley.
Bjorn's A-frame shack
sits on the edge of a stream.
I stall in my car,
puttering engine idling,
wipers squeaking,
waiting for the drizzle to dissipate.
I didn't call.

Bjorn might get angry
that I just showed up again.
But it's worth a shot.
There's not a chance I'll fall asleep tonight
without some herbal assistance.
I climb out the door
and dart through the mist.
The boards on the old porch creak underfoot
as I raise my fist to the door.
I pound the wet screen.
He opens it.
Electronic music spills out into the rain.
Heyyy!
Bjorn's bloodshot eyes squint
and a sloppy grin unrolls over his face.
He grabs me by the shirt.
Yanks me.
A chorus of snickers greet me
as I stumble inside.
His ragtag crew
camps out in a circle
around a neon green hookah.
Hooligans, Agnes calls them.
I quit going to school with them years ago
when Agnes hired Edvin to teach me.
Might be a better environment for you, lad.
She was right; it had been.
Until it wasn't anymore.
I haven't seen any of them
except Bjorn
 in a couple of weeks.
I've managed to miss them
each time I've come by.
They aren't really friends,

because they don't know anything about me,
just the stuff they've concluded on their own.
They're more like props in my life.
They are to me what Annika was to Ivan.
Where've you been mate?
You been hiding, Oskar?
Yeah, Oskar—where?
The last voice drips whiny with expectation.
She's the only girl here,
mousy-haired and sick-skinny.
Sana Stansdottir.
Bjorn's sister.
She's slept with all of his friends.
I was last.
He doesn't know.
Doesn't need to.
She thinks we're something—me and her.
Because I haven't spoken up
to tell her that we're not.
Sometimes clarification
takes more effort than I have.
I have a script I stick to with different people.
Sides of myself I keep separate from the rest.
It keeps the broken strings in check.
I play a part.
I don't feel like playing it right now.
So I stick to the main agenda.
G-g-gras? I ask Bjorn.
Already?
I nod.
Come on.
I follow him down a dark hallway
that smells like piss.
People or animals,

I can't be sure.
There's only one clean room here.
The underground bunker.
We jog down the stairs
to a door covered in foil.
Bright light floods the stairwell.
I squint as we enter the room.
Tiny greenhouses line rows of industrial tables.
Plants twist upward to fluorescent lighting so bright
I almost forget the gray
that awaits me outside.
In the back corner,
a tabletop showcases
a heap of tight green buds
laced with burnt sienna leaves.
They dry under warm ultraviolet rays.
Bjorn lifts a bud and twirls it
between his dirty-nailed fingers.
A smug grin parts his dry, cracked lips.
He outstretches his hand.
THC concentration in this batch is the highest it's ever been.
I don't know if it's a fact or a sales pitch.
But I take it, inhaling the bittersweet aroma.
Exactly what I came for.
He accepts the crumpled króna notes from my pocket.
You can still get in on this, mate.
I've got some men up north who want to buy in bulk.
I could use another leg man.
Mmm-ma-maybe.
It's what I always say.
Some extra cash flow
could connect the electricity at the lighthouse.
But I don't stay and discuss it.
I save business talk for another day

and leave out the back door
to avoid goodbyes with the others.
When I get back,
I park my car
down the road from the shop
and walk through the rain
to the empty lighthouse that has no lights.
I prefer the respite of the dark.

TWENTY-FIVE
Evie

*E*vie paced a groove in the wooden floor.

Though very little damage had been done inside the guest cottage—she guessed these buildings were built for frequent earthquakes—there was no way of knowing how it affected Papá with the internet down and no way to contact him. She'd asked him to add an international plan to her cell phone before they left the states. *Too expensive*, he'd said. *Just use your computer to talk to your friends.* It made no sense to her that he couldn't afford it. She checked at the guest office for a message. Surely he was wondering if she was okay. But there were no calls from him.

Something had to be wrong.

He wouldn't just forget to check on her. Or not come home after an earthquake. The moment the Wi-Fi started working again, a full three hours later, Evie started trying to video call his work computer from her laptop. But he didn't answer. The aloneness caved in on her then. A cold settled in that only the Florida sunshine could abate.

It had been two weeks since she'd spoken to Abuela, and Evie couldn't wait a blink longer. Papá made a promise they'd call her, and he wasn't here. No more waiting. She'd just find a way to do it herself. She pulled up an international calls app on her laptop and settled into the sofa by the front door as it down-loaded. When it was finished, she hammered the number into the keypad with frantic fingers, praying it would work.

The phone rang in Florida at Abuela's assisted-living apart-ment. As the echoing hum of ringing stretched on, dread piled into a heap in her gut. Maybe the whole world had been sucked inside the earth, leaving her tragically behind. She was living some Lifetime movie version of the book of Revelation. What saint would she pray to in end times?

Her finger hovered over the mousepad, ready to click *end*, just as a sleepy, raspy voice replaced the ringing.

"*Hola.*"

Relief coursed through Evie like rip currents, dragging her out into a sea of emotion. *Don't cry, Don't cry, Don't cry.* Tears pooled in her eyes, anyway. "Abuela, it's me." The words trem-bled over her lips.

"What time is it?" Abuela asked her in Spanish, muffled by the sounds of swishing blankets and pillows.

Evie glanced at the clock on her laptop. It was 9 p.m. in Ice-land, which made it late afternoon in Miami, probably during her nap time. Though she should feel bad for waking her, she didn't. Clocks had become irrelevant.

"I'm sorry to wake you, Abuela," she lied. "I just—there was an earthquake here. Papá isn't back, and I'm alone and I just needed to hear your voice."

"An earthquake!" Abuela's voice sharpened, suddenly more alert. "Are you hurt, *nieta*?"

"No, no. Nothing like that. It was minor, I guess. At least here where I am. But I haven't heard from Papá, and I don't know how bad it was wherever he is, and I can't get in touch with him." The words pitched high and squeaky at the end.

"*Escúchame, nieta,*" Abuela said, taking charge in that spe-cial way that always made Evie feel like everything would be okay. "Go to a center room in the house. Sit under the door frame until it's safe."

"I think it's okay now, Abuela. It's been hours since the quake. It wasn't—I don't even really know why I'm so upset. Papá is probably just working. I'm just alone all the time and…" Her voice cracked as the tears spilled hot down her cheeks. "I can't even speak the language here to make friends."

"Shhhh, *nieta*, shhhh. *Escúchame.* You're going to be okay. *Estará bien.*" The gentle lilt of her accent worked like a lullaby. Evie slumped against the sofa pillows and drew the blanket around her, pretending it was a hug.

"How did you do this," Evie whispered, "when you were my age?" She almost felt guilty for crying about it, because she would get to go home eventually. Abuela never had that luxury.

"Ah. It wasn't easy. I understood nothing, but I learned. You will, too. And then you'll be home. *Es temporal.*"

She hoped Abuela was right.

"Just try to enjoy your time while you're there, *nieta*. Explore."

She wanted to tell her about Oskar, but Abuela's tone had resumed its sleepy inflection. Then it occurred to her that she hadn't even asked Abuela how she'd been feeling. She was a terrible granddaughter.

"How are you, Abuela? Do you like it there?" She regretted the second question immediately. So stupid. She thought of the *clunk clunk clunk* of the roll-y oxygen tank next door.

"Ugh," Abuela grumbled. "They won't let me have my prayer candles. It'd be so much easier to find things if I could just properly pray to San Antonio."

Evie sniffled. "Why can't you have prayer candles?"

"They think I'm *loca* because I forget where I put things." Abuela laughed her raspy laugh, but without the usual humor. Anger pressed in on Evie's sadness. Abuela was just fine. The thought of people treating her like an elderly invalid pissed her off.

"When I get home, we're going back to your house. If Papá has to stay here, I'm going to move in with you." She knew she shouldn't make promises she didn't know if she could keep.

No, forget that. She was keeping this promise.

Abuela laughed again, but this time it was lighter. Happier. "Oh, Rhona. *No seas tonta.* Alberto needs you."

Evie swallowed a nervous lump in her throat.

Evie. Not Rhona.

She let it go. Abuela was sleepy. She'd woken her from her nap, after all. "I miss you, Abuela."

"*También te echo de menos.* Come Sunday after Mass, we'll paint."

Evie sat up from her spot on the sofa in the living room, dropping the blanket from her shoulders. Abuela knew she couldn't come over Sunday. She was a world away. Abuela was just too tired to think straight. "Thanks for talking to me, Abuela. Go back to sleep. I'll call you later."

"Okay. Sleep well. *Te quiero mucho, nieta.*"

"I love you, too."

See? Everything was fine.

When the doorknob clicked and turned at 1 a.m., she rolled off the couch and jumped to her feet in an adrenalin-fueled panic. Papá barreled in with a bag slung over his shoulder, hair disheveled, tired lines pulling under his eyes.

"I was worried sick!" Evie's words garbled as her lips stuck to her teeth. She rubbed her eyes. "Why didn't you call me?"

Confusion settled into his exhausted face. "Of course I'm okay, Evie. I told you I'd be working late in this phase of research."

"But the earthquake..." Evie's mouth went dry as ash. Was it a dream? Had she imagined the whole afternoon?

"Oh." He waved his hand in the air, dismissing. "I was at the research center in Reykjavik. We barely felt anything."

He dropped his bag on the floor and turned the coffee pot on. Evie just stared at him, something hot pinching deep in her chest where angry tears were always born. Never mind that *she had* felt something and had spent the entire day worrying he was swimming in magma.

"Did you feel it here?" he asked as he puttered around the kitchenette, pouring coffee, not looking at her. "I called the café. They assured me everything was fine."

"Wasn't bad," she lied. No way would she break down now and let him think she needed him.

"Did you call Abuela and tell her about the earthquake?"

She sunk to the sofa again. "Yes. From my laptop. Why?"

His forehead creases scolded her. "Please don't do that without me, *mija*. She called your mother in hysterics."

"How—?"

"Your mother called me. Said she was very upset and demanding she go pick you up, there had been an earthquake. We thought maybe she saw it on the news."

"I'm sure Rhona is exaggerating." Evie gritted her teeth. So he'd answered calls from her mother, but not from her. Just great. "Abuela was fine when we got off the phone."

He sighed, a big-chest rattling sigh. "I'm sure you think so, Evie. But she forgets things. She gets confused. And don't call your mother by her first name, *por favor*. It's rude."

It's ruder that you chose her to be my mother, Evie thought, grabbing her laptop from the floor.

"She said she's been trying to call you. Why haven't you called her back?"

"Because I can't talk to her like I talk to you." She'd try for flattery. Sometimes that worked with her papá, reminding him he was the favorite.

"Call her back, Evie. Tomorrow. You two need to discuss the plans for the school year."

So that was it, then. His exhaustion had made him drop the pretenses. He'd already decided he wasn't going back to Florida.

Evie clenched her teeth. She'd just have to be firm about her plans. "Are you staying here past September?"

He shrugged. "Nothing's set in stone yet. But you and I both know the magnet school would be great for you. And you already have portfolio work to submit with your application. Those paintings you've been doing are—"

"I'm going back to Florida. I'll move in with Abuela and finish at Saint Bart's."

He set his coffee down with excessive force. The dark liquid spilled over the cup lip onto the white countertop. "Evie—"

"I don't know how much time I have left with Abuela."

"—there's no money for Saint Bart's."

The new information blindsided her. The two of them stared at each other. She opened her mouth to speak, then closed it again, like a fish dangling from the end of a razor-sharp hook.

"I planned to tell you, but I kept hoping I wouldn't have to." He scrubbed his fingers over his eyes, posture drooping. It had never occurred to Evie that paying for Saint Bart's was an issue. It never had been before. They weren't rich or anything, but her dad had a good job. She'd never had to worry about basics. Education was a basic, wasn't it? "I was going to sell Abuela's house, because that would make it possible. But she isn't ready to let it go."

Sell Abuela's house? A burning prickle surged into Evie's throat. He couldn't pay for Saint Bart's because he was paying

Abuela's assisted-living rent. Evie remembered hearing him grumble about the cost when he set up the bank draft for payments.

The solution was crystal-clear. Abuela's assisted living rent wouldn't be necessary if she lived in her own house. And then it wouldn't have to be sold. And Evie could live with her there, and go to Saint Bart's. She started to tell him that, but he raised his hand to stop her.

"I know what you're going to say. The answer was no the first time you suggested it. And the answer is still no, Evie. I don't think you understand what's happened to Abuela's mental capacity. I have to do what's right by both of you. I know you don't believe me, but this is it."

Evie marched to her bedroom without a word, wishing she could smash something, cause an earthquake of her own that would finally shake him up to see how much he was hurting her.

"Evie," he called after her. "Don't be upset."

Too late. Upset was an understatement.

TWENTY-SIX
Oskar's Journal

Spending the week in a smoky haze
doesn't subdue the way
she hijacks my thoughts.
Neither does
the unhealed knot
on my head.
Not even Agnes's nagging about missing Edvin again
can take my mind off her.
I have nothing to say to Edvin Jonsson.
Agnes knows that.
He can come here a hundred times,
and a hundred times
my answer will be the same.
I drag my feet through the orchard,
cleaning fallen branches,
picking rotting cherries off the ground,
and glancing over the hill
for her red beret.
But it doesn't come.
By late afternoon
I take my ukulele to the fire ring by the lighthouse
at the water's edge.

The breeze from the sea
makes it colder on the cliff face than it is in the orchard.
A perpetual golden glow surrounds me
like a not-quite-adequate blanket
so I throw some damp wood
inside the stone ring
and light kindling.
Besides the warmth,
it creates a billowy smoke mask
to cover the smell of the joint from Agnes.
Not that she will leave the barn any time soon.
She is much too busy cooking and canning,
replacing what we lost to the quake.
Keeping her hands busy
as if that will undo
all the damage
we endured.
I have my own maladaptive coping mechanism,
and I take a long draw from it.
Honestly, I never intended
for this to be a habit.
I would've never tried it
if Bjorn hadn't given me that edible
without telling me about the extra ingredient.
I should've been fucking furious with him
for using me as entertainment for the group.
But something happened that night.
Through the funhouse goggles,
I finally felt distance
from the pain.
I was here,
but not.
Gone,
yet perfectly

rooted in place.
Escaped.

TWENTY-SEVEN

Evie

T hough she'd sent instant messages telling them about her new friend—a boy named Oskar!—Loretta and Ben were both ignoring her altogether now. Maybe they were on their honeymoon.

Evie had brushed her hair, put on makeup, and cleaned her room so that, while in view of the laptop camera, it looked spotless. She waited patiently, chewing her lip as she waited for the ringing to stop on the other end of the line. God, she did not want to do this. But she needed someone on her side. She'd take anyone at this point: even the enemy. When the screen filled up with a picture of her mother's expressionless face, her stomach rolled.

"Well hi there, Evie!" She smiled, but it was painted on and didn't touch her heavily mascara'd eyes. Evie could paint better smiles than that when she was in elementary school. "Happy Fourth of July!" Rhona's raspy cigarette voice frayed against her ears.

"Hi." Independence Day felt like a foreign concept to her right now, in more ways than one. Evie took a deep breath and tried to focus on the task at hand.

"Your face is looking thinner than last time I saw you!" This was Rhona's version of a compliment. *Hey Evie, you aren't looking quite as fat today.* "About time you called me back."

"Sorry." She shrugged. "Been busy."

As Evie racked her brain for a way to bring it up, an awkward silence stretched between them on the line. She couldn't decide if the connection had frozen, or if Rhona was just that bored to be talking to her daughter. Ugh, forget it. Maybe the call would disconnect and she could do this later. She glanced over at the Wi-Fi router. It blinked green, at full capacity. Such obscene misfortune.

Rhona flipped bleached hair behind her bare, spray-tanned shoulders. Evie bet she missed the Florida sunshine, where skin was bathed in ultraviolet kisses instead of orange pigment that smelled like surf wax. She stared into her mother's emotionless eyes.

Then again, maybe Rhona didn't miss anything from Florida. She was too busy recapturing the youth she lost when she reluctantly became a mother.

"I'm glad you're enjoying yourself," Rhona said, showing just how little she knew about her daughter. "Your father tells me you have a wonderful collection of paintings to choose from to submit with your application for Magnet Arts. Could I see them?" She craned her neck, focusing on the background behind Evie.

Ha. No dice. She'd hidden them before she bothered to make the call.

"They're drying," she lied. "Anyway, about that. I'm not going to Magnet Arts."

Rhona leaned in toward the screen, thick-lined eyes widening. "I'm sorry, what?"

Sé valiente.

"I said I'm not going. I'll find a way to go to Saint Bart's. I want to finish there."

"Oh, honey." Rhona's lips turned downward, but the rest of her face remained emotionless, like a mannequin. "I know it's hard. But think of it this way—you'd be leaving them all next year, anyway. You just get to do it a year earlier. And New York City!"

"No, I mean it," Evie interrupted, though her voice seeped out weaker now. Probably because she'd called her honey, like they were a long-lost mother/daughter duo who actually existed on the same wavelength. Like Rhona was worthy of calling her such a thing. "Papá and I will find a way to pay for it."

Rhona's nostrils flared. "I don't want to upset you, honey, but it just won't be possible with your father's finances. He has to pay for Abuela's expenses, the mortgage on the house in Miami, his vehicles, and my alimony."

Rage bubbled up in the back of Evie's throat. "Your alimony?"

Rhona hesitated, then nodded. "Yes, honey—"

"Please stop calling me honey," Evie spat. Could she be any more fake? Why was Papá paying her *anything*? She was the one who left. That money could go toward her tuition at Saint Bart's. "And what about you? Don't you have a real job finally? Can't you help out? You're my mother, after all. Or so you say."

Rhona's expression betrayed no hurt, which was disappointing. Trying to hurt Rhona was like punching a rock. You can't hurt someone who doesn't care.

"It's just not possible." She shook her head and it became a full body shimmy. "It's very expensive to live in the city. I barely earn enough to make ends meet."

So that's why she wanted Evie there. She'd probably get more money from Papá, child support on top of alimony. It was the same old story. Her mother had always put herself first, and that was never going to change. Not now, not ever. Tears prickled. Evie glanced up at the light in the ceiling, trying to suck the moisture back in her head.

"Don't be sad, okay? We're going to have a lot of fun when you get here." This whole act of *finally trying* was just what Rhona had to do to get paid.

Evie reached over and yanked the cord out of the Wi-Fi router. She was done with this conversation.

TWENTY-EIGHT
Oskar's Journal

~~She's got a way about her~~
~~Her eyes are like~~
~~Where did she go?~~
Every lyric I write
comes out like a cheap knock-off
of things already said
better
by somebody else.

TWENTY-NINE

Evie

After spending the day trying to drown her anger with paint, she hauled her awkward load over the hill, using her knee to push the canvases up as they slipped from her grip.

Maybe Agnes would be willing to work with her on this, or maybe she wouldn't.

But one thing was for sure: one way or another, Evie's paintings would be gone when her papá got in from work. She'd been thinking about it since she hung up with Rhona and she had decided. There was no way in hell she was using those paintings to get into a school she didn't want to attend.

Wind blew through the trees in the orchard, echoing its emptiness. Her pulse thumped in her neck as she searched around and behind her, welcoming the distraction from her shitty afternoon. Looking for him.

Ridiculous.

It wasn't like an earthquake had made them bond or anything. It was instinct. Survival. She needed to get over herself and stop making it more than it was. Gulping a breath, she opened the front door and prepared herself to see him. Agnes looked up from behind the stove as Evie stumbled in like a flamingo on ice skates, trying not to drop the three canvases in her arms.

The shop was spick-and-span again, all traces of earthquake gone.

"He's outside, lass." Agnes went back to stirring her recipe on the stove. "Over at the lighthouse."

Evie regained her balance and played dumb. "Who?"

A crinkle pinched Agnes's mouth. She wasn't going to play along.

Evie approached the counter. Maybe her expression conveyed how silly she pretended to believe that was. "Yeah, I'm not here for him. I actually came to make a business proposition."

"Oh?" One copper brow rose slightly above the other.

Evie dropped the canvases on the front counter, then rubbed the sore spot on her forearm where the wood had dug into her skin and left an angry red mark. "I noticed the other day that you have some paintings for sale. I was wondering if you'd be interested in selling mine."

A frown pulled Agnes's mouth into a semi-scowl.

"On consignment, of course," Evie quickly added. "You'd get a percentage."

"I don't know, lass. The villagers go to Reykjavik for art. We get lots of tourists here from the Ring Road, but they don't really come to buy paintings. Those back there have been collecting dust for months."

"Oh." Evie's stomach sank. "Maybe you could just display them? For a little while? If they don't sell, I could come back and get them." She spread them out on the counter, face up.

Agnes glanced down, and then did a double take. Triple take. She dropped the ladle in the pot and stepped closer to get a better look. The wrinkles around her mouth smoothed out as her lips parted. She stared, wordless, at the three paintings—the little boy in the orchard, the redhead with dirt under her nails, and the one Evie had painted today while she binged on the cherries Agnes had given her: a red-trimmed lighthouse standing bulwark at

the ocean's frothy tiptoes, with the aurora borealis swirling ribbons of green and purple through a glittery night sky.

Evie had never even seen the Northern Lights, but this morning, she saw them in her head as though she'd experienced their
glory hundreds of times. It was the kind of impossibility that
made her want to dart behind the counter and retrieve the poem
she'd found after the quake—if it was still there—and hold it up
to Agnes and demand *What does this mean? While cherries tell
tales?*

Agnes gawked, clutching the hem of her apron. "These
are…" Her thick neck bobbed a little as she swallowed.

"I'm not a professional or anything. I just do it for fun." Evie
fidgeted, embarrassed, not quite sure how to take Agnes's reaction. This had been a colossally idiotic idea. She didn't know
what she'd been thinking. Nobody wanted to buy her art. It was
forgettable to everyone but Abuela. Maybe she so desperately
needed to believe she was good at it that she'd invented this theo-
ry that the cherries were telling her how to paint.

"They're astounding." Agnes let go of her apron to trace the
canvas. "I'll display them."

"You will?" Hope and surprise sprouted anew in Evie's
chest.

"I can't promise they'll sell." Agnes cleared her throat. "But
I'll put them up in the sitting area. See what happens."

"Thank you!" Evie squealed, clapping her hands and bounc-
ing on the balls of her feet. If she was being honest with herself,
knowing Oskar would see them was the most exciting part. Maybe he'd think of her when she wasn't around.

"What are your rates?" Agnes asked, grabbing a pen, still
looking at the paintings from the corner of her eye.

"Rates?" Agnes may as well have spoken Icelandic. Evie
hadn't thought that far ahead.

"What would you like to charge for them, lass?" Annoyance
dampened her voice as she cocked her head to the side, wild red

flyaways surrounding her sweaty forehead like strawberry sprouts.

"Oh, that." Evie bit her lip. "I don't know. Whatever you think is fair?"

Agnes dropped her pen and propped her fists on broad hips. "You want to sell your paintings but you don't know how much you'll be wantin' for 'em?"

Okay, maybe she should've planned this better. The thought of actually selling them hadn't really been the point. She just wanted them to put them out of Papá's reach. "I don't know the going rate for things like this here. Maybe you set the price, and keep 10% of the sale." There was more of a question mark than a period at the end of her suggestion. Agnes peered down at her, irritation at her business sense—or lack thereof—pretty apparent.

"Okay, lass. Follow me."

They gathered the canvases and took them to the sitting area of the store. Agnes rearranged books on the shelves behind the couch. The same couch Evie had crouched behind with Oskar during the quake. Blood rushed to her cheeks and she pushed the thought away.

Once a space was cleared, Agnes placed a canvas there, under a recessed bookshelf light. She did it twice more for the other two, then stepped back and admired the painting of the little boy in the orchard, then the young woman in the dirt.

"What made you paint these?" Her voice seemed hoarse and distant, guarded.

Evie tried to decipher her reaction, to reconcile it with her own suspicions, but Agnes didn't give much away. "I have no idea. There's something about your orchard. It inspires me."

"Well, then." Agnes stared at her, lines creasing around her smile. "Check back as often as you like."

She returned to her post behind the counter. Questions buzzed on the tip of Evie's lips. *Do you know this little boy? Is he Oskar? Is the young woman you?*

While cherries tell tales... She hadn't been able to put that phrase out of her mind.

As much as she would've liked to stay and ask, the fear of coming off completely insane stopped her. So she nodded to Agnes as she left.

When the door shut behind Evie, the alluring pluck of strings slowed her feet through the orchard. The song echoed through the breeze and tapped her on the shoulder. Familiar—the tune she'd heard the first day she visited the shop. Her heart sped like a metronome set to *allegro assai*.

She turned and followed the sound around the foggy pond, through the cotton grass, toward the lighthouse, feet crunching softly beneath her. As she got closer to the smoke billowing from behind the painted white brick of the base of the lighthouse, the rise and fall of the song grew louder.

Evie couldn't walk away without getting a better listen. A few silent steps through the soft evening shadows confirmed her suspicion: Oskar was playing a ukulele. He sat poised on a rock, his back to her. She watched the muscles around his shoulder blades move under his gray shirt as he played.

Like a creep, she tiptoed to the side of the lighthouse, hiding in the shadow of it as she listened. He played it like he'd written it. She closed her eyes and smiled as the *ting-ting* of plucked strings took her someplace else: someplace she actually wanted to be. In that moment, she couldn't imagine the notes of any song coming from an instrument other than a ukulele.

THIRTY
Oskar's Journal

Smoke burns my eyes, so I close them,
joint dangling between my lips as I play.
The potency renders me weightless as I strum.
I play the song I wrote
like I've known it since birth.
But leave the lyrics here, in my journal.
I have to put the emotions somewhere.
Sometimes I wonder if they're imaginary—
these feelings trapped inside me—
until I give them life with ink or notes.
I write them down to make sure they're real.
She's the reason I finished the song,
my unattainable muse.
The way her hair moves on the breeze
inspired the opening;
her always busy mouth
wrote the notes for the bridge.
The sensation of her body pressed against me
as the earth shook beneath us
was exactly what I needed
to finish the chorus.
What a pathetic bastard

I have become.
Something rustles behind me
and my eyes fly open.
I twist my body
and glance over my shoulder.
There she is,
frozen on halted tiptoes.
I stare at her through a self-inflicted haze.
Her dark hair shrouds her shoulders.
Red beret hugging
the top of her head.
Red.
Why's it always red with her,
like she knows it's my favorite color?
Maybe I'm imagining things.
Or maybe this song conjures desires.
I nod at her
try to act nonchalant.
But underneath,
I'm chalant as fuck.

THIRTY-ONE
Evie

*E*vie was so busted spying.

"Um. Hi." Squeak. Wave.

So smooth, Evie. She pulled her beret down over the crown of her head, wishing it would swallow her up and spit her out in Florida.

Behind Oskar, brushstrokes of pink and purple and orange swirled under a hovering fog of slate, touching the horizon at the sea. She could actually see the ocean up here, and it came as a surprise to her. She'd known it was somewhere beyond the light-house, but she'd never ventured far enough to see it was this close, within walking distance of the orchard.

Flames from the firepit licked the sky, a sort of shaky haze shimmering at the meeting point of orange and gray. The sun never really set here, but it took intermittent siestas behind the dark clouds, creating a brilliant color palette in its shadows. She framed it in her memory, promising herself she'd put it on canvas later.

With a graceful, calculated slowness, Oskar lowered his ukulele to the ground next to him and pulled the cigarette—*or was it a joint?*—from his lips, dropping a tattooed arm by his side. His glassy eyes trailed to her feet and then back up to her face.

Silent. Waiting.

"That song you were playing…" Evie took a few tentative steps towards him, flip-flops sinking in the damp, dark pebbles. A whiff of something skunky, like the inside of his car, filled her nostrils. Things clicked together then—another layer of Oskar's mystique unveiled. Definitely a joint. Not only was she spying, she was catching him in the middle of illegal activity. She struggled to stay calm.

His blank expression remained as placid as the water in the volcanic crater behind them. Great. Where did she put that translation dictionary? She dropped it on the ground during the quake and hadn't seen it since. Evie held her hands up, miming playing an instrument.

"Beautiful." That was a pretty common word, right? She tried to simplify. "Good."

His lashes cast shadows on his cheeks as he drew the joint to his mouth, full lips curling around it in a gentle embrace. The fiery end brightened as he pulled a slow drag. Oskar blew a thick white puff into the air, and then outstretched a long, tattooed arm toward her. A curl of smoke extended from the cylinder between his fingers. It took Evie a second too long to get that he was offering it to her. God, she was so lame.

A nervous lump lodged in her throat. Last year, she had befriended her Biology Two lab partner, a girl named Angel, who made her love for marijuana no secret. *Angel is bad news*, Loretta had warned her. *Total drug addict, and she'll just try to pull you down with her. I mean, gawd, look at those awful dreadlocks, clashing with her Saint Bart's uniform like she stole it or something. You know you have to stop washing your hair for like, months, to get it to look like that.*

But there was never any pressure from Angel. Not that Evie got the chance to hang out with her. Loretta had always made sure to account for every waking moment of Evie's time at school. Funny how that used to piss her off, but now she would've given a pinky toe for a mere scrap of communication with her.

Oskar's eyes brightened to a silvery blue, joint dangling like a question mark in the air between them. This must've been the peer pressure the all-wise Loretta had been talking about. Loretta, the—air quotes—*friend* who was probably getting drunk and making out with Ben at the FloRida Fourth of July event in Miami at this very moment.

Evie stepped closer to Oskar. Screw it. When she took the joint from him, their fingers brushed, and the atmosphere grew twenty degrees warmer. *It's the fire*, she lied to herself.

Sinking to the coolness of the rock next to him, she left a foot or two of personal space. Then she put the end of the joint in her mouth. The minty sweetness of spearmint lingered on the end where his lips had touched it. Almost like kissing him, she thought to herself.

She took a puff, not even sure if she was doing it right, and held the smoke in her mouth, deciding that it wasn't that much different from the cigarettes she'd tried at a party last year. But she'd never inhaled those. Would he know if she didn't inhale? Her fear intensified as he watched her and waited. She took another bigger puff, just in case. And then she breathed in.

Razor blades.

Air with claws.

Fire.

Shit.

The smoke scraped down her throat into surprise-attacked lungs. She blew ragged puffs of pain through her mouth and nose, coughing like her Abuela's assisted living neighbor, the emphysema patient. In that moment, she wished she had her own *clunk clunk clunk* oxygen tank. She rocked harder than the earthquake and, in the process, accidentally dropped the joint on the ground.

Double shit.

They both dove for it at the same time, heads colliding with a thwack mid-air.

Awesome.

Oskar sat up, joint in one hand, rubbing his head with the other—just above the butterfly bandages closing the wound on his forehead—another injury he'd sustained because of her. His jaw clenched, and the fire lit the contours of his face. Shaggy loose curls, thick blond brows, and heavily lashed eyes. Oskar may as well have been a sculpture. If a mad scientist spliced DNA from ancient Vikings and Paul Bunyan, it might've rendered someone with a resemblance to Oskar. He was a living, breathing work of art.

As Evie's coughing fit died down, she searched her brain for a word or sign he might understand. Something that said, *I'm new at this.* In case he couldn't already tell. She gave him a double thumbs-up. Best she could do. "The rookie survived," she croaked, voice gritty as the rock beneath her. A grin cracked through his stern expression. His dimples glinted, and his eyes narrowed to amused slants as he pulled the joint to his lips again.

Those dimples. *Mother Mary.*

"Oh don't look so smug, Mr. Expert." Evie rolled her eyes, trying to stop the heat rising in her neck. His smile withered and he looked away. Withdrawing. A chilly breeze passed between them. Desperate to get it back, Evie extended her hand. Oskar glanced down at it and raised an eyebrow, eyes trailing upward until they met hers.

"What? I don't get another chance?" She wiggled her fingers in a gimme gesture.

Oskar smirked but relented.

A swimmy-headed residue lingered between them as minutes drifted by. Evie slid down into a nook on the rock. Sharp edges began to soften. Objects adopted a pleasant, gauzy glimmer like the tip of the flames. The horizon brightened to a more vivid version of itself, a chroma effect against the gray sky. Time lost its authority.

Oskar's hands rested on the knees of his worn-out jeans, long fingers dangling. A coiling spiral of smoke rose between the thumb and forefinger of his right hand. The muscles in his arm squeezed as he drew his hand to his mouth. Evie's gaze made the slow crawl up his neck, over a prominent Adam's apple, past the dark blond stubble on his jaw, and then...

He pinned her in place with his stormy eyes, exhaling sheets of clouds into the air, colors blurring through them. His lips parted further when the smoke dissipated, and he hesitated, as if on the cusp of confession.

She noticed his teeth then, for the first time. The top ones were straight and pearly, but the bottom ones sprouted from his gums at odd angles—crooked in an imperfect way that seemed like an afterthought, like God realized he made him too perfect and had to screw things up a little to even the score. They leaned into one another, like a white picket fence blown around by the wind. It somehow made him even more attractive. As she stared, she couldn't help wondering what they'd feel like beneath her tongue. What it'd be like to stumble over them, to trace the space between the two middle ones.

Had she felt Ben's teeth when they kissed? She couldn't remember. Oskar smiled then. An open-mouthed, purposeful smile. Something clenched in her belly, and the rest of her melted into a puddle of molten rock around it. Ben who?

"Sorry to stare." Evie shrugged, voice thick with a confidence she only had in her dreams. "You're really nice to look at."

Oskar sat motionless. She giggled, flooded with that same strange sense of bravery she'd felt when she'd tested him that day in the orchard. She sprawled across the rock like it was a hammock. She could say anything she wanted to him. Maybe she'd tell him she had been thinking about him nonstop since the day she first saw him. Maybe she'd walk right over and kiss him.

Then the reality occurred to her. Bolting upright, paranoia took the reins. *She was freaking stoned.* It was nothing more than false courage, courtesy of Bob Marley's favorite plant. Evie risked another glance at him. Oskar's face held no hint of recognition. He had no idea what she'd said anyway, so it didn't matter. She didn't have to be self-conscious.

But if she kissed him... she bet he would understand that.

THIRTY-TWO
Oskar's Journal

Have you ever heard of Bob Marley?
she asks, dark eyes glazed over.
I open my mouth,
then close it again.
I have to be more careful.
I almost let myself slip and speak,
which I promised myself I wouldn't do.
Of course I know who Bob Marley is.
Wait, she says, giggling,
Waitwaitwait—
She holds her hands up in the air,
I can totally explain this.
Rasta! she says,
flitting her fingers around her hair,
imitating dreadlocks.
Nothing?
Okay, I got this, hang on.
She holds an invisible guitar to her chest
and sings.
Adorably off-key.
Don't worry, bout a thing,
'cause every little thing, is gonna be alright.

Her hazy smile overpowers the fire.
You know that song?
Bob Marley?
She talks with her hands,
turns the volume of her voice up
as if that will make things clearer to me.
Me home is in Jamaica, mon.
She does the accent,
contorts her expression
playing a game of charades.
It takes massive amounts of willpower
to keep from laughing.
She goes back to the song,
mimicking the chorus,
This is my message to you-hoo-hoo.
She bobs her head in time with her words.
I can't keep a straight face
one second longer.
So I pick up the ukulele,
stick the joint in the corner of my mouth,
and play the melody.
She sits up straight and claps with glee.
Yes! I knew you'd know!
Everyone knows that song.
Even my abuela loves that song.
She watches me as I strum.
The way she looks at me
messes with my head.
Most people spare me pitying side-glances, at best.
She doesn't look at me.
She looks straight into me
and takes all the answers without asking.
Something tells me she enjoys it.
Shoving the thought away,

I let the embers jumping off the drying wood distract me.
When I peek up, she looks at her feet.
Caught again.
Even Sana—the only girl I've ever been with,
or even kissed—
doesn't look at me this way.
Being with her was never something to write about.
Sure, I wanted to do it at the time.
It was a sick curiosity,
a desire to know something everyone else already knew.
To be in on the joke.
But even the kissing was weird and wet.
Nothing I'm dying to relive.
If it was Evelyn…
Her upper lip forms a perfect lowercase m.
Mmmm.
A sound I can never play on my broken strings.
Her bottom lip puckers out,
a little indention squeezes the flesh where she bites it all the
    time.
She draws it between her teeth,
tempting me,
I'm certain.
Somehow I know kissing her
would never be awkward.
But it's not like I can ever find out.
I can't kiss her
after I've let this lie go on so long.
I can't tell her the truth
and double back on
the agreement I made with myself.
I flick the rest of the joint on the fire
and resume my strumming,
hiding between the notes.

THIRTY-THREE

Evie

*E*vie's emotions zinged all over the place as he finished the song.

One moment, she wanted to crawl in a hole from the embarrassment of getting herself into this situation. Two seconds later, she had to fight a tsunami of giggles that dammed up in her chest and tickled her throat to the point of pain. When Oskar caught her staring at him for about the fiftieth time, she lost control and let them bubble out in an endless string of silliness. His brows reached for the sky—which only made her laugh harder.

"You should see your face!" Evie cackled, grasping her midsection and doubling over. The rational part of her brain knew this was a side effect, but she couldn't reason it into submission. "It's like, whoa, who is this crazy American girl and why is she eye humping me to death?"

As if contagious, Oskar laughed. First a low rumble, then a sprawling richness that made the air around Evie sigh. Each chuckle encouraged another, a cacophony of ridiculousness that echoed well past expiration. When contented breaths replaced their laughter, the moment floated away. A deafening silence replaced it.

Paranoia taunted her—*say something!*

"I don't know why I just did that with you," she told him, feeling like she had to pierce the quiet, kill it like an enemy. "My abuela would be so disappointed if she knew." Evie stared at the ground, drawing circles in the black pebbled dirt with the toe of her flip flop. "She's not like, one of those holier-than-thou Catholics, but she's really big on the whole body is a temple thing. She loves Bob Marley, but she'd never like, smoke a doob with him. If he were still alive, I mean."

Evie glanced up at Oskar. He sat quietly, watching her. Seeming totally content to listen to her blab. "I stopped talking to a friend back home because someone told me stoners were bad news. But you know what? This is the best I've felt in a long time." Evie shook her head, imagining the friendship she might've had with Angel if she hadn't listened to Loretta. Angel probably wouldn't have moved in on her boyfriend, either. "Anyway, minds are changing about it in the States. It's already legal in some places. Once the economy gets bad enough, everyone'll embrace it. Because America has these so-called morals until there's money involved."

Oskar studied her through squinted eyes, probably trying to figure out what the hell she was even saying, but she couldn't stop flapping her jaws—safe in the promise that she could say whatever she wanted, and it'd be lost in translation.

"Americans are total money whores, you know. They'll do anything for it. My mother, for example, would rather force me to start over my senior year in New York City than give up her alimony." She threw her head back and let a bitter laugh escape, like releasing the carbon dioxide from a soda. "She left us when I was thirteen, approximately the moment I needed her most. But hey, at least she's getting paid, right?"

Oskar's face remained expressionless. Evie became more animated, talking with her hands. "This woman is ten years younger than my dad. They weren't even a couple. Just some random hookup, which is really gross if you think about it." She shook her head like she could wiggle the thought loose. "I try not to think about it. Anyway. Little ole me came along and almost ruined them both. Neither of them ever wanted kids."

She sighed, letting the harsh truth of that sink in for the millionth time in her life. Glancing up at Oskar, Evie continued. "She knocked on his door and asked for abortion money. So he married her and convinced her to have me. He's Catholic, too, you know. Catholics don't kill babies. The body is a temple. Good thing for me, huh?" Evie felt the overwhelming urge to cry, but instead, she laughed. Oskar studied her, so she looked away.

"She tried to be a housewife, but she sucked at it. She wanted to be an actress. I guess having a family made her miserable or whatever. She sunk into this deep depression and pretty much slept through my childhood. I'd come home from school some days and knock on her bedroom door for hours. If she answered at all, she'd just yell. So I started going over to Abuela's after school and on the weekends while Papá was working."

Evie's confession spun wildly out of control. She hadn't meant to tell him so much, but once she started talking, she couldn't stop. She was never this candid, even in confession with her priest.

She picked at her fingernails, risking a glance at Oskar. Through bloodshot eyes, he studied her, as if listening intently. The illusion of having someone listen, actually give a shit, gave her the courage to go on.

"She finally got in-patient counseling a few years ago, but afterward, she went to New York instead of coming home. To pursue her forgotten dreams, she said. She works as a stagehand now. I hope it's worth it to her, settling like that." The easy laughter turned to a bubble of regret in her throat. She didn't realize it would still hurt to say it all out loud.

"My dad actually gave me the choice: come here with him, or go to New York to live with her. So I chose him, like always.

But as it turns out, he's done nothing but ignore me since we got here, and he's going to make me go live with her, anyway. And if that wasn't already a big fat bucket of suck, my friends back home have already forgotten me too. Not one message from them since the first week I got here. You're the only person who's ever listened to me, and you don't know what a mess I am or you wouldn't, either." Her voice cracked on the last word.

Oskar leaned forward, invading her bubble of personal space. Something new settled into his features as he examined her. Her words may not have made sense to him, but her nuances must have. Maybe her teary eyes made him feel sorry for her.

Ugh. Pity. Not at all what she was going for.

On the bright side, though, he kept glancing at her lips. Six inches separated their faces. Maybe five. Four if she leaned forward a little more. Then three. Yep, he was definitely looking at her mouth. Two...

"Oskar! Come here for a minute, lad!" Agnes's voice boomed through the valley. Oskar jumped up like he'd been caught committing a felony. He darted to his feet and jogged away, toward the barn, without so much as a backward glance.

Mother Mary full of grace. She'd almost kissed him! A boy even less capable of getting to know her than Ben Benson.

Don't do drugs, kids.

When he disappeared from sight, Evie clambered to her feet and crept away.

THIRTY-FOUR
Oskar's Journal

Was she going to kiss me?
Or am I just baked?
Guilt churns in my gut as I stalk inside the barn.
I blink a few times, hoping my eyes aren't too red.
If Agnes asks, I'll just blame it on the fire.
Come in here, lad,
Agnes says when I reach the door.
Someone is here to see you.
My stomach plunges.
He's there, browsing the aisles.
I recognize the tan tweed overcoat and wrinkled trousers
that must've arrived in a time machine
from a dated sitcom.
He looks up at me through thick lenses
that make him look like
a scholar or a serial killer.
Oskar!
He pushes his wild gray hair off his forehead
and his face splits into a wide, Nordic grin.
Just the man I'm looking for.
Edvin Jonsson is just the man
I've avoided for two months,

ever since I refused the audition invitation
to the American conservatory
he went behind my back
and applied to on my behalf.
No way am I talking to him now.
I about-face and stalk toward the door.
Oskar.
Agnes's voice throws a force field
over all the exits,
daring me to try and walk away.
Mr. Jonsson came all this way to have a word with you
for the third time this week.
Best if you settle down and have a listen.
She motions toward the tables at the front of the shop,
the ones normally reserved for lunch patrons.
Reykjavik is hardly *all this way* from the orchard.
An hour, tops.
I'll only be a few minutes, I promise,
Mr. Jonsson pleads,
steepling his fingers in front of his chest.
The plea shimmers in his tired eyes.
It's maddening
trying to stay mad at someone
I never wanted to be mad at in the first place.
But giving in isn't an option.
Giving in means admitting defeat,
agreeing to leave
the land my father cultivated
with his bare hands,
the land my mother exhausted herself maintaining,
the land my little brother ran through—forever frozen in
    time as a child.
Leaving means leaving them.
And I won't go.

THIRTY-FIVE

Evie

*E*vie's social awkwardness knew no bounds, mouth flapping all night like a wind-up doll.

Hey hot guy, my mommy abandoned me. Thanks for sharing your weed. Let's make out.

Ugh. *Kill me now.*

She pushed her key into the lock, but the door flew open before she could twist.

Her papá's shadow fell across the open doorway. He looked older than he had just a couple of weeks ago. The excessive work aged him. She wouldn't let it make her feel guilty, though. Promises were promises and all he did was break them.

"Where have you been?" The corner of his left eye twitched—something that happened when he was pissed or stressed. Or in this case, both.

Evie swallowed a nervous breath. "Out." Was she wearing a neon sign that detailed everything she'd done today? It sure felt like it all of a sudden.

He narrowed his eyes and tilted his head. "Have you been crying?"

"No. Why?" Evie breezed past him, avoiding eye contact. She tossed her keys on the counter and made a beeline for her room.

"Evie."

She paused, waiting, without turning around. "Yeah?"

"Look at me."

He knew. He had to. But he never paid this much attention. Why now? *Because you smell like a Wiz Khalifa concert, Evie.* Slowly, she turned, trying to will her eyes clear and bright. She could probably nail her eyelids to her hairline and that still wouldn't make them open all the way.

"Why are your eyes so red?" He laced his hands together behind his back—stepping into Papá Mode. Great. All of the punishment and none of the benefits of having a father.

"Because the sun never sets here. Ever think of that?" Evie was going down anyway. She might as well let him know how disgusted she was with this entire situation.

The muscle in his jaw flickered several times before he spoke. "Where are your paintings?"

She shrugged, more surprised than anything that he'd noticed already. And that it was the most concerning thing to him at the moment.

"You don't know?" His eyebrows stretched upward. More pissy attitude.

"I sold them." She said it as matter-of-fact as she knew how.

"To whom?"

"The general store. The owner's going to consign them for me."

"I see," he said, arms dropping by his sides. "I thought you agreed to use them for your portfolio for Magnet Arts?"

Evie released a nervous snicker. Could she not just get away? The one time she didn't want to talk to him, he wanted to have a heart-to-heart. Nothing sounded better than crawling under a blanket and falling into a deep, give-no-shits sleep. But first, the Spanish Inquisition.

"I never agreed to that."

Just punish me and get it over with, she wanted to say, as she invoked any saint who may still be willing to listen to her. Let him yell at her about anything but that school. She wanted him to question her about the smell in her hair or the state of her half-closed eyes instead. But he didn't.

He walked to the counter and sorted through paperwork, maybe deciding how to punish her in a way that was worse than what he already had in store. But surely he'd come up short. There was nothing worse than pawning her off on Rhona.

Slowly, Evie tiptoed away, hoping he'd forgotten about her again.

"We're going to Mass first thing *mañana*," he called. She paused in her bedroom doorway. "We've neglected it since we got here. Confession, too. Time to remedy that."

Well, at least she had plenty to confess now.

"And leave me a note next time you plan to go somewhere."

"Sure thing." She punctuated her statement by stepping into her room and slamming the door.

THIRTY-SIX
Oskar's Journal

I lounge across my bed,
dark sheets wrapped around my ankles.
A little gnat runs across the ceiling
in a zigzag pattern,
searching
between the flakes of white paint.
I focus on that
instead of Agnes's nagging calls
from the bottom of the stairs.
If she thinks I am going to detail
my conversation with Edvin
she is sadly mistaken.
It wasn't as bad as I expected it would be.
He apologized
but maintained his stance
that I should attend conservatory
in the US.
I maintained my stance just as well,
wishing him away
so I could get back outside to Evelyn.
But when I went back,
she was already

gone.
Oskar! Get down here now!
I give up
and stumble down the stairs in a sleepy haze,
hair in a nest on the side of my head.
Those locks are out of control, lad.
The annoyance drips from her words.
I've half a mind to shear it in your sleep.
Go ahead and try, I think
but don't say.
And your clothes!
Draped over your body like it's a coat rack!
I can't fathom why a handsome lad
would present himself a slob on purpose.
You're seventeen years old, lad.
You can't pretend you don't know better.
I shrug.
It's all I've got for her right now.
Here, she says, pushing a clipboard at my chest.
I need you to take inventory of the shop.
Start with the souvenirs.
She motions to the area at the back.
I take the clipboard
and less than two steps
before I freeze in my tracks.
I stare at an assembly of paintings
that weren't there yesterday.
Come on now,
she grabs my shirtsleeve,
drags me to the back,
wake up and get to movin'.
Once we get to the back
I reach out and touch the paintings.
Wha-wha-what's this?

My mother. My brother. The lighthouse.
The American girl painted them,
Agnes says, voice only a touch above silent.
I've only seen one of them before.
My mouth hangs open,
jaw and senses unhinged.
I trace the rosy-hued textures
in my mother's cheek.
The paintings tell the stories I already know,
rendered from the point of view
of the *Aisling* tree.
Sadness sucker punches me in the face.
This is why I never eat the cherries myself.
The memories are too crisp.
That tree has seen so much
over the course of its life.
It watched my mother plant it in the ground.
It watched my brother sit in its shade.
It watched the abandoned Elska lighthouse
on the cliff in the distance
before other trees obstructed the view.
All of these paintings are fragments of the dream.
I thought I was the only one who could see it.
But this girl—
She painted the lighthouse
with the aurora borealis
promenading through the night sky
the exact way it looked the autumn I was ten.
I stand paralyzed
beneath the acupuncture
of vivid recollection.
At the lighthouse's doorway,
my mother reached for my hand.
When she smiled,

her green eyes flashed
with more animation
than the ribbons of color swirling above our heads.
Together, we climbed
the spiral staircase
leading to the lookout tower.
My father and Ivan trailed behind.
Footsteps echoed around us,
dampened only by Ivan's excited giggles.
Everything was new then.
The world was ours.
She wants me to try and sell her work.
Agnes's voice breaks the spell.
I told her nobody would buy—
I cut her off.
I will, I tell her,
I'll buh-buh-buy them.
Take it out of my p-p-pay.

THIRTY-SEVEN
Evie

On Sunday morning, a heavy weight in the pit of Evie's stomach pinned her to the passenger seat of Papá's rental car.

They weaved around the rural roads near the sea, distant waves tickling the edge of silence between them. The surreal landscape, a palette of grays and blues and blacks backlit by sun, could have been a painting instead of something real that existed outside the car windows. They drove almost an hour to the nearest Catholic parish with English and Spanish speaking services, in the opposite direction of Reykjavik.

St. John's Chapel sat atop a hill overlooking a fjord, a plain white old-style building trimmed in blue. Blue roof. Blue trim. Blue doors. Simple. Basic. It was almost cartoonish in comparison to the grand architecture of St. Michael's in Miami.

Evie squeezed her door handle.

"Have you examined your conscience, *mija*?" It was the first thing he'd said to her since *Get dressed, we're going to Mass.*

She sniffled, pretending she wasn't unnerved. "Yes, Papá."

He glanced at her crucifix—she'd put it back on, purely out of guilt—then nodded, and climbed out of the car.

The inside of St. John's was just as stark in contrast to St. Michael's as the outside. Simple wooden pews and kneeling benches lined the sanctuary. Muted, colorful light filtered in through the stained-glass windows. Gentle hymns in what must have been Icelandic drifted softly from an adjacent room.

The sweet aroma of incense and candles burned at the altar beneath a massive, ornate crucifix. Evie fixed her eyes on the creaky floorboards and greedily inhaled—another scent that reminded her of Abuela. Papá placed a gentle hand at her elbow and led her toward one of the old-fashioned confessionals at the back of the church. This was the punishment he had in mind.

She stepped inside, watching over her shoulder as Papá headed to the altar to pray. When she pulled the velvet curtain closed, she turned and choked back a scream. The priest was there, just like in any other confessional. But there was no screen separating them. Just a lone bulb shining down from above, like an interrogation lamp in a phone booth.

Sinking to sit on the wooden bench, Evie swallowed hard.

"Hallo," the priest said. Wrinkles circled his friendly blue eyes. A somber smile twisted his chapped lips. He hunched over in his booth, cloaked in a traditional black cassock, hands clasped in front of him as if he held some inherent goodness between his palms.

"Bless me, Father, for I have sinned." The words thrashed around, hollow in her throat. Evie made the sign of the cross. "My last confession was two months, three weeks, and one day ago."

At that Easter confession, she'd had the privacy of a screen, the comfort of the familiar priest she'd known all of her life, and nothing to confess but an unwillingness to forgive her mother.

Today was different.

Well, except for the forgiveness thing. She had even more resentment for Rhona now.

Though face-to-face with this priest, something dawned on Evie. She had more anonymity than she did in Miami. Could she tell Father Angelo back home that she'd stolen cherries, lusted for a boy she didn't know, exposed her temple to drugs, snooped in other people's belongings, and disrespected her father? Not to mention all the cursing, complaining and resenting she'd been doing.

Doutbful.

Once she left Iceland, she would never have to see this priest again.

Armed with that freeing knowledge, Evie didn't hold back the way she might've with Father Angelo. She treated him more like Oskar, and told him everything.

THIRTY-EIGHT
Oskar's Journal

I stare at the paintings on my bedroom wall,
trying to will them back to life.
The bell on the shop door
clangs against the glass.
I snap out of it.
My nerves shove me around.
I bound down the stairs,
forcing myself to breathe normally,
thinking maybe she'll be there.
But instead of Evelyn,
a short, square man
with dark hair and glasses
crowds the front of the shop.
He pleads with Agnes.
Can you contact the person who bought them?
I'll give him double his money.
Evie only sold them because she's angry with me.
It's really important I get them back.
A rock ripples deep in my gut.
Her father.
He wants her paintings.
Agnes glances up at me.

I shake my head
before rounding the counter
to pretend I'm busy organizing supplies.
Don't even think about it,
I tell her with my eyes.
Aye, I'm sorry, Dr. Perez.
Seems it was an independent buyer
on his way through town.
'Twas kismet.
But if I see him again, I'll ask.
I'll let him know how important your daughter's paintings
    are to ye.
His heavy shoulders slump.
Guilt tries to creep in,
but I am certain those paintings
mean more to me
than they do to him.
And no matter her reasons,
Evelyn doesn't want her father to have them.
So I don't, either.
I have her money when she's ready to pick it up,
Agnes tells him.
I look out the window over the sink.
My stomach plummets to my feet.
There she is,
in the parking lot
in the passenger seat of a little white car.
She stares down at something in her hands,
turning it over and over.
Look up, I think as loudly as I can.
But she keeps her eyes glued to her lap.
Can we order more canvases? he asks.
Same order as last time, but twice the quantity.
Agnes nods in my peripheral vision.

Aye, I can do that.
She takes notes on a yellow legal pad by the cash register.
Look up, I think one last time.
We can have them in a week.
Giving up, I turn away from the window
and find her father staring at me.
His dark eyes narrow
as if he's just figured something out.
But that's probably just my guilty conscience.
He can't know I have the paintings.
He's never even met me.
Thank you for your help,
he says, never taking his eyes off me
until he turns to go.
I'm dizzy from holding my breath
when I finally exhale.
You heard the man,
Agnes says when he's gone.
They're important to him. You should consider—
NO WAY IN HELL.
It's the most fluent thing I've said
in I don't remember
how long.

THIRTY-NINE
Evie

"They've sold them already." Papá harrumphed into the driver's seat and slammed the door.

"Already?" Little sprouts of hope bloomed in Evie's chest. She couldn't believe it.

Nodding and grunting, he started the engine. "She's going to track down the owner, though, and get them back."

Evie sunk down into the seat, quickly deflated, hoping Oskar had at least seen them before they sold. She wondered how much they'd gone for. Maybe she could sell enough of them to pay her own way to Saint Bart's.

But then something occurred to her: if she went to Saint Bart's, things would probably never be the same again. Based on the complete lack of contact she had with Loretta and Ben, she might not even have any friends when she went home. Nobody except Abuela, which was how it had been all along until junior year, anyway.

"Who's the boy in the window?" Papá asked as he backed out of his parking space.

Evie looked up, toward the shop window in front, and saw him. A little gasp thumped her lungs. Oskar stared right at her. She cleared her throat and shrugged, trying to be cool about it, even though she couldn't look away. A moment later, he was gone from the window. "He works there."

It's not like she'd ever be able to talk to him again after last night.

She marinated in a puddle of shame. Well, it was sweat, but it felt like shame. She reached up and bumped the knob on the car heater, turning it down slightly below fires of Hell. Last night came back to her in fuzzy blips. She cringed inwardly. She'd made a complete ass of herself.

"You friends with him?"

Evie scoffed. "He doesn't even speak English, Papá."

"Doesn't mean you can't be friends, *mija*. Boys and girls can talk with more than words. And his face said a whole lot while he watched you out the window."

"You're *loco*, Papá." Evie tried to ignore the flood of excitement this observation unleashed. She stared down at the prayer candle in her lap that she'd picked up at the church gift shop after the service. She knew the moment she saw it that she had to have it.

Papá peeped at her out the corner of his eye as he drove. "Be careful with that. I'm not sure what the rules are for burning candles at the guesthouse."

"Okay," she said. But she had no intention of burning it. She'd gotten it for Abuela. She just had to figure out how to get it to her without telling Papá.

"Why Saint Anthony?"

"*San Antonio* is the patron saint of lost things, Papá. I'm pretty lost."

He had nothing to say back to that.

They pulled into the guesthouse, and Evie wasted no time shutting herself in her room. It was the first day her papá didn't have to go to work since they'd arrived, but she didn't feel like hanging out with him now.

FORTY
Oskar's Journal

Sweat drips into my eyes.
I drag the mattress up the last set of stairs,
 roll it up like a burrito,
and shove it through the opening in the floor.
The floor-to-ceiling panoramic windows
drench me in gray light.
Being in the Elska lighthouse
feels different after seeing her painting.
All of our hopes were pinned in this building.
We could see everything so clearly
this high up.
But it never lasted.
We always had to come back down.
It had been their plan to live up here.
He promised he'd fix it up for her.
But he never got further than the plumbing.
I glance over at all of his old records stored on shelves,
covers all faded from the glare of sunlight.
The crank-style phonograph
he rigged up to play 33s
sits next to them
in protracted silence.

Pabbi found a way to listen to his music
even with no electricity.
I tamp down the loose bricks with my heel
on the floor of the lookout room
and drop the mattress on top of them.
It's finally warm enough
to make this my bedroom
for the summer.
If I could hook the power up
this could be my bedroom year-round.
Maybe I'd finally be awake to witness
a magnetic midnight—
that time of night when the earth
is aligned perfectly
for the best possible viewing of the auroras.
It's the clearest and brightest moment in the cosmos,
when the answers to everything are finally attainable.
Or so the story goes.
Pabbi was obsessed with that story,
used to tell it to us over and over, and get mad if we
    interrupted.
I collapse on the mattress and stare out to the point
where the North Atlantic horizon
nudges the gray clouds.
I remember when this room
felt like a place we could all live.
The dusty old loveseat pressed in the corner,
with its bleached out floral print,
used to be vivid as spring.
The cushions were so comfortable,
sitting on them was like getting a hug
from a piece of furniture.
I remember lounging there with Ivan
watching our parents dance

to haunting love songs
while white crests
broke silently in the distance.
But the day our electricity
got turned off
at the shop,
I remember him screaming at her.
Telling her it was all *pípa draumur*.[12]
Something that would never happen.
We couldn't pay the bills we already had.
The trees were young and barely produced.
We'd never have enough to keep the shelves stocked.
We'd never make enough to see the dream realized.
Look around you, Maggie!
he screamed in her face.
Spittle flew from his lips.
I'd never seen him so helpless, so angry.
We have nothing!
But looking back now, I know he was wrong.
So tragically wrong.
We had everything.

---

[12] pípa dramur (**pee-puh dra-*mure***): [Icelandic] *pipe dream.*

FORTY-ONE

Evie

*E*mbarrassment overruled Evie's curiosity for the rest of the week.

As much as she wanted to see Oskar after what happened, she couldn't bring herself to go to the store and find out how he'd react to her. Instead, she stayed in her room. By Friday, she set up her last canvas to paint.

Out of cherries but full of inspiration, she tried to recapture the scene by the fire. It hadn't left her mind all week, even as she tried to drown it with books and music.

Fleshy hues on the tip of her paintbrush became a tattooed arm on the canvas. The honeyed glow of a fire illuminated long fingers strumming a ukulele against the gray fabric over his chest. Muscles in his forearm clenched tight as he pressed chords into the fret board.

She couldn't sell this one. Stupid to waste her last canvas like this, especially when this subject wasn't coming through for her nearly as crisp as the others had. Which made no sense, considering she was right there to witness it herself.

While cherries tell tales…

That mysterious poem again. Maybe she needed cherries to paint accurately. She could never be good enough on her own.

She kept vacillating between methods—show the brushstrokes? Or blend them in? This was the exact same problem she'd had with her self-portrait in class.

Maybe it was because her brain was fogged over in that moment by the fire in the same way her brain fogged over when she tried to visualize herself accurately. Or maybe she was losing touch with reality, holed up in her room like this. When her papá came home at night, she pretended to be asleep. She barely opened her laptop, for fear of her mother pinging her on video call or messenger. If the conversation about school never took place again, she'd never have to go. Weak plan, but that's all she had.

Papá had kept his promise and called to video chat with Abuela after Mass, but it took her nurse fifteen minutes to figure out how to set it up on her laptop, and the video kept cutting out once it was set up.

They'd given up and called her on Papá's international work phone.

She was more coherent for the brief conversation, which eased Evie's worries a little. The sleepy confusion from their previous chat had tugged at the back of her mind. What if Papá was right? What if Abuela really was incapable of being on her own?

Evie had taken her phone to the bedroom and quietly told her she was sending her something, to look out for it in the mail. But in order to send it, she'd need Agnes's help. Which meant going back to the general store, and possibly facing Oskar—after getting stoned and trying to kiss him. She wasn't looking forward to that, not one bit. But it had already been almost a week, and Abuela was expecting something from her.

The sooner she got that prayer candle to Abuela, the sooner Abuela could start praying for both of them.

FORTY-TWO
Oskar's Journal

The sofa at the back of the shop
molds a divot around me as I sit,
shifting the shrink-wrapped pack of canvases
between my hands like a Weeble wobble.
I can't stop wondering
why she hasn't come for them.
Or to collect her money.
What if she left Iceland?
Her father hasn't been by again, either.
I made it weird between us that night.
Weirder than it already was.
An antsy uneasiness vibrates in my fingertips
as I seesaw the canvases back and forth.
The toe of my boot taps the floor
in a nervous thumping
that echoes through the quiet of the shop.
Oh for Christ's sake, Oskar. Just go see her!
Agnes's annoyed voice bellows,
and she tosses a spoon in the sink with a crash.
You're making me nervous!
I lurch forward as her voice grates my already frayed nerves.
For once, Agnes has a good idea.

And the canvases are the perfect excuse to knock on her
   door.
Maybe it's time to tell her the truth.

FORTY-THREE

Evie

Evie rubbed her lips together, smoothing the sticky lip gloss. The mascara weighed heavy in her eyelashes, out of place. Taking a breath, she pushed through the front door of the general store, hand over the stenciled *GRIMMURSON'S* on the glass.

Just act normal. Be cool. No big deal.

The scent of baked goods and cherries welcomed her in. It smelled so much like Abuela's kitchen she had to stop and take a few deep breaths of the sweet warmth. Agnes looked up from behind the counter where she was breaking down cardboard boxes.

"Well, there you are! Did Oskar find ye?"

Evie stopped cold and clutched the Saint Anthony candle to her sweater.

"I didn't know he was looking."

Agnes frowned. "He was bringing ye your canvases."

"To the guesthouse?" Evie tried to push the shock back down and put a lid on it. She couldn't even imagine what she would've done if he'd knocked on her door. She shrugged, pretending not to care, but glanced down to make sure her heart wasn't jumping inside her shirt like a frog. "I didn't see him."

"Aye, well. Must've changed his mind then. I guess ye'll be wantin' your payment for the paintings." She wiped her dusty hands on her apron and thudded over to the cash register, pressing a few keys until it dinged open.

Evie stepped up to the counter and set the candle down. "So someone bought all three?"

Agnes seemed to hesitate before nodding. "American dollars, I presume?"

"Yes," she said, eyes getting bigger as she watched Agnes count out five twenties, a five, and three ones.

"They sold for forty US dollars apiece. One-twenty for all three. Minus the ten percent, you get one hundred eight."

Evie took the bills and shoved them into her pocket. "Thanks." She did some quick math in her head, excited about the money, but aware she'd have to sell a lot more to make the eight thousand dollar tuition at Saint Bart's for her senior year. Not to mention supporting herself as an emancipated minor.

"Your father seemed pretty set on gettin' 'em back. Mind tellin' me why you sold them?" Agnes had a maternal, authoritative presence. Evie didn't really want to tell her, but not telling her didn't feel like an option, either.

"I didn't want him to have them."

Agnes chuckled. "That much is obvious, dearie. But why?" She leaned against the counter and crossed her arms.

"He wants me to go to this school in New York City. Instead of finishing my senior year back home." She shrugged, expecting Agnes to chime in and agree with her father. Adults always banded together like villains. "It's this snobby magnet arts school."

"Well, you're certainly talented enough."

There it was: the corroboration. Worse than a backhanded compliment. Suddenly, though, Agnes seemed to be much more interested in Evie. Her eyes widened, less sleepy. Her posture straightened, her frown lifted a touch.

"I don't create well under pressure," Evie defended. "It has to be on my own terms."

"I see." Agnes quirked a brow and pointed at the prayer candle. "What's this?"

"Oh." Evie hesitated. "I was, uh, hoping you could help me mail this to my grandmother in Florida. I'd like to buy a postcard and maybe send her something homemade. From here. Something that'll keep in international mail."

"Hmmm." Agnes glanced down into the glass display case below the register, filled with pies and scones and breads. "How about the cherry walnut bread? Just baked it this morning." She took the loaf from a pan below and set it on the counter between them. "I can wrap it up nice. It'll keep for a week or so. Best to expedite the post, though."

She nodded. "Okay."

Agnes grabbed a roll of foil and started wrapping it up for her. Evie glanced over her shoulder, up at the loft area. Wondering.

"He's probably at the lighthouse again," Agnes said, without looking up. She had pulled a flattened cardboard box from beside the counter and was folding it into shape. "Spends all of his time out there lately. Just like his father used to."

"His father?" She stared at Agnes. "Does his father work here, too?"

Agnes glanced at her, then began sealing the bottom of a shipping box with packing tape. It screamed across the bottom flap, and Evie jumped. "Not exactly." Agnes set the bread inside the box, and then rolled the prayer candle in bubble wrap. "Why Saint Anthony?"

Evie wanted to hear about Oskar's father, but Agnes kept changing the subject. "Oh. She forgets things sometimes. She's in an assisted living facilty. Not a nursing home or anything. It's like her own apartment, she's just a little more supervised. Anyway, she's a devout Catholic, but she has no access to prayer candles. They have church there at the community center. It's a lot different than what she's used to."

"I see."

"The act of burning a prayer candle means a lot to her faith, but nobody cares, apparently."

"You mean nobody but you," Agnes said.

Evie grinned. It made her feel good that someone else noticed, that Agnes was listening to her. "Are you Catholic?"

Agnes chuckled. "No, lass."

Evie frowned and looked down, tracing the wood grain on the counter, unsure what Agnes's laugh meant. People liked to judge the religious types. She wanted to establish herself as Different From Them. "I'm Catholic, technically. I mean, I believe there's a God. I just think everyone observes faith differently. I don't really think God's as concerned with making us jump through hoops and follow antiquated traditions as much as religion would have us believe." She looked up at Agnes, who now studied her with slightly narrowed eyes. "What about you?"

Agnes went back to packing the box. "I believe in the earth, lass. The cycle of life through the universe."

Oh. So maybe she was one of those Celtic women—or a druid, like in *Outlander*. She remembered the symbol on the rock beneath the tree, and on Oskar's arm, and on the poem Agnes had stowed away beneath the cash register. And even on the wall in the shop. She glanced up at it. Oskar had said it was a rune— or rather, he'd pointed to the word rune in the translation dictionary.

Evie tried to imagine for a moment what those religious practices entailed, how different they were from the ones she observed.

"You know, maybe we're both right," she told Agnes. "Maybe every faith is just a piece of the puzzle." Evie thought of those giant jigsaw floor puzzles she and Abuela used to put together when she was younger, before she started painting. It always interested her how every piece was beautiful in its own way, but never as lovely and complete as it was once it became part of the whole. "Maybe nobody has all of the answers, all of us just have part of them."

Agnes pushed the box to the side and grinned. "I like the way you think, dearie. What else for you?"

Evie walked her fingers along the postcard carousel next to the register. Images of the northern lights, geysers, and volcanoes stared back at her. Puffins perched on a cliff by the sea. She settled on one of the orchard. In bold red letters, it read: *GRIMMURSON'S ORCHARD, lone outdoor cherry orchard in all of Iceland*

And why, she wondered, was this the only outdoor cherry orchard in Iceland? Could nobody compete with Agnes's cherries?

"I'll take this one," she said, holding the postcard up. "Can I borrow a pen?"

Agnes slid one across the counter to her, and she scribbled a quick note.

Dear Abuela,

Iceland is a beautiful, lonely place. I wish you were here.
This cherry walnut bread is from a *maravillosa* little
Icelandic general store. And in case you forget how much I
love you, here's *San Antonio* to help you remember.

Te Quiero, Evie

"Do you have matches?" Evie asked, looking up. It'd be silly to send her a candle with no way to light it.

Agnes pointed to a display at the front of the store. "What we have is over there."

Evie grabbed a small matchbox with a lighthouse on the front and handed it over to Agnes to put in the box. She wrapped and sealed everything. As Agnes rang up her order, Evie took a few deep breaths, once again reveling in the delicious aroma of the shop. "It smells like her kitchen in here," she said.

"Your grandmother's?"

Evie nodded. "We always make cherry pastelitos together. Every summer. All the neighborhood kids smell them cooking three blocks away, so they show up in droves. By the time they're ready, we have an eager line on the porch."

"That popular, eh?" Agnes grinned. "I don't suppose you'd like to share the recipe?"

Evie shrugged. "Nothing to them, really. Just a handful of ingredients." She took a marker and wrote Abuela's new address on the sealed box. After paying for her order and postage, she tucked her wallet back into her back pocket.

"Thanks for everything." Evie turned to go, wishing for a little more time. Wishing Oskar would show up. She'd put on all of this goopy mascara for nothing.

"Wait, lass."

She glanced back at Agnes.

"Which ingredients?" Agnes placed her hands on her hips, grin wedged between her rosy cheeks. "Maybe you could stay and show me."

A smile spread over Evie like sunshine. "I could do that. But they'll never be as good as hers."

They only tasted like magic when Abuela's soft, wrinkled hands made them.

Agnes motioned her around the counter. "Well, we could try. Come on over here. I could use a new recipe."

FORTY-FOUR
Oskar's Journal

A hundred heartbeats
stand between me and her moss-green door.
I grip the canvases.
Maybe I'll say…
"Hi.
Sorry I didn't tell you until now, but
I understand everything you say."
But there are so many difficult sounds,
and sorry is hard enough to say as it is,
for anyone.
I know it'll never come out right.
Or at all.
But it has to be done.
I step to the door.
And knock.
The seconds unroll in my head
lengthening into minutes
that lengthen into regret.
She isn't even here.
She's a tourist.
Hardly any time
And she'll be gone.

If she isn't gone already.
This is an exercise in futility.
I get in my car and drive away.

FORTY-FIVE
Evie

*H*er loneliness was showing and she knew it.

She couldn't help it, though. Agnes listened to her in a way that her mother never did. It didn't even matter that Agnes was a little gruff around the edges. She told her about how she'd spent so many days in Iceland alone, and how it was only half-way over. Then it would be off to New York, if that's where her parents forced her to go.

"So tell me, lass, what's so bad about New York?" Agnes asked as they spooned cherry filling into pockets of the pastelito dough.

Evie shrugged. "My mother is there."

Agnes's eyebrows stretched skyward. "And that's a bad thing?"

"She's horrible." Evie reached over and folded the pastelitos, showing Agnes how to seal the edges with the tines of a fork. "Just close them like this."

"At least you have your mother," Agnes said, picking up on her directions right away. "My mother died when Maggie and I were verra little. I don't remember her, not even as well as Oskar remembers Maggie."

Evie's ears perked up. "Who's Maggie?"

"My sister. Oskar's mum." Agnes grabbed a clump of confectioner's sugar and rubbed her fingers together, sprinkling bits on the sealed pastelitos, just like Evie'd shown her.

Evie paused, hand suspended with a pinch of sugar. She pieced things together. "Wait, so Oskar's your nephew? He's Scottish?"

"Half. His father was Icelandic."

"Was?"

"Aye. They both passed," Agnes said, voice taking on a somber tone.

Evie stared at her, hands covered in dough. "That's tragic." Her mouth opened and closed several times. "What happened?"

Agnes hesitated for a few long moments before responding. "Car accident. It was a head-on collision. Took both of his parents, his little brother, and my husband. Oskar and I were the only survivors in the vehicle, probably because we were sitting in the very back, on the third-row seats."

Evie tried to process this for a few minutes, eyes darting around the counter as she arranged and rearranged the pastelitos on the industrial pan. "I'm so sorry," she finally said quietly. "I had no idea."

"'Twas five years ago. I became his caretaker after it happened. Moved to Iceland and took over the orchard."

Evie's brows creased. "You didn't already live here?"

"Nay. We were here for a visit when the accident happened. We were all headed to Reykjavik for a concert. Oskar was supposed to perform for school." She concentrated on the pastelitos and sniffed loudly, maybe trying to suck the emotion back into her head. It was quiet for a few long minutes between them.

"Tell me about this recipe, lass. Is it one of those that's been passed down over generations?"

"Oh," Evie sighed, feeling both reluctance and relief at the subject change. "My grandmother learned to make these when she was a teenager. She came to the United States from Cuba on

Operation Pedro Pan—the biggest movement of unaccompanied minors across American borders in history—and she lived in a Catholic orphanage with a bunch of nuns. She always made pastelitos with her own family in Cuba, but there, they're made with figs. The cherries are a Catholic thing. On Saint Mark's Day, the nuns brought in barrels of cherries. Instead of making pie, Abuela taught them how to make the pastelitos. They were a hit, so it stuck."

Agnes smiled. "That's lovely, dearie. And how about you? When did you learn?"

"I've been making them so long that I don't even remember the first time. A lot of my childhood was spent in her kitchen. I still remember the way the treads on the step stool pressed against my bare feet."

"You know, you and Oskar have quite a bit in common." She grinned. "Pinned between two cultures the way ye are."

Evie swallowed. She'd hit the jackpot of information about him today. "I heard him play the other night."

"Oh, yes. The boy has taught himself to play every instrument he touches, out of sheer willpower. Music has always been his way of communicating with the world. And his voice—sweet heavens! It's the most beautiful thing of all, if he'd just use it. He's a true bard."

Evie opened her mouth to ask what she meant, but the bell on the door clanged against the glass and Agnes startled, knocking the rolling pin into the floor. It sprinkled flour everywhere. Oskar walked in holding two bundles of canvases in his hands, stopping mid-stride when his gaze traveled to Evie.

Evie forgot what she was going to ask.

FORTY-SIX

Oskar's Journal

Well there ye are!
Agnes blurts.
She seems guilty.
I'm suddenly terrified
of the unknown words
spoken in my absence.
Put the canvases on the counter
and unload those crates of milk in the cooler
she says to me in Icelandic,
recovering.
You missed the grocer's delivery.
I know she's not happy
to have to keep up my lie.
But I'm thankful that she does.
I tense my jaw and do as she asks.
So, Evelyn says, lowering her voice,
but not quite low enough,
Why doesn't he speak English
if his mother was Scottish?
I glare at Agnes
through narrowed eyelids
and lean against the heaviness of that word.

Was.
How much has she already told her?
Agnes ignores me
as she shoves a pan of pastries in the oven.
He doesn't care to learn.
The boy's daft at times, love.
Stubborn as an old mule.
Her facial expression changes then,
as if she's just had an epiphany.
She holds one finger up.
You know what, though?
He might want to learn, if you're doin' the teachin'.
Evelyn glances up at me
under shy lashes.
I turn and go back to unloading crates.
Oh, I'm probably not qualified.
She laughs.
Nervous.
Brushing away flour from her shirt.
I speak a lot of Spanglish.
Agnes calls out to me,
speaks in Icelandic.
*Oskar, the girl here would like to teach you some English
    words.*
She points at Evelyn, smirking.
H-h-hætta, I say through my teeth.
Stop.
Evelyn's eyes widen as my voice fills the shop.
She turns to Agnes.
What did you say to him?
*I told him you're interested in teaching him some English
    words,*
she declares with a victorious grin.
And he said he'd love that.

Evelyn's big brown eyes
grow wide as the open oven,
face radiating a similar heat.
Oh. I guess I could do that.
I don't miss the way she lights up
under all the makeup on her eyes.
Here. Agnes hands her the translation dictionary.
Why don't you study this a little?
Evelyn laughs.
I'll have to study it a lot.
But uh—she shifts nervously—*I better get going.*
Agnes leans down and whispers something to her,
probably just to get under my skin,
then hands her a bag of cherries from under the
    counter.
Here, lass. For helping me today.
Evelyn takes them
and her smile
and goes.
The moment she's gone, I turn to Agnes.
You sssaid you weren't muh-muh-muh-meddling.
She smirks at me, unapologetic as I've ever seen.
I'm not meddling, lad. I'm helping you keep up your lie.
Which, might I remind you, I could change me mind about
    any time!
She's bluffing, I'm sure.
I wave her off.
Let's just settle this right now, she says,
stomping toward the door Evelyn just exited.
I step in her path.
Yell:
I d-d-don't like being ta-talked about like I'm not
    even here!
You're not here, she tells me. *You're a ghost.*

Incapable of appreciating things or being happy in the
      moment.
Just like your father.
Agnes returns to her post.
She dusts flour piles off the counter
onto the floor
for me to sweep.
She's taken with ye.
Said she heard you play.
So that's what this is about.
I'd be lying if I said I didn't want her around.
But she's not one of those attainable girls.
She's one you write shitty poetry for
and deliver it in an imaginary heart-shaped box.
She's one you work to try and deserve
but never actually get there
because you're too damaged.
Maybe if I'd handled it differently,
from the beginning,
I'd have a chance.
But I didn't.
It doesn't matter
how fixated I am on her.
We live on different spheres.
I clean up the shop and leave.
On my way out, I tell Agnes,
I'm n-n-not like him.
Don't ever sssay tha-tha-that to me again.
Then, instead of going to the lighthouse,
I go to Bjorn's.
And find Sana.

FORTY-SEVEN
Evie

The morning mist in the orchard gave Evie the strangest sensation.

Aside from the distant, gentle lapping of water and the slurp of her shoes on the damp ground, a dreamlike quiet settled around her on the hillside. Sunlight scorched the edge of the low-lying clouds as she waded through them. She squinted, trying to see the barn.

Excitement had kept her from sleeping most of the night. She'd tossed and turned, curiosity running wild, wondering what Agnes had planned. *Come back tomorrow morning around nine,* she'd whispered. *I have a surprise for you.*

Maybe she was going to teach her some Icelandic recipe in exchange for the pastelitos. Maybe she just needed some help around the store. Or maybe—and this was what had her the most nervous—she wanted her to sit down with Oskar and teach him some English words. Agnes's invitation came right after Oskar said he'd like to learn.

Somewhere around 2 a.m., she'd downloaded a copy of Icelandic for Dummies and read until she fell asleep.

As she approached the barn, the quiet rumble of two voices filled the air—one female, one male. Agnes and Oskar. She followed the sound around the barn and into the parking lot, where the two of them were loading crates into the back of Oskar's car. They both stopped talking and looked up.

"Well, good morning, lass!" Agnes beamed. "We're going on a little trip today. Would you like to come with us?" She placed the last crate into the space left for it. Oskar narrowed his eyes at Agnes. He shoved his hands into the pockets of his zip-up hoodie and retreated to the driver's side of the car, not looking at all excited about the prospect of Evie going anywhere with them.

"Oh." Evie hesitated, glancing at Oskar as he climbed in and shut his door. "Where are you going?" She couldn't shake the feeling that he wasn't happy about her being there.

"Kolaportid, dear. It's Reykjavik's big flea market. We go one Sunday a month to sell product and invite people out to the orchard. We've met a lot of customers that way." Agnes brushed her hands off and shut the back hatch.

Though she'd left her papá a note that she'd be with Agnes, she didn't mention going anywhere. Not that he'd particularly care or notice that she was gone since he'd probably be working until late. And it's not like she had anything more interesting planned. "As long as I'm not in the way," Evie said finally.

Agnes laughed. "Of course you won't be in the way. We could use the extra hands unloading! And you said you haven't been far from your guesthouse—I thought this might be a way to get you out of your rut." She opened the back door and motioned her in. "Come on, lass."

A prickle of anticipation tingled through Evie's arms and legs. She'd spent the last couple of weeks avoiding sightseeing of any kind because she didn't want to do it alone. Now she didn't have to. She climbed into the backseat behind Oskar. Looking at the back of his head was a lot less intimidating than sitting next to him. She set her purse on the floor at her feet and fastened her seat belt, the cold metal of the buckle nipping at her shaky fingertips.

"Foggy morning," Agnes commented as they pulled out onto the road.

"So pretty," Evie sighed. Oskar looked up then, caught her eye in the rearview. She glued her gaze to the window and pretended not to notice. The sheer absence of other people struck her the most as they traveled. Once they passed the guesthouses and the small supermarket where she'd gone with her papá to buy groceries, the landscape opened up into a sprawling, beautiful emptiness. Other than the tarry black road carved through the rise and fall of the mossy hills, and the occasional car passing in the opposite direction, there was no evidence of civilization.

As the road navigated away from the coast, large, volcano-shaped rock outcroppings jutted up and reached for the sky, bathing in the fog as they went.

"What are those things?" Evie asked when they'd passed the third one.

"Elf houses," Agnes answered, grinning over her shoulder.

Evie raised an eyebrow.

"The Icelanders love their elves. Road workers are careful never to disturb them, else they come back the next day and find all their previous work undone."

Evie caught Oskar looking at her in the rearview again. "Does Oskar believe in elves?"

Agnes giggled. "Not since he was little, lass. But his father believed. He even built a little house for them out of loose rocks on the far edge of the orchard's property, in hopes they'd bestow their powers on the trees and help them grow."

"Seems like it worked. You have the *lone outdoor cherry orchard in all of Iceland*," she said with air-quotes as she recited the postcard she'd sent Abuela.

Agnes shrugged. "You can grow anything if you know how to converse with nature."

Evie watched Oskar in the mirror as they rounded a bend, working his jaw and concentrating fiercely on the road. Suddenly she lurched forward. The seatbelt locked and kept her from smashing into the back of his seat as the car came to a halt.

"Och! Close one," Agnes said, a trace of panic in her voice. She gripped the dash. Outside the car, five or six ponies crowded the valley of a hill. One errant pony, roan colored and fuzzy as a pair of fleece socks, had wandered into the road.

Oskar pulled onto the shoulder of the road and put the car in park. He unbuckled and climbed out, leaving his door open.

"What's he doing?" Evie's mouth hung open as she caught her breath.

"Shooing him out of the road. Wild ponies can cause accidents if a driver comes along who isn't being careful."

They watched as Oskar slowly approached the little pony. He held out his hand to it, as if presenting a peace offering. "Are they dangerous?" Evie asked.

Agnes shook her head. "They're pretty docile. Used to humans in these parts. He isn't afraid of them."

Oskar seemed to know exactly what he was doing as he stroked its mane and led it back to its herd. Evie had never seen something quite so adorable. The pony wasn't bad, either.

A thought struck Evie as he got back in the car. "Was it a pony that caused the accident that…"

"No, lass." Agnes shifted and fiddled with a hairpin at the back of her head. "'Twas an American tourist who caused that accident."

Evie's heart dropped to her feet. "God. No wonder he hates me." She tried to meet his eyes in the mirror as he pulled back out onto the road, but he wouldn't look at her.

"Oh, he doesn't hate you, dearie. He's just a grump. Kolaportid usually puts him in a bad mood because he has to be around people."

"So he doesn't like people in general?" Evie noticed more cars and colorful houses as they drove into a little town. Road signs welcomed them to Selfoss. Oskar followed the arrow pointing toward Reykjavik, off Route 33 onto Route 1.

"He's just shy, lass. Especially around girls. But I think he likes you," Agnes whispered conspiratorially. "He just doesn't want you to know yet."

Evie tried to deny passage to the blush rising up her neck as she watched him, wondering if he could sense that they were talking about him. Oskar's Adam's apple bobbed and his grip on the steering wheel tightened. She took the opportunity to ask one of the many things she'd wondered about him. "So he doesn't have a girlfriend, I guess?"

He glanced up at her then. Evie swallowed and looked away, to Agnes's grinning expression. "If he did, he wouldn't tell me about it."

Evie laughed. "Fair enough."

"What about you?" Agnes asked, turning around in her seat to face Evie. "Do you have a gentleman waiting for you at home?"

Evie exhaled and slumped in her seat. "Gentleman? Definitely not." She thought of her Ben troubles as they meandered through the small towns leading toward Reykjavik. Tourist camper vans and petrol stations dotted the landscape as they approached more heavily populated areas on the Ring Road.

She thought of how Ben had gone right for her bra the moment he kissed her. She knew now, after lots of lonely introspection, that wasn't how it was supposed to be. Maybe Ben's age just made him immature. She wondered...

"So how old is he?" Evie asked Agnes.

"Seventeen," Agnes said as she glanced at Oskar. Evie wasn't sure, but she thought he seemed uncomfortable. His jaw clenched and unclenched nonstop in the rearview.

"Same as me," Evie said, a little shocked. He seemed far more mature than the other guys her age she knew. Especially Ben.

For the remainder of the ride, Evie tried to keep the conversation on Oskar. "I loved hearing him play the other night. He's really good."

"Aye," Agnes said. "I tell him that all the time. The lad's a clever musician. He worked very hard. His teachers always loved his determination."

Evie stared out her window at the horizon. Sheep farms rested on hillsides, little white puffy dots moving around in the distance like dandelions blowing in the wind.

As they got closer to Reykjavik, the houses became more brightly colored, like even the paint there was happier. Traffic picked up as they entered the town limits. Modern architecture and carefully landscaped roadsides greeted them. Evie hadn't felt so overcome with awe when she'd left the airport with her papá. She had just propped her head against the passenger window and closed her eyes.

She'd missed all of this beauty before.

FORTY-EIGHT
Oskar's Journal

We park in our usual spot at Kolaportid.
I waste no time getting out of the car.
The forty-five-minute ride
felt like hours,
listening to them talk about me
like I wasn't even there.
I know it's my own fault for being in this position.
But it's not like I can do anything
to change it.
Not now.
As much as I'd like to.
I load the crates on a cart
and try not to watch her
watching everyone else.
She observes the world with a wide-eyed wonder
I haven't felt in a long time.
This place is huge,
she says to Agnes as we walk inside.
Aye, you could get lost in here.
We blend in with the early crowds,
make our way to the booth
next to a coffee stand in the back corner

near the exit.
Agnes's baked goods sell quickly here.
Though the market is open until five,
We're usually out of everything by two.
The three of us stack jars,
arrange breads,
and line bottles of homemade cherry wine
on the wooden table.
Evelyn holds a bottle of wine in her hands,
traces the *awen* on the label,
dark eyes narrowed in pondering.
I see this symbol everywhere,
she says absently.
Agnes changes the subject.
Have ye ever been to a place like this before?
Evelyn grins and leans against the table,
glances around,
sets the bottle down.
This looks like the flea markets back home,
she says.
Just quirkier.
Quirky is a good word for it.
The warehouse building teems
with equal parts
junk and treasure.
Why don't you wander around, lass?
Just follow the signs for the south entrance
if you get turned around.
She looks unsure.
Go, Agnes nudges her,
I can tell you want to.
We'll be fine here.
She nods, tosses her purse around her shoulders.
I watch her as she walks away.

She stops at the nearby tables,
pointing, asking questions,
giving each person
the privilege of her infectious smile.
You better go with her, lad,
She's headed for Cyrus's booth.
Sh-she won't stop, I tell her.
The sssmell will keep her from it.
But of course, Cyrus calls out to her.
He twirls a toothpick between his fingers,
holds out a sample for her.
I can read his lips from here.
You try, he says.
Evelyn takes it from him.
Better hurry, Agnes says as she labels jar tops.
I hate being puppeted like this.
But I'd also really rather not
have her throw up in my car.
I jog over to her.
It smells weird, she laughs.
Don't eat that, I want to say.
Instead, I take the toothpick from her,
pitch it in the trash next to the booth.
Her eyebrows climb up to her hairline.
Oskar! Cyrus bellows.
His white handlebar mustache wiggles as he laughs,
curls on the ends with his smile.
You'll make her sick, I tell him.
in Icelandic.
I stutter and hope she didn't notice.
What was that? she asks him.
Hakarl, Cyrus explains. *Fermented shark.*
We kill. Bury. Four months later, dig up.
Hang in butcher two more months.

Slice it up. Serve to you.
Evie's mouth hangs open.
Her face goes a little green.
Cyrus takes great pleasure in feeding it
to anyone he can.
He's a silly old man who likes to joke around,
but he also loves the shit.
It's rancid.
Evelyn looks up at me.
Her face brightens into a show-stopping smile.
My hero, she says,
and hooks her arm through mine.
You're just gonna have to come with me
and keep me from eating
something gross.
The heat from her body diffuses into mine at the point of
     contact.
I try to find a balance for my arm between loose and rigid
but settle somewhere in the neighborhood of limp noodle.
Now would probably be a good time to tell her.
Maybe I could break out in song,
like we're in a musical,
since singing is the only time I don't stutter.
I grit my teeth, imagining the horror that'd be.
We walk through the aisles of tables,
and I steer her toward the back row—
to the area where the artists gather
to sell their wares.
Oh, look! She grins, pointing to a row of paintings.
She stops beside a particularly bright one with Latin flair.
I love that this one has people who look like me.
Not a lot of that here, I've noticed.
She looks up, glances around.
That's because she's one of a kind,

and I wish I could tell her that.
She drags her feet as she studies each piece.
I slow to her pace.
Seems like I'm out of place everywhere I go.
I can relate to that more than she knows.
She studies each piece with a critical eye,
leaning into me to observe from a different angle.
I started painting because Abuela did, she says.
*When Abuelo went back to Cuba, she thought he was coming
    back.*
*Years went by and it became clear it wasn't going to
    happen.*
They'd been together since she got here.
They fell in love as teenagers,
and living without him was hard on her.
*So she started painting as a means of therapy, as a way to
    hope.*
She stops in front of a painting of a fishing boat tethered to a
    rock.
She handed me a paintbrush that winter after my mom left,
told me to listen to the music and paint what I felt.
*We listened to Bob Marley and painted the cold afternoons
    away,*
and something came alive in me.
*I realized I could translate the emotion of the song to the
    canvas.*
She was like—Oh, you're better at this than me, nieta.
And she pretended she was jealous,
but I know it was an act.
If it weren't for her,
I would've never known I was good at it.
I would've never known I was good, period.
It kills me, the look in her eyes.
I hate the doubt I see there.

She pulls me along and we keep walking,
our connected arms as outwardly natural as a real couple.
But inwardly, I'm hyperaware of her proximity and the
    chagrin of my limitations.
Anyway, my paintings have never been as good as they are
    here.
But I don't think it's me.
I think it's you.
Her eyes burn brightly
beneath the fluorescent lights
when she looks up at me.
My brain buffers,
so we keep walking
while
it
catches
up.

FORTY-NINE
Evie

*E*vie's heart beat wildly with her arm locked in Oskar's.

She didn't know what finally made her bold enough to reach out and touch him, but he didn't stop her, and he hadn't pulled away. That was something. He was warm and smelled like soap. They walked together through a doorway to another part of the market where strands of clear lights draped from the ceiling like a waterfall.

The tables on each side of the walkway were piled high with pottery, clothing, and jewelry. They stopped and dropped arms to examine the junk. One table, manned by a woman with bright pink lipstick smeared across her front teeth, had big jars of glass marbles just like the ones Miss Izzy had. Evie pointed to them.

"There's a lady in my hometown that uses those to see the future," she said to the seller.

"Oh, yes! They look beautiful in bowl with candle. Or in aquarium!" As she made her sales pitch, Evie couldn't stop looking at the lipstick. She wondered if she should tell her. Instead, she bought a small bag of them and dropped them in her purse. Evie glanced up at Oskar as they walked away. "The lady back home—Miss Izzy—told me I'd meet a guy who was very kind and handsome. Maybe there's something to them." Her cheeks burned as she said it, even though she knew he couldn't understand her.

The sediment on the tables got more eclectic as they continued on. Old coins, feather hats, and wooden shoes. Toilet paper rolls made into Christmas ornaments. Blue wigs of varying lengths. A horse costume. Dinosaur bones that were probably not actually dinosaur bones, considering they were packaged in plastic eggs.

They riffled through the piles. Evie giggled at the weirdness of it all. She loved the spirit of the Icelandic people—they were all so happy to be alive, it seemed. They ate their rotten shark and sold their strange wares and ate candy bars with black licorice inside, as if that was exactly how the world was supposed to be. For the first time, Evie was glad she got to live in their world for a little while.

More than anything, she liked watching Oskar interact with people. Agnes made it sound like he hated everyone, but his behavior illustrated something else entirely. He said very little, but there was a definite kindness and respect in the way he communicated, thanking the hot chocolate lady with his eyes and quiet smile as he bought a cup for each of them. Evie sipped it—no black licorice in it, thankfully—and grinned at him as they made the full circle back to where they'd started.

It didn't seem like they'd been gone that long, but by the time they made it back to Agnes, there was nothing left but a roll of labels. She'd sold all of her products.

FIFTY

Oskar's Journal

On the drive back
I realize how trapped I am in this situation.
As much as I'd like
to come right out and tell her,
the truth is hard.
She's been telling Agnes
all about the weird things we found.
I'm sorry you had to sell everything yourself.
I came to help and then we disappeared.
Agnes waves her off with a heavy hand.
No worries, lass. I'm just glad you had a good time.
Agnes never cared about the help.
But I have to admit it—I had a good time, too.
I wonder how much more fun I might've had
if I'd made myself talk to her.
Say all the things I've been thinking.
There's no use wondering.
Oskar saved me from eating rotten shark.
I'll definitely thank him for that once I've taught him some
    English.
Agnes laughs uneasily.
My lies make her uncomfortable, as they should.

I'm flat-out lying to this girl.
It's no longer just an omission of truth.
I have a question,
she says to Agnes.
Agnes twists her body around to look at her.
What is it then, lass?
I sense her hesitation
in the way she lowers her voice,
averts her eyes in the rearview mirror
and toys with the roll of leftover labels in her hands.
This symbol on all your products…
She looks down at the roll.
The three lowercase letter i's…
What does it mean?
Agnes clears her throat.
I glance over at her.
She wrings her hands out.
She's nervous.
Why?
Oh, that, she finally says.
It's called an awen.
It's a Gaelic symbol.
Means poetic inspiration.
Evelyn's eyes narrow slightly in the rearview,
like she's remembering something,
calling it back for comparison.
In a microsecond's time,
she glances up.
Catches me staring.
I look away.
Is that why Oskar has a tattoo of it?
Agnes nods.
That awen means a lot to our family.
We come from a long line of dreamers.

Agnes glances at my arm and then to the backseat again.
So you noticed his tattoo, huh?
She chuckles.
It ruffles my nerves
because I feel like I'm on display.
I think I have a crush on him, she mumbles.
I'm suddenly incapable of rational thought.
I hit a pot hole and the whole car stutters.
Agnes gives me a brief, scolding glare.
It hurts my face not to smile.
As we pull into the guesthouse drive,
Evelyn hands Agnes the roll of labels
she's been holding.
Agnes tells her: *Come to the shop tomorrow and we'll bake.*
She grins, ear to ear.
This is never going to get easier.
Agnes is making sure of it.
She waves goodbye to us and shuts her car door.
You have to tell her, Agnes says as we drive away.
Listenin' to her confess all those things is downright
   voyeuristic.
It's not that I don't know that.
She likes you, lad.
It's now or never.
If you can't tell her the truth, you need to leave her alone.
Which will be impossible
with Agnes inviting her to the store all the time.
The inevitability rolls in on me like high tide.
I can't let myself get any closer.
I'll just have to stay busy.
Keep my distance.

FIFTY-ONE

Evie

*S*he remembered that word from the poem.
the powers of awen
engraved upon rock...
What powers, exactly?

Evie wasted no time opening her laptop when she got inside the guesthouse. She typed the word into the search engine, and time itself took a bated breath as more than two million search results populated her screen.

The first result was Wikipedia.

Awen is a Welsh, Cornish and Breton word for "(poetic) inspiration." In the Welsh tradition, **awen** *is the inspiration of the poet bards; or, in its personification, Awen is the inspirational muse of creative artists in general.*

Okay, Agnes had told her that, nearly verbatim. And she had called Oskar a bard just the other day—Evie remembered wondering what the heck that meant at the time.

But it was the second result that sent a shiver tingling down her arms.

It was the website for the order of druids in the UK.

She clicked on it and realized immediately where the powers came from. The awen was also their representative symbol.

Agnes was a druid.

And maybe Oskar was too.

"I think there's something in those cherries," Evie told Agnes with a conspiratorial grin, showing off her latest painting.

The awen was living up to its name, because every time she ate cherries, inspiration flowed like a volcanic eruption of creativity. Evie knew now that it wasn't an accident. She just wasn't sure how she fit into all of this. She'd spent hours on the druid website, trying to make sense of things.

Druids were spiritual beings, extremely in touch with the forces of the earth. They believed in the power to influence others, to influence outcomes, through meditation and spells and fellowship with nature. It was when she'd read the line about how druids *have conversations with nature* that everything clicked into place. She read about their rituals—the sacrifices of their own blood and sweat they used to fuel their spells, and the importance of gratitude in everything they did.

Evie glanced up at the framed poem on the wall and read it again.

Bless this orchard
As we sow
Limbs and bark of
Ev'ry row.

From midsummer

To Samhain
Gestate cherries
Red from green.

Take blood and sweat
For ripened fruit
Our sacrifice
And gratitude.

That's why these cherries grew in Iceland for Agnes, but no-body else.

"You're really very talented, lass," Agnes said, bringing her back to the present.

Between the fibers of her canvas, colors swirled together in-to a lifelike composition of the scenery beyond the barn. Shrouded within a secret cove, a pond the color of jade stretched beneath a low-lying layer of clouds. Puffy white flowers grew in the tall grass surrounding it. The razor-back cliff rose up and shrouded them from the sea. The lighthouse stretched skyward on the horizon, like a steeple marking holiness. The sky sang in hues of pink and orange and lavender.

But it wasn't the exceptional landscape that made *this* paint-ing feel special.

In the middle of the pond, a graceful woman draped her arms around the neck of a tall man who held her in an embrace. Her chin lifted toward the sky, and her thick red hair wisped down her back, grazing the surface of the water.

Evie had never met these people, but she knew they were in love.

On a small rock to the left of them, two white-haired boys dipped their toes in the water. She'd been working on this one ever since she opened her new canvases, a little bit of progress each night.

"It's lovely." Agnes took it to the back to the shop and propped it below the recessed lighting on the bookshelf. She stood back and examined it for a minute. Evie may have been imagining it, but she thought Agnes had tears in her eyes.

"The man," she said, running her fingers over the bumpy paint of his close-cropped blond beard, "reminds me a lot of Erik."

"Your husband?"

Agnes grimaced, and Evie wondered if maybe she shouldn't have asked. She could tell Agnes didn't like talking about the accident that had taken her family away. Now that she knew the story, she understood Oskar's guarded behavior a little better too. How hard it must've been to lose everything, and then fall under the guardianship of a family member from a different country.

She thought of Abuela again, as a teenager. Abuela had nobody but the nuns.

"No, lass. Finn was my husband. Erik was Maggie's husband. Oskar's father." Agnes opened a drawer next to the sink and pulled out a silver gilded photo frame. She handed it to Evie. "This was Finn."

He was stout and round with a head full of red hair and a face full of smiling beard, perfect teeth peeking through. He held a giant salmon up—it must've been two feet long, maybe more. "He caught that on Loch Ness on holiday. I'll never forget how happy he was then. He was a truly contented man. He loved his family." Agnes sniffed. She took the frame back from Evie and put it in the drawer.

Evie didn't know what to say, so she said nothing. She glanced out the window, looking for Oskar. She'd been back every day this week, learning new recipes and helping Agnes around the store. Most days she stayed until the shop closed, sometimes later if they were waiting on something in the oven. Oskar had kept to himself, though, since the day they'd gone to Kolaportid.

Whatever bonding she thought might've taken place between them had seemingly evaporated by the next day.

He hung around in the shop, mostly ignoring them when he wasn't in the orchard. If he really wanted her to teach him some English words, he hadn't shown any immediate interest. For some reason, she didn't believe he was really down with the idea to start with. His tone that day—whatever he said to Agnes—didn't seem like agreement. It sounded like a hiss.

On those late nights she stayed, she'd watched Oskar leave and head to the lighthouse, or go up the stairs to the loft and disappear. Curiosity tugged at her, and she wished she had an excuse to go up there and see his room, to see the place where he slept. She wondered if his room was clean or messy, what texture his sheets were—did he prefer flannel or silk against his skin, or just plain old cotton percale? Maybe he slept in pajamas, maybe it was boxers, or maybe it was nothing at all.

Agnes spoke and heat blasted Evie's face, bringing her back to the moment. "I hated him with a fiery passion, that Erik." She tensed her jaw.

Evie found it hard to believe Agnes could hate anyone. "But why?"

"Well, he took my sister awa', of course. Came to Scotland on holiday and left with her as a souvenir. She was positively mad about him, lass. She left me behind, and it left me heartbroken." She trailed her fingers down the painting, sighing deeply. "Growing up, it was just she and I, y'see. Our mother died when we were young, our father was in prison. Our mad old aunt raised us on her orchard—she was a witch in more ways than one—and she died, too. So when Maggie left Scotland, it was just me, until I married Finn. I was angry for a lot of time. By the time I forgave her and came here to visit, I only had seven days left with her. Turns out, all that time she'd just been trying to make this place look like home." Agnes slung an arm toward the window.

"With the cherry orchard. Planting an environment like the one we grew up in. She was as homesick for me as I was for her."

Evie searched her brain for the right words but came up short.

"Aye, well," Agnes said, seeming to shake it off. "She gave me Oskar. I love him as if he were my own. Don't tell him I said that, though." She elbowed Evie with a chuckle.

Oskar strolled into her line of vision then, ladder hoisted on his shoulder. His mouth pulled down at the corners, eyes glued to the ground. He moved with programmed purpose, like he'd flipped an autopilot switch. Arms and legs followed a pattern. Robotic. He was just going through the motions. She'd seen someone else in her life behave this way, but it made her stomach hurt to even make the connection.

No. It was different. He'd lost his family. He didn't give them away on purpose like her mother had.

"I know you said it was a long time ago, but he seems like he carries so much pain." Agnes followed her gaze out the window. "When I heard him play that night by the fire, it came through in the music."

They watched him together.

"Music has always been his therapy, lass. After the accident, though, he lost his drive to play. He just needs a swift kick in the pants. I tell him all the time he's wastin' that talent. He doesn't want to play for anyone but himself now."

Evie gave Agnes a side-eye. She didn't believe talent was ever wasted. Why was playing for himself not enough? It was his. He didn't owe it to anyone. "I get where he's coming from," she said. "I never wanted to share my paintings with anyone except Abuela until I found your cherry orchard."

Agnes turned to look at her through beams of dusty sunlight, serious expression etched into her plump features. "You only wanted to share it with your grandmother, lass, because you knew she'd love anything you painted."

Evie thought about that for a moment. She guessed Agnes had a point.

"Everyone needs validation. Someone to believe in them." Agnes stooped and hoisted the large green tub of cherries from under the counter and plopped them next to the sink. "This orchard wouldn't even be here if nobody had believed in my sister. Erik did that for her. He spent his life's savings to buy this property when it was still a barren lava field and an abandoned lighthouse. Maggie thought the springs running beneath it, mixing with magma deep in the earth, would create the perfect soil environment to grow cherry trees, like the ones we grew back home. So she bought that tree there." Agnes pointed to the tree at the top of the hillside, towering above the others at the back fence. "The *Aisling* tree, from a greenhouse in Reykjavik. Planted it. Fostered it. Believed in it. When it began producing, they bought more. They kept adding to the orchard every planting season."

The word rang a bell for Evie. "What's *Aisling*? Is that a specific strain of cherries?"

"'Tis what Maggie named it, lass. It's Gaelic. Means *vision* or *dream*. For her, it represented everything this place could be, and did become, even though she didn't get to witness it herself."

Evie thought for a moment. The other poem she'd found was about that tree. "So it's special. Is that why you tell people not to pick from it?"

"Aye." Agnes looked away quickly and busied her hands, putting away utensils and wiping up crumbs. Evie picked up on her skittishness, but said nothing. "'Tis a good reminder, lass. When you believe in something, it bears fruit."

Evie gathered her courage to ask Agnes about the poem that *had to be* a spell. Had to be. But then she glanced out the window again and met Oskar's gaze. She tore her eyes away as he headed for the door and charged inside with another full bucket. He froze at the counter, looking past both of them to the back of the shop. Evie followed his gaze to her painting.

He glanced over at her, and then back to the painting, tensing his jaw. Annoyed? God, she couldn't keep obsessing over everything he did like this. "So what are we cooking tonight?" Evie asked, pointing to the tub of cherries, trying to appear busy and completely oblivious to Oskar's presence.

A slow smile spread over Agnes's face. "Not cooking tonight, lass." She nodded to Oskar. "I have a project for you two instead."

Evie glanced over at Oskar, hands becoming insta-sweaty. "Uh," she fumbled with her fingers. "For *us*?"

Agnes nodded, hoisting the tub onto her hip. "Follow me outside."

Oskar stepped aside and motioned for Evie to go first behind Agnes. She gave him a weak smile and shoved her damp hands in the pockets of her jeans to hide the fact that they were shaking.

Out back, Agnes led them away from the orchard and the sea, to a spot about twenty meters from an inland misty pond. She set the large bin of cherries on the ground in front of two chairs, a bucket-like contraption with a crank, and a garbage pail. Evie studied the equipment, confused and nervous. Oskar looked away.

"Och, you two look like frightened sheep." She laughed. "Relax. Ye'll be making wine today. But it gets verra messy, which is why you have to do it outside. You'll sit here and punch the pits into this pail," she motioned to the garbage container, "and then drop the cherry inside this cheesecloth liner in the wine press. Once it's done, Oskar will press the juice in this bucket here, we'll cover it for a bit, and then add the additional ingredients when the time arises." Agnes demonstrated how to use the corer to remove the seed of the cherry, pointing it toward the waste bucket. It made a snapping noise and shot the pit across the mossy ground. "Aye, well, you get the idea." She grinned. "Any questions?"

The two of them stared at each other, then at Agnes.

"Oh," Evie said, "do you need to tell him how to do it in Icelandic?"

Agnes cut her eyes at Oskar, and Evie thought she sensed a little irritation. "No, dearie. The demo was for you. He knows how to do this." She winked, spun on her heels and left the two of them alone.

FIFTY-TWO
Oskar's Journal

She sits next to me on a chair,
our backs to the fleeing sun.
Her toes tap inside her flip-flops
to an imaginary beat
as she works.
Every time the wind blows
I smell her hair.
I wish I could bury my face in it.
Tell her how beautiful she is.
Like some romantic hero.
But that kind of shit
doesn't happen for guys like me.
I've tried to stay away.
Foil Agnes's plan.
Yet here I am.
She sneaks a cherry.
Plops it between her lips with a grin,
like she's just done the most criminal thing in the world.
I chomp on my gum to hold back the laugh.
I can't believe you don't make yourself sick eating these, she
    says.
I haven't eaten a cherry since I lost them.

It's better to avoid the tartness
of taste and memory.
I wish you could talk to me.
She mutters it, under her breath, as she looks at the ground.
My silence is an elaborate net of lies I've trapped myself in.
It doesn't even feel like my choice anymore.
I've been learning some Icelandic words, she says.
Reaching into the bin in front of us,
she grabs a cherry
and holds it up by its stem.
It sways a little in the breeze,
sunlit dew gleaming.
Kirsuber.
I don't know if that pronunciation is right.
It isn't.
A grin takes my face by force.
That's another one I know!
She points to my mouth.
Bros. Smile.
She air-quotes the translation
with stained fingers.
Like that will help me understand it.
You should bros *more.*
Smile.
You're crazy hot when you bros.
Pink dusts her cheekbones and I break our eye contact,
returning to the task at hand,
pretending not to pick up on it.
Ripping the hearts out of these cherries
is a great metaphor
for my life.

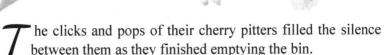

FIFTY-THREE
Evie

*T*he clicks and pops of their cherry pitters filled the silence between them as they finished emptying the bin.

Evie was glad she'd worn a black shirt. The apron Agnes lent her wasn't catching all the cherry juice. It splattered the knees of her jeans and the tops of her feet. Oskar wasn't much better off.

"You look like you just came from a murder scene." She laughed, pointing a thumb at his white t-shirt, soaked with red dots of varying sizes. He looked down at it, and then at her from the corner of his eye.

Her leg was starting to get a cramp from holding it rigid. Sitting so close to him, she was terrified her thigh muscle would get lazy and accidentally lean against his leg. She glanced down at his jeans. His stiff knee—the one closest to her—trembled. She smiled, glad she wasn't the only one worried about what her leg was doing.

They both reached for the last cherry on the bottom of the container, and their knuckles bumped. Evie drew her hand back, letting him have it. He discarded the plucked stem into an overflowing waste can at their feet, shot the pit in with it, and dropped what was left of the fruit into the press.

Oskar stood and tucked the cheesecloth that lined the wine press into the top of the container. He placed a five-liter bucket beneath the spout and began twisting the crank. His arms clenched as he turned the handle, tattoo moving with the motion.

"I can't stop wondering if that tattoo means you're a druid," Evie said quietly. "Maybe you've put a spell on me."

He glanced up at her briefly, then back to his work. Evie watched his hands, stained a bright shade of pink. His nail beds were a deep crimson. She noticed then that he must bite his nails. They were jagged on the ends.

He looked up and caught her staring.

"*Hönd*," she blurted. "In English, it's *hand*. Very similar."

Lame. Embarrassment dumped warmth down her back. She wanted to put her own sticky *hönds* over her mouth so it'd stop talking.

As he turned the crank the last few times, he had to really muscle through to churn out the remaining juice. When he did, he cranked too hard, and the pressure sprayed Evie with a blast of cherry juice. She froze, recoiling from the cold, and looked up at him in shocked amusement.

An accident, obviously, based on the *oops* expression he wore. But laughter rumbled out of his throat, deep and authentic. It might have been the prettiest grouping of notes she'd ever heard. She could paint warehouses full of canvases based on that sound alone. She wanted to hear it again, put the song on repeat.

"You think it's funny, huh?" Evie stood and grabbed the empty container on the ground. Cherry juice rolled around in the bottom. He shook his head and backed up, chuckles still simmering.

An evil grin spread across Evie's lips. With a flick of her wrists, she flung it at him. It soaked his shirt, covering the remaining white with red and sprinkling sticky liquid on his neck and into his blond hair.

Things devolved from there.

He grabbed a handful of the squeezed juice—from the bucket that would become wine—and flung it at her, splashing her left ear. Wind whooshed past her head and Evie unleashed her laughter as he chased her round and round the wine press. She took off her apron to use as a shield but dropped it in the scuffle.

She squealed when he landed a shot, giggled maniacally when he missed.

They were wasting all their hard work, but she didn't even care. For a moment, she forgot that he'd never breathed a word to her, because this playful side of him needed no translation. She understood it just fine.

When she lunged to get away from one last effort, he grabbed her and pulled her toward him, spinning her around at the waist. They stood there, inches from each other. His hands swallowed her hipbones where they rested. Their laughter faded to loud breathing as they surveyed the damage. Evie's hair and clothes were wet and sticky. Oskar had a streak of red on his left cheek that dipped down into his deepest dimple. She swallowed hard. What would happen if she climbed up on her tiptoes and licked it?

Her pulse throbbed in her neck.

God, she could not think things like that. What if he was, like, one of those mind-reader people like Miss Izzy and could see that thought swimming around behind her pupils? The disarming look in his eyes only worsened her paranoia.

His fingers squeezed, as if using her to hold himself upright. She tilted her chin, sure he was going to kiss her. Any second now. She locked on his eyes and waited. *Now would be good.*

But then she sensed it—a subtle backing away, a microscopic release of his grip. His eyes, after what felt like years of contact, slowly drifted. He was chickening out. *But why?* Evie thought she must've done something wrong. Maybe he'd mistaken her nerves for rejection.

He dropped his hands and pointed to the water, about twenty meters behind her.

"*Vv-vatn.*" He said it barely above a whisper, with a slight stutter, but it brushed chills over Evie's skin. It was the first time he'd ever spoken directly to her.

"Water?" Evie exhaled the question mark. He nodded and turned toward the pond, motioning for her to follow. He didn't have to say it twice. She'd follow him into a volcano for five more seconds of his hands on her hips like that.

Their shoes crunched the gray-green moss underfoot. It reminded her of the pine straw that fell in Florida marshlands, except it was longer, and it curled against the earth at rounded angles. It was as if they were walking around in some prehistoric bird's nest. She glanced up at the color-wheel sky. Anything seemed possible in a place like this.

A damp warmth hovered in the air as they neared the pond. Bordering black pebbles separated the mossy grass from the still, jade liquid. They walked through a wet cloud, and Evie breathed the vapor. She realized then that the fog shrouding the water wasn't fog at all, but steam.

Cotton grass swayed at the water's edge, and even as the sun hovered teasingly over the horizon, never to actually dip below, the sky turned a sleepy blue—dreamlike against the green of the water.

Oskar stooped on a sloping rock that kissed the edge of the pond. He rinsed his hands. Evie sunk next to him and did the same. The heat surprised her; she'd expected it to be warm, but not quite this warm. Swirls of pink left their hands and melted away, disappearing beneath the surface.

Her heart had begun to slow down after all the running and laughing. But then...

Oskar reached behind his shoulder and tugged his shirt over his head, then tossed it on the ground. Evie's breathing went into shutdown mode for fear that inhaling and exhaling would somehow blow the moment away. He stepped out of his boots, dropped his jeans to the ground, and kicked them to the side.

Holy. Boxer. Briefs.

She glued her moon-sized eyes to the landscape of their secluded little valley, concentrating on the contrast of colors and ignoring the demands of her greedy peripheral vision. He stretched his hand to her. Waved her toward him and pointed at the water.

Don't look at his crotch. Her gaze panned downward. Yep, she looked at his crotch. When she looked back up, he was staring at her. He saw her look at his crotch.

"You're *loco*," she said, forcing herself to focus on his eyes. They were more blue than gray, now that she really looked at them. Or maybe it was the dim daylight causing the shift in hue. The pond stilled, anticipating. "Who knows what's swimming around in there?"

He shrugged and dove in with a laugh. Warm water splashed on the shins of her pants. She imagined her painting—the comfort of the family who swam in the jade pond—and wondered what his reaction to it meant. Did her paintings give him the same sense of nostalgia as they seemed to give Agnes?

Oskar's head broke the surface with a wet explosion and he stood up. Droplets rolled off blond curls made darker by the water. She made a mental note not to let her eyes dip below his neck. She'd already memorized every line in his chest, spent nights tracing them on the canvas in her bedroom; there was no need to look now. He raised a hand and motioned her forward again.

"Fine," Evie huffed, drawing a circle in the air with her hand. "But turn around."

A smile stretched between Oskar's dimples and he obliged, ripples cascading through the water with his movement as he gave her his back. Evie focused on the *awen* on his arm as she shrugged out of her shirt and jeans, hurrying before she could change her mind.

Her purple striped bra wasn't awful, but the tattered black underwear with one frayed leg hem was another story. Sweet saints above, she could not let him see those. Nerves flooded her all the way up to her neck. She swallowed repeatedly, trying to choke it back. Then she yanked her ponytail free and put the band around her wrist. Huddling on the slick rock at the water's edge, she dipped her fingers in the opaque liquid, face-to-face with her timid reflection. She tried to reconcile the things happening right now.

Life.

Life was finally happening.

She curled into a ball behind her legs when Oskar peeked over his shoulder.

"Nuh uh," she commanded him with a gesture. "Don't look."

Grinning, he turned back around.

Okay, maybe he understood her a little bit. She pulled her long dark hair around her shoulders, using it as a curtain to hide her bra. Maybe it was the same as a two-piece swimsuit, but they both knew it was underwear. Which somehow made it more intimate, more personal. She plunked her thick legs in the water and slid forward, letting the hot liquid swallow her whole. Her toes met a bumpy, springy bottom. Her face must've betrayed her surprise, because he turned and grinned at her as she pressed up on her tiptoes, wading further toward him on a surface that felt like hardened mini-marshmallows.

"Oh my God, Oskar, what is in this water?" She squealed as she cupped a handful of floating white crystals that resembled sea salt, water dripping through her fingers. A red halo surrounded her as the cherry mess rinsed from her skin. Oskar took a step into her outstretched hand. She drew back and dropped the crystals when her fingers bumped the taut flesh of his belly.

She looked anywhere, everywhere else as they waded deeper into the water.

Lavender streaked the sky. Hues of blue and green and purple curled around them like pastel watercolors.

She waded out until the water stopped just below her bra. She splashed it up on her chest and shoulders, rinsing off all the stickiness. Her long locks floated around her, swirling like a mermaid's. "The minerals are gonna dry my hair out." She pressed the wet ends to her chest, only for them to float away again a moment later.

He moved closer, causing a strange current of electricity between them. Ignoring him was impossible. She trembled in her wet skin. His minty breath overpowered the mineral scent of the water, and she inhaled as inconspicuously as she could. She'd never had such a craving for spearmint gum in her life. She was close enough to him to notice there was a slight dimple in his chin, too. Another step and she could have touched it with the tip of her nose.

She looked up and caught his gaze roaming the front of her body. Flustered, she crossed her arms awkwardly in front of her, trapping her hair in place. He reached down and picked up her right hand. His callused fingers sent chills squirming over her wrist as he pulled the ponytail holder free.

Before she could think or breathe, he lifted her hair off her shoulders and gathered it behind her head. A fizzy effervescence tingled outward where his fingers raked her scalp. She looked down and her chin bumped his collarbone as he wrapped her hair into a bun and twisted the band to hold it in place. Weirdly impressive that he even knew how to do that.

"You worried about my hair drying out, too?" She laughed a little, hoping it would hide the quiver in her voice. When he was done, he dragged his fingers around to the sides of her neck and cupped her head, tilting it toward his face. His lips parted as he traced her jawline with his thumbs.

"Please just kiss me this time," she whispered. "I'm so tired of waiting. And hurry, before I bail."

Something warm and overpowering grew there between them like an unspoken promise. But—no. This boy couldn't be the real thing. This was a summer crush, someone she'd forget about until she was rocking on a porch in her eighties. This was stupid. She searched for a word, a gesture, a reason to back away and stop it from happening. But a disconnect between her brain and body prevented it.

Oskar peered down at her, a storm raging between his long lashes. Evie was doomed. Fighting her feelings for him was as pointless as trying to stop a volcano eruption with a metal trash can lid. Heat rode a current from his hands to her skin, melting into every cowardly cell, disabling them. The lid just kept getting hotter. It was time to let go.

His lips parted, and there was no sound but his breath, then her breath, and the faraway echo of water lapping at their waists. Through a wispy white curtain of steam, his mouth met hers. Velvety soft, his lips moved like gentle brushstrokes. Her eyes fluttered shut as he painted streaks of pink and green with his spearmint tongue.

Her damp flesh pressed against him, erasing all the negative space between them. If the two of them had been a painting, there would not be one inch of canvas untouched by all-consuming color. Evie's arms floated outward, buoyant and un-aware they were still connected to her. Everything burned. A fire raged in her lips and chest and hips and toes. She traced her hands up his waist, over the lines she'd been thinking about touching since she'd first painted them.

This. This was how it was supposed to feel.

Somewhere in the distance, a grumbling sound brought Evie back to earth. Slowly, reluctantly, her lips let go of his, and she pulled back and opened her eyes. The air stilled and cooled.

"Damn," she whispered, trailing her hands down his chest and into the water.

He grinned like he understood it was a compliment.

Then, the grumbling again. It swirled somewhere above their heads, churning on the breeze.

"…here to see you! And there's gnats in the juice! Daft children couldn't be bothered to cover it!"

They both turned their attention toward the voice.

Agnes stood over the wine press, looking in the bucket, fists punched firmly on her sides. "Did ya not hear me?" she called to them, and Evie thought she must be talking to her, since she was speaking English. She sunk down into the water, hiding her bra.

Agnes said something to Oskar then, something harsh and heavy with k's. She pointed to the bucket of cherry juice and then back to the cellar door at the base of the barn. She rambled in Icelandic, words that made Evie think it sounded like she was choking on something.

Oskar moved past her in the water and climbed onto the rock. Evie couldn't stop her eyes from tracing the curve of his bottom under his wet boxer briefs as he stood and pulled his pants back on. He shoved his feet into his boots and his head into his sticky shirt as he walked toward the bucket in question. Evie watched as he lifted it and carried it into the cellar.

"And you!" Agnes pointed directly at Evie. "Your father called looking for you." She threw her hands up in the air, as if overwhelmed by irritation, and then turned back toward the barn.

Despite the frustration in her voice, Evie could've sworn she saw her smile.

FIFTY-FOUR
Oskar's Journal

She tasted like cherries.
Nothing like that other girl.
The one whose name fails me now.
That always feels like a list item.
Something I did to prove
I'm a regular guy.
Even if I don't speak like one.
Kissing Evelyn could be a list item
on a list of things I've been missing all my life.
She kissed me like she meant it.
I want to do it again.
And soon.
I jog up the steps of the cellar,
water dripping down my legs under my jeans
and I see Bjorn.
Standing at the top of the stairs.
His eyes squint, like the sun is in them, but it isn't.
Talked to Sana lately?
Unmistakable anger infuses the syllables.
The pitch is off.
I shrug.
He must know.

She must've told him.
Seems you liked my sister a few nights ago.
I stop on the top step.
Narrow my eyes at him.
That isn't what happened with her.
I ended it, finally.
His truck is parked on the far side of the lot,
facing the water.
*But you had your tongue down that girl's throat a minute
    ago.*
How long was he watching us?
I look over his shoulder, toward the water.
Evelyn is gone.
Her clothes are gone.
Before I have time to prepare a defense
or even say anything back,
his fist blasts the side of my face.
I fall backwards.
Down the stairwell.
And crack my head on the cellar door.
Darkness swims the currents
behind my eyelids
and the last thing I hear is his warning.
Stay away from my sister.
I lie there on the cool concrete
for an indeterminate amount of time,
sometimes thinking, sometimes dreaming,
a constant dull ache pinching the back of my skull.
It's Agnes's shrill voice that brings me out of it.
Oskar! Where'd you get that goose egg?
Did somebody hit you, lad?
I sit up and rub my face.
Why'd he hit you, lad?
That hooligan never comes 'round unless he wants some

thing.
I shake my head and wince from the pain.
Ffffell, I say.
Aye, like hell you did.
She tugs me by the shirtsleeve until I'm on my feet
and up the cellar steps.
I scan the empty landscape around us.
Don't worry, she's been gone awhile,
Agnes says, tugging me harder.
Come on, we need to get some ice on that.
I slump on the sofa in the back of the store
while she gets the ice.
This is just the kind of thing that proves you should be away
    at school
instead of here scrapping with those losers.
Agnes hands me the ice bag
wrapped in an old tattered towel.
I won't tolerate this brand of behavior.
Why'd he hit ye, then?
I grit my teeth.
D-d-don't worry about it.
Her eyes turn violent.
I most certainly will worry about it!
Ye let that boy know he isn't welcome here anymore!
I'll have him arrested if I so much as hear that ratty truck of
    his putterin' by.
I don't doubt her one bit.
She's a force to be reckoned with.
And the girl! Did ye tell her the truth yet?
I look down.
Shake my head.
Well, that's fantastic.
She's been confessin' all sorts of things in your presence,
thinkin' you don't comprehend it.

She's learnin' Icelandic just so she can talk to you.
What do ye mean kissin' her like that
if you don't intend to tell her ye understand her just fine?
The vein in Agnes's forehead pulses.
I don't like her being mad at me.
Especially because I know she's right.
I never meant for any of this to happen.
But this girl—she lays waste to me.
She questioned if I'm a druid.
For once,
I wish I was.
So I could track down a spell
to turn back time.
And start over.
I'll tell ye right now, I'm tired of lying on your behalf.
When she comes back, I'll tell her myself.
Agnes stomps off.
I can't let that happen.
Wwwait,
I call behind her.
She turns back to me,
crosses her arms over her chest.
I'll tuh-tuh-tell her.
Just let mmme do it in my own tuh-time.
Agnes shakes her head.
I don't believe ye will.
She narrows her eyes at me.
I pro-pro-promise. I mmmean it.
Agnes stares at me for a moment,
expression changing from anger to determination.
Fine. I'll keep my mouth shut and let you do the tellin'.
Thank—
She holds her hand up to stop me.
Only if you'll reapply to the schools on Edvin's list.

My mouth falls open.
It's such a low blow that I don't know what to say.
Essentially, it's blackmail.
But there's no way to argue my way out,
and she knows it.
Fffine, I growl.
I march to the sink and drop my ice pack there.
On my own tuh-tuh-time, I repeat.
And leave.

FIFTY-FIVE
Evie

*E*vie woke the next morning with a smile on her face.

For the first time since they'd arrived in Iceland over a month ago, she was happy to wake on the squeaky twin mattress. She reached under her pillow and felt around for the heart-shaped piece of metal attached to a corroded chain. When her fingers tripped over it, she grinned wider.

It had caught on her toe when she climbed out of the spring yesterday. She took it as a sign from the universe, God, or whoever was calling the shots, that Miss Izzy's predictions had been right. That magic was real and existed ever-present in her life, no matter where she was on the map.

A heavy-handed knock landed on her door.

"Evie?"

She sat up and bunched the eye mask on top of her head. "Come in, Papá," she said, her voice raspy with sleep.

He cracked the door open and hovered in the threshold. His forehead creased with wrinkles. Uh oh.

"Did you submit your portfolio yesterday?"

Evie opened her mouth to speak, then closed it again. Her face must've given her away.

His voice changed then, and she knew she was in for it. "*Ay ay ay*, Evie. Yesterday was the deadline. I've been forwarding you the reminders all week! Your mother filed your paperwork for you, but you have to send them the portfolio."

She shrugged, a sigh of relief swirling in her chest. She hadn't even checked her messages this week. She'd been too busy with Agnes and Oskar. "It's no big deal, Papá. I didn't want to go there, anyway."

"It is a big deal. Magnet Arts is your best chance at going to a good school for your senior year. If they don't accept the portfolio late, you'll have to settle for public school. Wherever your mother's apartment in Queens is zoned." He started to leave, pulling the door shut behind him.

"Papá, wait!"

The door inched open and he waited, jaw working overtime.

"What if… what if I stayed here with you? I could maybe go to school here. We could bring Abuela up. She could hang out here with me whenever I'm not in school. She'd love it here."

She was done begging for Saint Bart's. What would she be going back to there, anyway? The only thing she missed about home now was Abuela. Maybe home was never a location, but a feeling, a togetherness. If nothing else, being alone all summer had taught her who mattered and who didn't.

He narrowed his eyes. "I thought you hated it here?"

"I did. At first. I guess you could say it's grown on me." She looked down, trying to hide the creeping blush. She didn't want him to know why it had grown on her.

He squinted at her. "Well, I'm glad you've made friends with the boy up the road, *mija*, but staying here is not part of the plan. My contract expires at the end of September. And school will begin for you in two weeks, rather than four, if Magnet Arts doesn't accept your portfolio late. The public school's calendar year begins sooner."

She started to protest about Oskar—how did he even know? But the two weeks part claimed all of her attention. Two weeks was not long enough. She'd just gotten settled here. She wasn't ready to pack her things and head home—wherever that was supposed to be—yet.

She remained steadfast. "I'll do some research on the schools here. There's a high school right in the village. I could probably walk. Abuela could—"

"Bringing Abuela here is out of the question, and you know it. She can't be left unattended. I spoke with her nurse yesterday, and she's been having episodes."

Evie's heart plunged to her feet. "Episodes?"

"She loses things all the time, and now she's in denial about it. She's blaming the nurses, accusing them of taking her things. It means the dementia is progressing."

Evie stood up then, anger pushing her fully awake. "Maybe the nurses are taking her things. We don't know for sure that they aren't."

"I do know it for sure," he said. "Call your mother today and make a plan for getting your artwork in. I have to go to work. You and I will discuss school at dinner."

The door shut behind him with a thud.

Tears prickled at the corners of Evie's eyes. How could he not believe Abuela? Why would he take some stranger's word over hers? Of all the times her father had stood her up this summer, she'd never once done the same thing to him.

But tonight, he would just have to eat dinner alone.

FIFTY-SIX
Oskar's Journal

Five years without eating cherries
and all it took
was a kiss from a girl
to make me go back on that.
I'd forgotten how sweet they were
until I tasted them on her lips.
I take another one
from the dish.
Little details from the past
swim to the surface in my mind
as I get lost in the spell of her painting.
Is this what she saw when she ate them, too?
I don't know how it's even possible.
Four bodies in the water.
A silver locket
that broke as we swam that day.
It fell from my mother's neck,
uncatchable.
Into the abyss of jade.
The white crystals clumped
beneath my father's nails
after he'd dragged his hands

along the bottom,
searching.
My brother's toothless smile
as he cannonballed
into the warm water.
All of them
unaware.
They only had days left on earth.
All I can think
is how unfair it is.
How we're just sitting ducks,
waiting to be picked off.
Snuffed out.
Surprise attacked.
Agnes wants me to *be* something.
Contribute.
But maybe I don't want to give anything
to a world without them in it.
I gather her paintings
and take them all to the lighthouse.

FIFTY-SEVEN
Evie

*I*t'd be embarrassing to face Agnes after what happened yesterday, but it was worth it.

She pushed the door open and strolled in carrying her laptop, lugging her messenger bag full of art supplies over her shoulder and her empty canvas under her arm. She'd have to come up with a portfolio today if she was going to buy herself a couple of extra weeks in Iceland. She read the requirements for the first time this morning: she'd need a graphite sketch, a life painting, and a piece that accurately reflected herself as an artist. She planned to snap a picture of her latest painting at the shop, too.

Agnes came out of the storeroom carrying a cardboard box.

"Oh, good afternoon, lass! You're just in time to help me add yeast to the wine."

She dropped the box on the counter with a thud, and motioned Evie to follow her out the back door. Maybe Agnes was just going to pretend she had forgotten about what she'd seen. Evie was one hundred percent okay with that.

She set her things down on the counter and trailed behind her out the door, around the side of the barn, down the cellar stairs, and into a dank room that smelled like moss. Agnes pulled a dangling ceiling chain, and with a click, a lone light bulb cast a bright yellow glow on the small, dusty workspace. The bucket full of cherry juice was covered in cheesecloth and sealed around the lip with twine. Agnes untied it.

"We're going to add this," Agnes said, pulling a small packet from her pocket, "to the juice. Then it'll have to sit for a few weeks."

A sadness pulled Evie's smile down as they stirred the solution into the cherry juice.

Agnes, noticing, asked her, "What is it, then, lass?"

Evie shrugged. "I just realized I might not even still be here when it's ready."

"Oh." Agnes clapped her on the back with a little more force than Evie expected. "Well, I'll just have to mail you some." She winked.

At least Agnes wasn't mad at her for kissing Oskar. That had to count for something.

"So how much longer will ye be here?"

"Papá says a couple more weeks. Maybe longer if things work out. Feels like I just got here."

They exited the cellar and went back into the shop. Evie looked up at the back wall and noticed that her painting was gone.

"Did you sell my painting already?"

Agnes glanced at the empty easel and her brows pinched, seemingly as surprised as Evie. "Yes! To a tourist," she said, covering her mouth as if she were going to cough. "Said it was beautiful. Let me get you your money." She waved her over to the cash register.

For the first time, Evie considered what it'd be like to really make a living as an artist. While Agnes got her payment together, Evie peered out the window into the orchard, wondering if he would act different around her today. Or maybe he would just pretend like nothing had happened, the way Agnes did. God, she hoped not.

"He's not here, lass," Agnes said. Evie looked back at her outstretched hand, money dangling for the taking. "He's off with his teacher. Applying to schools."

Her heart sank as she took the money. It reminded her that she had to face her own issues regarding school. If she didn't submit a portfolio to Magnet Arts now, she'd have to leave Iceland two weeks sooner. She grabbed her things and moved to a table in the dining area.

"Do you have Wi-Fi?" Evie asked Agnes, opening her laptop.

"Aye," Agnes nodded, going back to unloading a box. "Password is my last name—McNally. M-C-N-A-L-L-Y."

Evie typed it in and connected, getting two more bars than she got at the guesthouse. She stared at the messenger app for a moment before clicking on it.

3 unread messages.

Ben Benson: We need to talk. (6 days ago)

Ben Benson: I know you're probably busy n all. But I'm kinda havin a hard time with this thing. Us. I like you n everything but your just so far away. Maybe we should just play it by ear til you get back. (6 days ago)

How charming. He was dumping her via messenger when she wasn't even online. Evie hoped he'd checked the app every day for the last six days, biting his manicured boy nails and wondering why his messages hadn't been marked read.

It was stupid for her to be mad. After all, she'd kissed someone else. And had spent the last few weeks completely crushing on Oskar. It hit her then that she should've been the one to dump Ben first. That's what she was mad about. She hated he got to be an asshole *and* pull the plug on their sham of a relationship. She should at least get to do one of those things.

She clicked on the next one.

Loretta Devereaux (active): Here's the thing. Ben and I are dating. He said we should wait to tell you until you get back, but

I wanted to be upfront with you so you could be prepared for it. I care about you and your feelings, so it's only fair. You guys hadn't exactly made it official or anything. I hope you aren't mad at me.

Evie narrowed her eyes on the message. Loretta cared about her feelings. Ha. That was a good one. A real gold nugget. This settled it for her, though. She was definitely not going back to Saint Bart's, even if a bag of money fell out of the sky into her lap.

"You all right over there, lass? You look upset." Agnes's voice shoved her out of her own head.

"I'm fine." She wiped her eyes. She wasn't crying so much as she was leaking anger. Of course, none of this was a surprise—she'd known it already. It didn't make the confirmation suck any less.

She clicked off the app and pulled up video chat and dialed Rhona. She would just get all the sucky things over with at one time. When Rhona answered, the screen opened up and her made up face came into view. Her hair was freshly colored, all black outfit neatly pressed. She almost looked glamorous, even if she was just the stage hand. It was such a stark contrast from the ratty-t-shirt-wearing mother she remembered from a few years ago.

"Oh, hi Evie. Just getting ready for a show," she said, leaning over to the mirror next to her computer and finishing off her lipstick.

"I just wanted to let you know I'll submit my portfolio today or tomorrow," Evie said, flat.

Rhona yanked her gaze back to the screen. "What do you mean? The deadline was yesterday."

"I missed it."

Rhona rolled the lipstick back into the tube and capped it, then tossed it a cosmetic bag. "That's just great. They probably won't take it. Deadlines are deadlines, Evie. It's a very competitive school."

Messenger dinged in the bottom corner of Evie's screen. 1 message from Loretta Devereaux. Evie minimized the notification.

"Fine," she huffed, looking back up at her mother. "Then I won't bother."

"Yes, yes you will bother. Just take pictures of the things you already have and send it over to me now. You don't need to do something new. I'll take it by there myself in the morning and see if I can talk to someone. Explain you're out of the country." She flicked her fingernails like everything was such a bother. "I'll make up something. Tell them you had a Wi-Fi issue up there and couldn't get it in on time."

Evie gritted her teeth. "I don't need you making excuses for me."

Rhona's eyebrows raised ever so gently. "Obviously you do. Let me help you, Evie. Stop resisting me at every turn." She glanced at her watch. "Look, I have to go. Send it over tonight. I'll call you tomorrow and let you know what they say."

Evie clicked end without saying goodbye. She opened Loretta's message.

Loretta Devereaux: You not gonna say anything back?

Evie typed the words into the reply box so hard it sent zings through her fingertips. Agnes looked up from her spot behind the counter.

Evelyn Perez: Did you tell him he's a Zip-It? Or does that kind of thing not bother you anymore?

The reply was instant.

Loretta Devereaux: You're being unfair.

Evelyn Perez: How am I being unfair?! You're the one who made fun of how dumb he is, then gave me advice on how to handle my relationship with him, then moved in on him the second I left!

Loretta Devereaux: It's unfair because you can't expect everyone's world to stop just because you're gone. You're only one person. And Ben isn't dumb. He's just different. I can't expect everyone to be as smart as me, lol.

Something hot and sharp stabbed the inside of Evie's throat. She wanted to tell her she'd met someone. That it didn't matter, because she felt nothing when she was with Ben, anyway. But it would all sound like bullshit, something prideful to save face.

When it came down to it, Ben was never the point.

Evelyn Perez: You're right. You just like having people you think are beneath you so you can boss them around. That's what you did with me.

Loretta Devereaux: WTF are you even talking about right now, Evelyn? I get that your feelings are hurt, but you don't have to be a bitch.

Evie's mouth popped open like a letter O. Without missing a beat, she typed her response.

Evelyn Perez: My name is Evie. That's what my friends call me, anyway. I should've known you weren't my friend when you tried to change me. I'm not coming home to Florida. And thanks to all of this, I don't even have to be sad about it. So thank you for that, at least.

The message was marked read. Loretta didn't reply.

Feeling energized for finally standing up for herself, Evie clicked over to Ben's IM window.

Evelyn Perez: Here's a tip: YOUR means something belongs to YOU. For example: Your girlfriend, Loretta, told me everything. YOU'RE is a contraction that means YOU ARE. YOUR never means YOU ARE. Used in a sentence: You're a dick. Don't ever contact me again.

Her hands shook as she hit send. She slammed the laptop closed and met Agnes's eyes across the counter.

"Would you like some hot cider, dearie?" Concern pinched the corners of her mouth.

"No, thanks." To her surprise, her voice wasn't uneven. She was one hundred percent recovered to chill. "Could I store my laptop behind the counter, though? And maybe set up in the orchard to paint? I have a lot of work to do."

Agnes nodded. "Of course."

Evie rose from her spot at the table and headed toward the counter. She thought for a moment. Maybe she'd just come clean with everyone. "I ate some of the cherries from the *Aisling* tree. I'm sorry I didn't tell you before."

Agnes didn't look the least bit surprised. "I know, lass."

Evie paused, weighing in her brain how much she could safely admit. "I didn't know I wasn't supposed to at first. I knew it was special somehow when I saw the rock with the *awen* on it. Then, the day of the earthquake, I saw that poem with the same symbol. You didn't want me to see it because it's a druid thing. A spell, right? Like the one on the wall." She pointed to the framed poem. Light reflected off the glass. "That one makes the orchard grow, right? I Googled it."

Agnes fidgeted and cracked her knuckles, like she was popping all the tension right out of the air through her fingers. After a deep breath and a paralyzing bout of silence, she stooped beneath the counter and rummaged a bit until she came up with a piece of parchment paper. It was black around the edges, like it had been ritualistically burned. She extended her arm, and the breeze from the air vent made the page flutter between them.

Evie didn't realize her hand was shaking until she reached out to take it. The paper was warm between her fingers, as if it had its own life force. She'd forgotten how red the words were, and wondered for the first time if it was written not with cherry juice, but with blood.

She read it again, stumbling over some of the unfamiliar words.

O mór Alban Hefín
Lend us your draíocht
With powers of awen
Engraved upon rock.

I scatter these ashes
On mourning tree roots
Infuse here an essence:
Their spirits through fruits.

May love here still flourish
And comfort our loss
By the otherworld's link
With harvest and blás.

When sea winds blow gently
Through midsummer's veil
Preserve here the stories
While cherries tell tales.

May only the purest
Inspired eyes see
The memories kept here
By the Aisling tree.

"The spell was for him." Agnes's voice broke open on the last word. "I wrote it myself the day we scattered their ashes over the roots of the Aisling. Only ashes are powerful enough to create a connection to the Otherworld, ye see. Those visions were supposed to be for him, a safekeeping of their memories and in-spiration to go on, but he's a stubborn lad. He'd never eat the cherries himself."

Every word seemed to writhe out of Agnes's mouth, and Evie got the distinct impression that she was telling her more than she was supposed to.

"You don't have to explain it all," Evie said, swallowing the lump in her throat. "I figured most of it out. I remembered the line about *the memories of the Aisling tree.* And *while cherries tell tales.* And when you told me the thing about it meaning dreams, I wasn't sure if it was the dreams of your family, or if the tree itself maybe had its own dreams and memories. I just needed to know I'm not crazy. I'm sorry for pressing—"

"It's okay." Agnes cut her off, wiped her hands with a towel and tossed it aside. "The spell found a way. Just promise me one thing." Her eyes glassed over with unshed tears.

Evie nodded, waiting.

"Keep sharing those dreams with Oskar."

FIFTY-EIGHT
Oskar's Journal

Princeton, Boston,
Philadelphia,
London.
Four applications take me two hours to complete.
Edvin won't let me quit early.
I'm already pushing the final deadlines.
The café walls close tightly around me.
We could've done this at the buh-buh-barn, I tell him.
You need distance, Oskar.
Distance
is all I ever feel.
Except when I'm around her.
Edvin asked me about her on the way over.
On Agnes's insistence, I'm sure.
If I still had a dad,
would the conversation have been so awkward?
She's pppretty, I said,
and left it at that.
Lots of pretty girls outside Elska.
I just shrugged.
When we're done, he drives me back in silence.
The whole way, I hope he drops me off.

But of course, he comes inside.
To see Agnes.
Conspiring is no good unless you have an accomplice.
Their eyes meet across the counter, and I see it happening.
The slow burn catches and a flickering flame grows.
It's not that I'm not happy for them.
Or Agnes, in particular.
I just wonder how
she's over the pain
and I'm not.
I'll never be over it.
Agnes points to the window,
a conspiratorial smile lighting her face.
She's in the orchard, lad, painting.
My gaze follows her gesture.
Dark hair waves
from under the branches
of my tree.
Wow, Edvin says. *She's something.*
I'm well aware.
And right now, all I want to do is kiss her again.
Her lips are the only place
I've ever felt something that made me forget.
Even for just a moment.
I let the wind toss the door against the barn
as I head toward her.
Hoping I don't lose my nerve.

FIFTY-NINE
Evie

*T*hat bruise on his face gave a little more color to the black-and-white mystery Oskar had been since the moment she met him.

Evie couldn't imagine who'd want to hit him. Certainly not Agnes. She was a robust woman, but Oskar was big and broad in a way that would make even the toughest guys think twice about throwing a punch. Nothing about his demeanor said he'd ever hit back, though. He was strong but silent. Intimidating but gentle. A definite duplicity existed in him.

They both stared at her painting.

Beneath her trembling brush, a new image took shape. If it was the tree's memories coming to life on her canvas, she wanted to know what it was trying to tell her. What had Agnes meant by *the spell found a way*? Found a way to what?

A woman with long copper hair was walking away, toward the barn on the horizon of the painting. Around the periphery of the canvas, branches with cherries jutted out. As if the artist doing the painting was the tree itself. Evie felt like she could be the artist or the subject in this one; she, too, would be walking away soon.

Her heart had been beating itself bloody against her ribcage ever since he'd walked up. Something had changed between them. There was a closeness that wasn't present before, one that could only be shared when two people had felt the inside of each other's lips. It was like having a secret that nobody but them could ever know, even if they told the world about it. Which made it even more devastating that her time with him was ticking down. It made her want to turn around and kiss him right then, because in a few weeks, she wouldn't be able to.

"I'm probably going to have to leave soon." Her statement shattered the quiet. Even the breeze stilled against the sadness. "My father is sending me to New York to live with my mother."

As usual, he said nothing. She didn't expect him to. He stayed so motionless that she peeked over at him to make sure he was still sitting there. His eyes stayed trained on her painting.

"Guess I should learn to speak better Icelandic if I'm going to tell you goodbye." She put the final touches on her painting and dropped her brush in the water cup, and then twisted her body to face him.

The air was colder today than it had been in days past, which felt appropriate somehow. It was easier to be sad when it was cold, to fold in on herself and hide beneath layers.

If only there was a world where Oskar and Abuela and the Florida sunshine could co-exist.

SIXTY
Oskar's Journal

I've been thinking about running away.
She draws her knees under her sweater,
stretching it out.
I try not to think about
the golden skin
under that woven pale fabric.
But I fail.
Silly, because I'm probably too old to run away.
If she ran away,
maybe she'd stay here.
With me.
I let that thought
plant a shaky smile on my face.
It wobbles
under the force of my pulse,
like it might
slide
right off my face
into
my
lap.
Something simmers

in the air
between us.
It's weird, right?
She rests her head on her knee,
long locks draping down,
tickling the ground.
Her big dark eyes study me.
This thing between us.
We can't even have a two-sided conversation.
But we can kiss like we did yesterday?
There she goes again,
picking apart my thoughts.
I erect a stone fortress in my brain,
trying to keep her
from seeing the things
going on behind my eyes.
And speaking of that—I shift.
Fluff my sweatshirt over my waist.
God. I have never kissed anyone like that.
I think of the most repulsive things I can conjure.
Rotten cherries.
Bjorn's bathroom.
Agnes's angry face.
There.
That's better.
If Agnes hadn't come outside...
She lifts her head, leans in, whispers,
I wouldn't have stopped.
I would've let you do whatever you wanted.
My throat aches as I swallow.
Candid is a new thing for me.
Everything anyone has ever said to me
since the accident
has felt like a code

that needed cracking.
People dance around the truth with me.
Not her, though.
There's no guesswork.
She invites me to look into the window
of her most private thoughts.
Would she be so honest if she knew I understood?
I'm guessing not.
Her cheeks deepen in color
and she looks away,
back to her painting.
Looks like New York is a sure thing now.
But I can leave next year.
Maybe I'll come back here.
And bring Abuela with me.
She shifts in her sweater cocoon.
I know that's smarter than running away.
But I hate having to give Rhona even a year of my life,
when it takes a year away from Abuela's.
Rhona couldn't give me any of hers when I was growing up.
It's too late now.
My stomach hurts for her.
I lost my mother, too.
But even now, I know she loved me.
Still loves me,
if there's really a place
beyond the grave.
In a way,
her loss is worse than mine.
Because she never had it to begin with.
It's like a void, you know?
I wish I could fill that void for her.
For the first time,
I consider something I said I never would.

America.
Would I feel differently about it
if she was there?
Would she?
There are two ways I could ask her.
The first is with my lips.
The second,
also with my lips.
I lean in.
Take her by surprise.
It's even better
than the instant replay
my mind's been suggesting.
I never wanted to eat cherries again.
But here,
against her mouth,
I remember the sweetness.
The love that once filled this orchard.
Maybe it exists beyond the property lines.
A sneaking suspicion creeps up behind me,
like the prickle of someone's stare.
I pull away.
Glance behind me
at the window of the barn.
Agnes and Edvin scramble
to turn away when I see them.
Fury replaces the hope
almost instantly.
This is exactly what they want.

SIXTY-ONE
Evie

They attended Thursday night Mass together because Papá had to work the weekend again. Evie had submitted her rushed portfolio to Magnet Arts but hadn't heard anything yet. She'd stopped worrying about it.

The past week had been better than all the others put together. Oskar let her talk to him; he never interrupted her. She unloaded, and he was there for her. And even though he didn't understand her, it was okay, because just being there was enough. Maybe it was her imagination, but he did always seem to kiss her at exactly the right moment. On some level, he understood.

So much kissing had happened that week. Under the shade of the trees. Behind the barn. In the cellar as they checked on the progress of the wine. She'd be content to spend full days doing nothing but kissing.

Well, maybe she'd do even more than that, but it never came up. Part of her wondered if that meant he was a gentleman, or if there was something wrong with her that he hadn't even tried. No hands in her shirt. No groping. No taking without asking. Always in her hair or on her hips. Intimate without crossing any lines.

"You've been spending a lot of time at the orchard," Papá said to her as they left the church. She jumped, paranoid that he'd somehow read her mind. "With the *muchacho*, I guess?"

Evie fixed her gaze on the blurry landscape beyond her passenger window and rolled her eyes. This was not a conversation she was interested in having.

He tried again, failing to take the hint. "Does he know you're leaving?"

"We don't talk about it." Evie turned and glared at him. "We don't talk at all. He doesn't speak English, remember?"

"That doesn't seem healthy." Papá's worried look gave her a small pang of satisfaction. She opened her mouth but closed it again, instead reaching forward to crank up the local radio station. Some song about boys smoking in the woods thumped in the speakers. Which, of course, made her think of Oskar. Things had changed since that night by the fire. No, maybe they didn't talk, but she was starting to believe that he knew her in a way nobody else ever could. And knowing how soon their time together would be finished made her angry with her father all over again.

Screw it. She'd just say it.

"Going to live with someone who never wanted me in the first place is probably not exactly healthy either."

"Evie."

"Don't worry about it, it's only a year, right?" She waved him off. There was nothing for her in Florida but Abuela, but maybe she'd hop in her car and drive straight to Florida. He couldn't stop her if he was in Iceland. She had a year to figure out if she wanted to go to college, or maybe she'd get a job and save enough money to move Abuela to a retirement home in a new city, where they'd both start over. Hell, maybe she wouldn't even finish her senior year. Maybe she'd get her GED and call it a day.

"Let's spend some time together before you have to go back," Papá said. "You've been gone so much lately."

His hypocritical complaint cut her so deep she refused to even respond.

She wanted to spend her last week with Oskar. She might never see him again.

As Evie was packing some of the things she knew she wasn't going to need for the next week, Papá knocked on her bedroom door.

"Come in."

He poked his head in the door, a smile hugging the corners of his mustache. "I have to leave for a work dinner *en un momento*, but Abuela's nurse finally figured out video chat. Want to come say hi?"

Evie dropped the books in her hands into a storage container and followed him into the kitchen. They sank to the dinette table together. The dark-haired nurse smiled into the screen.

"Oh, Evie! She's going to be so happy to talk to you." She stood up from a desk, holding her computer against her midsection. The background swirled behind her as she moved down a bright hallway.

Evie's pulse hummed in every pressure point in her body as she waited, watching the nurse knock on the door, go inside, and set the shaky screen on a table. When Abuela came into view, Evie held her breath.

She'd never seen her look so tired. Her usually smooth salt-and-pepper hair was falling out of its bun, frazzled. Half up on one side, half down on the other. Behind round frames, her dark eyes seemed vacant. Awake, but unaware. She looked around for a minute before stopping on the screen. Instead of looking at the camera, she searched the picture on her own screen instead. After a moment, a slow smile crept onto her face. Her eyes flickered with recognition, and she drew wrinkled brown hands to her face. They trembled against her cheeks.

"*Nieta.*"

The word nearly wrecked Evie right then, but she held it back. If she were seeing Abuela in a week, instead of her mother, it might be easier to leave Iceland.

"Hola, Abuela."

They talked for a few minutes. Evie told her about New York. She tried not to sound as disappointed as she felt, but Abuela picked up on it immediately.

"Maybe I'll come and see you there," she said. "You can show me the Big Apple."

Evie nodded, knowing that would probably not happen, and the realization churned tears into her eyes.

"Will you get to be in shows?" Abuela asked.

Evie's eyes narrowed on the screen, searching the depths of the vacant look that had returned. Before she could say anything, Papá cut her off.

"Mamá, you're getting confused again. That's Rhona who wanted to be an actress. Not Evie."

"Oh, Alberto, be quiet. I was talking to Rhona, not you!"

The argument became louder and more heated as it progressed. She was exhausted just watching them. But more than anything, she was sad. How could Abuela mistake her for Rhona, even for a moment? Maybe she could jog her memory somehow.

"Did you get the package I sent, Abuela?" Evie interrupted. She felt a little silly for not checking on that sooner.

Abuela looked up at the screen again, train of argument lost for a moment.

"You sent her a package?" Papá asked.

Evie nodded. "Did you get it?"

Abuela looked around, as if she would find it next to her. "Yes, yes of course," she said, uncertainty trembling in her smile. "*Gracias.*"

"What did you send?" Papá asked, an edge of irritation in his voice.

It's not like she had to tell him every single thing she did. It didn't concern him. Nothing but his job concerned him.

"Baked goods," she answered, purposely leaving out the contraband items. She was certain he wouldn't be happy about those, if he knew.

"The bread was delicious, Rhona." Abuela kissed her fingers with a grin. Some recognition set in, but not enough. At least she had received her package.

Evie's throat burned.

"We have to go now, Mamá," Papá said to her. Running diversion. "But we'll talk again this week, okay?"

Abuela nodded. "*Adios.*"

The nurse leaned over and picked up the laptop, Abuela's face suddenly replaced by a scrub-top pattern and a swirling background again. Once in the hallway, the nurse spoke to the camera.

"She's just having a difficult day today," she said, false reassurance selling itself out in her voice. "We'll try again later in the week."

Papá nodded. "Thank you for doing that."

"No problem."

Evie had approximately thirty seconds before she melted into incoherent sobs, so she stood and headed toward the door before it could happen.

"Evie, wait—" Papá called to her as he disconnected the call. She didn't wait, though. She grabbed her hat and scarf and headed to the only place that felt safe anymore.

SIXTY-TWO
Oskar's Journal

When I come downstairs from my room,
carrying my ukulele bag over my shoulder
I find Agnes's note next to the cash register.
Gone to a show with Edvin, be back late.
At the back of the store,
a painting sits on the easel
in a pool of recessed lighting.
It's the one she was working on yesterday,
when I crept up behind her
and inhaled her words before she could speak them.
It's a hand,
dripping with water,
holding a locket.
A silver locket with a broken lobster clasp.
As far as I know,
my father never found it.
But maybe he did.
Maybe he gave it back to her.
Maybe she was wearing it that day,
and I just didn't notice.
Maybe it was stowed away in her purse,
some future trip to a jeweler

that would never be taken.
I hoist it from the easel
and haul it out the side door,
locking up behind me.
As I pass the pond
on my way to the lighthouse,
I hear something.
Quiet crying.
I freeze when I locate
the source of the sound.
The retreating sunlight hides her
in the shadow of a large stone.
She's on the ground at the water's edge,
face buried against her knees,
dark hair cloaking her like a curtain.
Once I'm in front of her,
I don't remember the walk over.
Like I usually don't remember
the ride home from Bjorn's.
Muscle memory.
I just go to where I belong.
As I kneel in front of her,
setting the painting
and my ukulele
on the ground,
she looks up.
Her eyes have puffy wet rings around them.
Tangled lashes mat against her lids.
She wipes the end of her red nose
with her sleeve.
She didn't remember me.
Her voice quivers.
*It's been less than six weeks, and she didn't even know my
   name.*

I reach for her,
and she dives into my arms.
Papá was right—she's deteriorating fast.
She mumbles against my chest,
words barely coherent.
By the time I leave New York, she'll forget I ever existed.
She shakes against me,
and we stay like that for a long time,
on the wet ground,
huddled together against the icy breeze.
When she finally pulls back,
I want to kiss her,
but I don't.
Instead, I wipe the wetness
from her eyes with my thumbs.
She rewards me with a weak smile.
Abuela is the only person who ever really knew me.
She pulls her hair off of her face,
twirls it into a rope,
and lets it drop over her left shoulder.
I'm not myself with anyone else.
My mother. My friends. My Papá.
But Abuela is the only person I didn't have to pretend
    around.
With everyone else, I'm a fraud.
I'm weak and I fake it and I'm too cowardly to just say what
    I'm thinking.
She's wrong, though.
She's the most real person I've ever met.
I could tell her that right now.
I feel the weight of the do-or-die moment.
The heaviness subsides
as it passes me by.
If I tell her now,

after all this time,
that I understood her all along,
it'll only ruin everything between us.
We don't have much time left as it is.
I can't hurt her more than she's already hurting.
But maybe I can make her understand
somehow
she isn't alone.
That I'm here for her.
I pull my ukulele out of the carrying case.
Prop it against my chest,
and play the opening melody
of a song
I know she'll know.
Her frown lifts by millimeters
as the notes surround us.
I sing the words in my head.
No woman, nuh cry...
She sniffles as I play,
smiling through her tears.
She makes me
want to play
on and on
until everything's better.
When I finish the song,
she dives in.
Kisses me
until we have to come up for air.
She glances at the painting
that I propped against the rock.
What are you doing with my painting?
she asks, breathless.
I stand and reach for her hand.
If I can't tell her

the whole truth,
maybe I can show her
some of it.

SIXTY-THREE

Evie

*E*vie held his hand as they walked around the pond, his ukulele slung between them, her painting under his other arm.

He led her to the lighthouse and opened the heavy arched door, motioning her inside. This was significant. Agnes had told her this was his private place, his hideaway.

She stepped into the trapped briny air. A faint light spilled in from the top of a massive spiral brick staircase. He took her hand again, and they walked up the steps for miles. Orange light poured in through the portholes extending every few feet all the way to the top. When they reached a landing, Evie looked through one of them, squinting against the retreating sunset as it kissed the ocean goodnight.

She followed Oskar up a ladder into a square-shaped hole.

What she found there made her equilibrium swirl. It was like crawling into another world.

The room that housed the light itself—which Agnes mentioned hadn't functioned in years—had been converted into a living area overlooking a panoramic view of the sea. Floor-to-ceiling windows faced them, 180 degrees around. Piles of music books were organized on makeshift bookshelves where the old light used to be. An ancient record player sat in one corner, next to a cabinet full of vinyl records with framed photos on top. Instruments were scattered about—a drum on an empty shelf, guitars of various sizes in separate stands on the floor, a harmonica tossed on a mattress that was covered in a down blanket and armloads of mismatched pillows. The place could've been a two-page spread in an Ikea catalog if it weren't so dusty. The Musician's Loft by the Sea, they'd call it.

Behind them, a wooden door led to a small bathroom. Evie turned, admiring the view, but what hung on the back wall stunned her into silence.

Evie turned to him, a shaky realization tingling through her words. "You bought my paintings?" Every single one of them hung neatly on display, with the exception of the one he'd set on the floor at their feet. An inexplicable fluttering took root in her chest. Tears filled her eyes.

She wandered around the small space, mouth agape, touching the paintings, running her fingers over the vinyl records, picking up a photo that rested on top of the cabinet.

Inside a gold frame, six people stared back at her. Two of them she recognized. Agnes stood on one end of the pose, younger and thinner, clutching a short, stout man with a mustache—the man from the picture she'd shown her. Finn. Beside him, a tall and skinny bearded man with a severe frown draped a lanky arm around a beautiful red-haired woman with a silver locket around her neck. It took Evie less than a blink to realize they were all subjects from her paintings. The two young boys who stood in front were Oskar and his brother.

Evie's hands shook. Oskar reached over and took the frame from her, and then set it back on the shelf. "That's your family." Her whisper wasn't a question. He nodded like he understood. "That's why you bought all my paintings."

The spell found a way.

When Oskar didn't cooperate with Agnes's plans, the tree had shared waking dreams of his family with her instead. It wanted her to know. Wanted her to paint them for him. Despite all of her Cs in art class and uncertainty about herself as an artist, she knew she was the only person who could've painted these images for him.

For the first time since she'd lounged on Abuela's porch swing, she was in exactly the place she was supposed to be. Maybe everything really did have meaning. Maybe losing Ben and Loretta and being forced to Iceland for the summer was exactly what was supposed to happen. Fighting it had made no difference, because here she was. And somehow, standing in front of her now, with big tattooed arms and messy hair and crooked bottom teeth and perfectly asymmetrical dimples, was her silver lining. Maybe they couldn't talk to each other, in the basic sense of the word. But they both spoke the language of cherries.

She stepped into him and kissed him until she couldn't breathe.

They wound up on the mattress, rolling around until darkness fell—which happened sometime after 10 p.m. now, as the summer faded and the earth hurtled toward the fall equinox. Everything in this beautiful, foreign landscape happened fast and intense. Summer burned bright every single evening, until the seasons whiplashed into change.

His hands stayed in her hair—the kind of restraint she didn't know boys were capable of. When they came up for air, a lazy smile stretched across Oskar's lips. He lit the wood stove next to them with a long match from the bookshelf, and then shut the iron door. Warmth swam through the cavernous space of the lookout tower.

Evie collapsed backwards on the pillows and looked up at the sky. She noticed a green tinge faraway, above the clouds, so she focused on it for a moment, testing her imagination. She watched as the green grew into a swirling ribbon that cut across the sky and disappeared again.

Another match struck next to her. Oskar shook the fire away and took a drag, cherry end burning brightly as he did. Nerves flooded her belly when he passed it to her. She could've said no. She'd already done it once; she knew what it was like, so she couldn't blame curiosity anymore.

It wasn't curiosity that beckoned her this time; it was the desire to join him in oblivion. To forget that this had to end. She took it from him and drew a deep breath. Followed by raucous coughing. She could never make this look cool. Once her lungs had settled, she turned her attention skyward again. Through patchy clouds, she could make out constellations with the accuracy of an amateur astrologer. Miss Izzy had taught her a little bit about the stars.

"That's Orion's belt there." She pointed. "And there's Cassiopeia. Or is that Taurus?" She squinted, amazed that she could identify the same constellations from Iceland that she could from Florida. The world seemed smaller when she looked up at the sky, which ironically made the things she wanted seem more attainable. Made the distance feel less impossible.

The clouds floated apart, slowly, as they watched, inhaling and exhaling. Coughing and giggling. As the sky opened up to an orchestra of starlight, the edge of color that had hinted before stepped out to center stage.

"I didn't know you could see the Northern Lights in August," she said. Though she'd never seen them in person before, it didn't feel like the first time. She'd painted them just weeks before, and the memory residue lingered in her brain as a result. Oskar moved beside her, but she couldn't tear her eyes away from the sky.

A gentle melody played on the strings of an acoustic guitar, the same song he'd been playing the first night she heard him by the fire. As he played the song, the green ribbons twirled slowly, dancing with lavender partners to the tune. Evie lifted her hands above her head and made a triangle, closing one eye and framing snapshots of the cosmos—to paint later.

All of her worries were like the distant stars. She knew they existed, but somewhere far away. Nothing mattered in that moment but the warmth and the starlight and the music. And, she had to admit, the boy.

Evie turned over on her side and shifted her gaze to him. She propped her head on her hand and admired the way his forearm flexed as he strummed the strings. He held it differently than he'd held the ukulele, but the song was the same.

His lashes kissed his cheekbones, eyes closed, mouth slightly open, as he melted into the melody. He played with the desperate intensity of a true artist, someone who had to play to survive. Evie knew that feeling. It's exactly what music did to her, exactly the feeling she had when she painted. Her paintings in Iceland were the only ones not composed to music. Maybe that was because he was meant to be her music. She knew his songs before he ever sang them. Knew his pain and his passion without him ever putting them into words.

When the song was over, his eyes opened and a hazy smile brightened the darkness of the room. It was the kind of smile you only share when you know exactly what the other person is thinking. That terrified Evie, because if he could read her thoughts...

Oskar made no move to close the distance between them. Instead, he stood and went over to the old phonograph and vinyl collection. He sunk to the floor in front of the cabinet and began flipping through until he landed on one with a shiny red cover. He placed it on the turntable and began cranking the handle coming from the back of it. It made a clicking, popping, squeaking sound as he worked. When he met resistance, he stopped.

He dropped the needle, and the song began to play through a gentle crackle of static. He crawled across the floor, onto the mattress with her. Evie concentrated on the sky again, to keep herself from saying or doing anything stupid. Though she'd been with him all evening, for some reason, this moment felt heavier than the rest. Like one move would propel them in some direction they couldn't come back from.

The acoustic song on the phonograph played distant and quiet, and not in English. But there was something beautiful and romantic about it. She wished she knew what they were saying. She turned her head and met Oskar's gaze.

"Agnes said you sing," she said. "*Syngja.* Is that the right word?" She knew it was right, because she'd read her downloaded copy of Basic Icelandic for Idiots a dozen times now, and that word was one of the easier ones. She always doubted herself when she had to say something he'd actually understand.

Oskar just stared down at her, gray eyes piercing her through the darkness. He lifted his right hand to her face and covered her eyes, gently brushing his fingertips over her lids.

"You want me to close my eyes? Okay." Evie obliged, settling into the nook of his shoulder.

When the chorus of the song reached its peak again, a deep baritone rumble moved through Oskar's chest and into Evie's ear. Suddenly his mouth was making sounds and singing along to the words in the most hauntingly beautiful cadence she'd ever heard. She didn't need to know what the words meant to feel them. The vibration of the syllables traveled through every nerve ending in her body, and before the song was done, she opened her eyes and lifted her head to watch him sing the last measure. Eyes closed, throat moving, lips dancing.

How was she supposed to say goodbye to him?

Leaving Iceland would be almost as hard as leaving Abuela had been. She had belonged here this summer just as much as she'd belonged in Florida before she left. She didn't want to think about where she'd belong next. She just wanted to stay here in this moment with this boy who listened to her and made her feel.

The song stopped and the needle made a clicking noise as it returned to its resting point. He opened his eyes and looked at her, holding her gaze only a moment before she rested her head on his shoulder. Green flames sizzled through the sky above, as if the whole world was on fire because of this thing between them.

"Is it possible to love someone who doesn't understand your words?" She said it aloud, to nobody. But suddenly he shifted and answered with his lips. Under his mouth, she heard the colors of the aurora and felt the music on the tip of his tongue and tasted the starlight that wrapped them in its arms.

For the first time in all their make-out sessions, his hands ventured lower than her hair. Down the sides of her face. Over her shoulders, across her collar bone, down her sides. His fingertips hovered just beneath the hem of her shirt as he pulled away from her mouth. Distant galaxies twinkled in his eyes as he asked an unspoken question.

He was the kind of boy who would never touch her without asking, who would never assume he had a right to her body unless she expressly gave it to him. And it was that very thing that made her want to give it to him even more.

Evie tugged her shirt up and over her head and dropped it beside them on the floor. He closed his eyes then, and put an ear to her chest. With his index finger, he tapped a rhythm on her arm. Thump-thump, thump-thump, thump-thump. Listening to her heart.

When he rose up and reached behind her to unhook her bra, she let him—not thinking, just living in the moment. Translation was unnecessary when meaning was written in everything else.

SIXTY-FOUR
Oskar's Journal

There's a time of night
when the globe's position
reaches a height
of burning disposition.
It pauses and gazes
between observer and sun.
Lights the sky with green blazes
until it is done.
Clarity puts on a show
of unfathomable light.
Here in this moment
with her,
I finally feel
the magnetic midnight.
Hands and lips
and hips and fingers,
buttons, clasps
and hooks don't linger.
Sweaters, denim, lace and cotton
On the floor, happily forgotten.
On top of the world
And away from the din

Voltage swirls beneath bare skin.
Orion watches with Taurus the Bull.
The earth shifts on its axis,
breathless.
Jealous
of our
gravitational
pull.

SIXTY-FIVE
Evie

*M*orning sunlight trickled in through the panoramic windows, and Evie thought the sun must be exhausted from all that shining with barely any break.

Oskar's chest rose and fell under her left cheek. A smile took over her face and she buried it in his neck to hide. If hell was the punishment she faced for last night, it had been worth it.

She nestled there, under their cocoon of blankets, listening to his soft snoring. She felt different. Loretta tried to tell her months ago that she wouldn't feel different when it finally happened, that it was no big deal. But just like everything else Loretta said, she got to label it with a big fat bullshit in all caps. BULLSHIT.

Loretta had wasted her v-card on the wrong person—maybe that's why she didn't feel different. Suddenly an overwhelming gratitude filled her, and she thanked the God who'd surely disown her that she at least hadn't wasted it on Ben.

It had been special. With a boy she was falling in love with—she was sure of it—as impossible as that sounded. She'd only met him a little more than a month ago.

And then reality hit her between the eyes—she only had a week left with him if Magnet Arts didn't accept her late portfolio.

How many more nights like last night could she cram into a week? And then what? It's not like they could talk on the phone. Or write letters. *No, no, no, no.* She tried to wrestle the sadness into submission, refused to let it in.

But it wouldn't leave her alone. Neither would her bladder. Reluctantly, she sat up and searched the floor for her sweater. She leaned over and grabbed it from the floor and tugged it over her head, stretched out as it was, and tiptoed to the bathroom.

After clicking the switch several times, she remembered there was no power, and shut herself in the dark. She winced at the soreness and the fear that he might hear her peeing. Which was stupid, after what they'd done. She felt around in the dark for toilet paper, and then the flush handle, which thankfully worked just fine.

Cracking the door open to let some light in, she turned on the faucet and let the cold water drizzle over her hands. She splashed some on her face, even though it smelled more strongly of sulfur than the running water at the guesthouse. She smoothed her wild hair down with a little water and twisted it around her left shoulder, hoping she didn't look too hideous. People didn't just wake up looking like rock stars in real life. She tiptoed back to the mattress.

Correction: Oskar looked like a rock star, even while he slept.

She kneeled down next to him and studied the planes of his face, the color of his complexion under the sunlight, trying to decide which combinations of pigment she would use to create that perfect shade. He opened his eyes and caught her staring. Which wasn't creepy at all. *Mother Mary.*

Before she could say anything to defend herself, he smiled and scooted backwards, holding the covers up and making room for her. One glance under the blanket lit her face on fire.

She scooted in next to him, back to his chest, glad she had her sweater on. Things felt too exposed in daylight. He curled his arm around her waist and fit himself to her back. A smile warmed her from head to toe as she concentrated on the way every part of him touched her, the way his legs tangled with hers. Soon, his breathing turned heavy against the back of her head. He was asleep again.

A gentle gold lit the face of the sea and highlighted the clouds on the horizon. She'd be content to sit in this lighthouse and paint everything in and around it until she ran out of supplies. Or breaths. There was something so romantic about the place, books and instruments strewn about. The old vinyl collection he kept. Oskar was a deep soul, and here in his world, she understood him. They understood each other.

The edge of a red leather bound notebook stuck out from under a corner of the blanket. It was the same one she'd seen sitting next to him that night on the rock by the fire. Lines and bars were doodled in ink on the front—musical measures scribbled with haste. Curiosity lit a dangerous fuse in her fingertips. Did Oskar have his own book of spells?

She flipped it open and read the first few lines on a random page.

I can't think when she looks at me like this.
It's like she can pick apart my life
with her inquisitive smile.
Like the universe may tell her
whatever she wants to know
because it's just as brainwashed
by the way stolen cherries stain her mouth
as I am.

Evie just stared at the perfect all-caps handwriting, noting the date at the top—three weeks ago. Musical notes were scribbled in the margins, with doodles and drawings of cherry duos. She read the lines again, heart seized in her chest. Could he have written this? In English? It had to be someone else's, right? She flipped pages forward, towards the back, looking for the last entry, stopping on today's date.

There's a time of night when the globe's position...

Something moved into her periphery so fast it blurred. Oskar's hand yanked the book from under her fingers and sat up, pulling the covers off her legs. The chill in the air waged war on her skin as she turned to him, heart banging clues into her brain.

He clutched the book to his chest, staring down at the blanket pooled in his lap.

"Is that... Did you write that?" Her voice came out like a harsh whisper.

He wouldn't meet her eyes.

"Oskar." She tried again, leveling her tone with a gulp of cold air. There had to be an explanation for this. "Look at me."

He peeked up through the messy blond bed hair falling in his face. For the first time, something registered she hadn't seen before. Recognition. She told him to look at her, and he did. He understood.

"Those are English words." And all signs suggested he had written them. What had he written in it last night? After...

Some irrational impulse made her want to rip the journal out of his hands and run away with it. Like a third grader. He must have sensed this, because he clutched it so tightly that his knuckles paled.

There was no sound between them but some obnoxious clock, pounding the seconds away in a tempo too quickly to be accurate. Evie had some vague sense of awareness that it was coming from her chest.

Then, something louder shook the floor beneath them—a booming echo from below. The sound of a latch, then a heavy door swinging open on newly replaced hinges, followed by thudding footsteps.

"Oskar!" Agnes's voice. Then another.

"Evie!" Papá was with her.

The circumference of Oskar's eyes grew three sizes as they shared a knowing look. Shoving the lie between them to the side for the sake of survival, they darted to their feet and began throwing clothes and shoes at each other.

Evie shoved her legs in the crispy cold denim legs of her jeans. She snagged the hem of her sweater trying to zip them. Footsteps got louder as they climbed. She yanked the blanket up, searching wildly for her underwear. Cotton panties peeked from under a pillow. She grabbed them and shoved them in her back pocket, then upturned everything in a two-foot radius looking for her bra.

She noticed the ash tray with the cached joint and spent condom in the middle, and she threw a pillow over it. The voices were so close now that she knew any minute, she'd have to face her father—braless and barefoot—in her den of shame. This was a Defcon 1 on the OMGWTF-o-meter.

Oskar dove onto the mattress, fully clothed now, and closed his eyes.

What in the actual hell was he doing?

Glancing back and forth between him and the hole in the floor that would yield two angry heads at any moment, she realized his plan. One she wondered if he could've communicated to her just as clearly as he'd been writing in that journal. She took the hint and dove down beside him, leaving a foot of space between them. She closed her eyes and tried to slow her breathing.

This was as good a plan as any. If they thought the two of them had just fallen asleep, it wouldn't be a big deal. Clothes were on. Only their feet were showing. She could tell her papá that they'd passed out listening to music.

"Here they are," Agnes said, and Evie fought every impulse to open her eyes. "They're asleep." Evie could hear the sense of relief in Agnes's voice, as if she expected to walk in on another scene entirely. The scene from two minutes ago.

"Evelyn Isolina Perez! *¿Qué demonio estás haciendo aquí con este muchacho?*"

This was bad. He'd gone 100% Spanish on her. And calling her by her middle name—Abuela's name—was enough to remind her of all the stupid things she'd done in a very short period of time. Her eyes snapped open.

Papá stood over her, lines etched into his hard face, mouth fixed in such a severe frown that it sent a wave of nausea through her. He breathed like a taunted bull, ready to charge. Evie sat up and looked around, as if realizing for the first time where she was. She'd have to be an excellent actress. Her life depended on it.

"Papá?" She infused as much sleepy rasp into her voice as possible.

He reached down and grabbed her arm, pulling her to her feet in one swift move. It was not at all gentle. He'd never laid a hand on her before. She glanced back at Oskar, hoping for... what? Him to come to her defense?

Instead, he lay motionless on his stomach, eyes still closed. If she didn't know the truth, she'd think he was asleep, too.

"Dah, the lad's a heavy sleeper," Agnes said, giving the side of the mattress a swift kick. "Oskar!"

Evie avoided Agnes's gaze like the plague. Something in her voice, the way she yelled at Oskar, made Evie think she knew the truth already. "I'm... I'm sorry, Papá. We were just listening to music and we fell asleep." Evie rubbed the imaginary sleep from her eyes so she wouldn't have to make any uncomfortable eye contact. "We watched the Northern Lights last night—they were beautiful."

If she just acted normal, carried on routine conversation, he wouldn't suspect a thing. She grabbed her flip-flops from the floor and sat down to pull them on. His silence—his lack of yelling, specifically—set her nerves on edge. Quiet Papá was much scarier than Yelling Papá. She risked a peek at him.

Something glassy shimmered in his dark eyes. Puffiness surrounded them. She'd never seen him cry, but Evie wondered if this is how it would look before he did. Or after he already had. His jaw tensed as stared daggers right at her. She focused intently on his feet as she stood up again.

He knew. That had to be it. And she'd disappointed him so much he was going to cry.

"I'm sorry," Evie said again. "I shouldn't have fallen asleep. Are you... are you okay?" She stole another quick glance through her lashes before returning to her intense study of the scuffs on the toes of his shoes. He sniffed once, loudly, and seemed to compose himself before answering.

"No, I'm not okay. We have to go. Something's happened with Abuela."

Terror crawled over the back of her neck. Evie forgot for a moment how much trouble she was in. She needed to gauge the severity of the situation, to see if she needed to be as worried about Abuela as her instincts suggested, so she met his eyes head-on, full eye contact without looking away. Tears brimmed there again. This time, he didn't try to stop them.

Yes. The answer was yes.

SIXTY-SIX
Oskar's Journal

The Thor *eitsu* no longer exist.
I'm a coward.
I would've faked sleep until they were gone,
but his news shakes me out of my resolve.
There's been an accident.
The look on her face
when she saw my journal
was nothing
compared to the one
she wears now.
She crosses her arms over her chest.
She isn't wearing her bra.
Which is also my fault.
Because I shot it across the room last night,
like a slingshot
to make her laugh.
Her laugh
is the most enticing piece of music
I have ever heard.
I am desperate to hear it now.
Instead I hear only pain.
What kind of accident?

I want to rewind time.
Back to last night.
No, before last night.
To all those opportunities I had
to tell her the truth.
Make a different decision.
A better one.
A fire, her father says.
Confusion wages war
on her beautiful face.
A fire?
He nods, working his jaw.
Those pendejos let her have a candle.
She turns to Agnes,
and they share a horrified look.
Some inside joke
that isn't a joke at all.
It caught a curtain on fire.
Evelyn's legs shake.
Burned up half the building.
It's a miracle her neighbor's oxygen tank didn't explode
and kill them all.
She glances over at me,
eyes glassy and spilling.
Her lips tremble.
She looks back at her father.
What about Abuela? Is she...?
He clears his throat,
continually shaking off
his own urge to cry.
In the hospital.
I don't know how bad yet.
Our flight leaves this afternoon.
She slaps a hand over her mouth,

and for a moment,
I think she might collapse.
Agnes stands frozen,
as paralyzed by the situation as I am.
Her father stares past her.
At something on the floor.
I follow his gaze to a pile of red lace.
All the blood in my body
makes a mass exodus to my feet.
In less than a blink,
I'm against the wall.
His fists clutch handfuls of my shirt.
Some of my skin, too.
His hatred pinches me
in a completely deserving way.
I'm at least a head taller than him,
but I have no doubt
the force of his fury
could break me.
His bitter coffee breath
pins me against the cold stone
and I shiver.
Te mataré.
He spits it through his teeth.
It's a promise of some kind.
Whatever he said,
I believe him.
Behind him,
she flails her arms and screams at him
in Spanish.
She's so animated
with anger and fear,
so convicted by whatever she's saying,
that I wish I understood her words.

I hate being shut out of this conversation.
And then it hits me.
That's exactly what I've done to her.
Everyone STOP. Get out, or I'm calling the Lögreglan!
Under the demand of Agnes's voice,
he lets me go.
My feet touch the floor again,
and I realize they hadn't been a moment ago.
Tell your nephew he is lucky he'll never have the chance to
    see my daughter again.
He grabs Evie's arm
so forcefully that she whimpers,
and then shoves her through the exit in the floor.
She gives me one last fleeting glance before descending the
    ladder.
All the pain I've caused registers there,
scrolling between us like sky writing.
¡Dale! ¡Apúrate!
He yells again and shoves her downward,
following immediately behind.
Agnes's chest rises and falls
as she scans the room,
sees the evidence lying on the floor.
She turns to me,
voice dripping with disdain,
and says,
I hope you're happy.
As I swallow the bitterness,
I realize something.
I was happy.
Last night.
But like everything
I've ever let myself love,
it's gone now.

SIXTY-SEVEN
Evie

*E*vie packed up everything in her summer room that she once viewed as a cell.

Now she only wanted to stay here and pretend the rest of the world didn't exist—but only if she could just go back and un-make some mistakes. If Abuela didn't survive, she'd have to carry that blame alone. *Screw the rules*, she'd thought when she sent her that candle. *God,* how could she have been so stupid? Her stomach coiled into tight knots as she filled her last suitcase.

She pulled the only remaining sweater from the closet and stared at the two paintings she hadn't sold. The very first one, of Oskar in the orchard, and then the one she'd painted after that night by the fire: his arm, strumming chords.

She couldn't let her father see these.

The walk of shame down all those flights of steps had been the longest of her life. Her arm would be bruised from Papá's grip, she was certain. *I'd march you straight to church right this instant if there were time*, he'd spat in her ear in Spanish. Her eyes burned just thinking about it. She decided, in that moment, that maybe Quiet Papá was less scary after all.

At least I was smart enough to use protection, she'd wanted to say. In what universe was he anyone to judge her, anyway? Abuela, though—she'd have a right to be disappointed in her.

She'd been the one to have the sex talk with her when she was thirteen. *Don't you dare take it lightly, nieta*, she'd said.

What if Abuela didn't make it? What if she did, and Papá told her everything?

She lifted her pillow and noticed the silver locket, where she'd kept it since she found it in the water. She had assumed it was a sign from the universe—some magical message like the ones from the tree, telling her Oskar was going to be her first love. After seeing the pictures inside the lighthouse, she knew that it had belonged to his mother.

It wouldn't be right to keep it.

She glanced up at her paintings, not knowing what to do with them, either. Every worry in her head began to snowball. What if she never saw him again? Swallowing a lump in her throat, she walked over and quietly clicked the lock on her door. She slid the locket in her back pocket and gathered the paintings, dropping them on her stripped mattress while she raised the window. Without thinking, she crawled out, and then reached through and grabbed the paintings when her feet hit the ground.

Maybe he'd understood her all along. Her assumption was that he didn't speak English, but maybe he just didn't speak it aloud. She didn't understand why Agnes wouldn't have just told her that, but there had to be a reason. Those words in that journal were English. And if he didn't write them, who did?

She had to know the truth. Or at least let him know *her* truth. Whatever it was between them was real, and she couldn't walk away from him without saying it, without telling him she didn't regret a single thing that happened between them. Her feet crunched the crispy grass in the path she'd worn between the guesthouse and the orchard in the weeks since she'd first seen it—seen *him*. He was always the reason she went. It was never the cherries, or the lure of the orchard, or the smell in Agnes's shop. Those things were just added bonuses. Excuses to keep going back.

She rushed into the shop but found it dark and silent. The closed sign was turned. Only the side door was unlocked. Her eyes scanned the shelves in the dim light—one lone bulb in the souvenir section at the back of the shop cast a glow. Despite the perfect alignment of the products on the full shelves, the deep shades of red against wood grain, it all looked hollow and empty without Oskar and Agnes.

"Oskar?" she called, though her voice was hoarse and weak. She called again, this time a little louder. "Agnes?"

Nothing.

She set her paintings down and took the stairs, two at a time, holding the cool rail to help her climb. She called for them again as she made it to the top. But she only met more silence and a deeper darkness.

Tears welled up as scenarios played in her mind. She was running out of time, and if they weren't here, then she might not have a chance to tell them goodbye, to see them one last time and clear things up.

She flung the first door open, and light spilled onto the cat-walk of the upper level. Inside, vacant instrument cases lay strewn all over the floor, along with sheet music and half empty water bottles and discarded clothes. A forgotten bed frame held no mattress. It hit her then—this was his room, but he'd taken his mattress to the lighthouse. Maybe she'd find him there.

Evie grabbed her things at the bottom of the stairs. She crashed back through the door into the orchard, searching, the paintings constantly slipping from her grasp. She stopped and used her knee to pull them back into her arms every few feet as she ran. Her Papá would be looking for her any minute now. He'd notice she was gone, and this would be the first place he'd look.

She jogged past the pond where they'd first kissed. The wind swirled in her ears as she approached the lighthouse, but the sound of conversation interrupted the wind. A voice got louder as she approached, one she'd only ever heard once, but in a language this time that ironically seemed foreign to her ears.

"She's a t-t-tourist!" The voice exploded. Evie stopped cold. "It's d-d-d-done."

"Oskar, you have an opportunity here to do the right thing, to make it right before it's too late. Don't ye see that?" Agnes's back was to Evie, but she could tell by her posture she was pleading on her behalf. In English, of course. He understood. He always understood.

"There's nnnothing to muh-muh-make right. It's nnnothing. She was always going to lllleave." He shrugged off Agnes's suggestions with such adamancy.

The most horrible part was that it was true.

He was right; she was always going to leave. As the wind continued to batter her, she could barely feel it. Everything went devastatingly numb as the realization blew through the valley of her heart, leaving wreckage in its path. All of the things she felt over the course of the summer. The things she felt last night… it was nothing to him. None of it was real. He'd known she was leaving, and he let it happen anyway. He didn't even care enough to make sure they got to say goodbye.

Evie sucked in a breath and steeled herself, letting the numbness propel her forward. She dropped the paintings at her feet. They made a thudding noise against the rocky footing. Agnes and Oskar both turned and saw her there, faces suddenly frozen to stone.

"Liars. Both of you." Her voice cracked when she said it, dangerously close to tears. She wouldn't let them see her cry. All the fury she felt over hearing him so callously shrug her off— she'd slept with him, for God's sake!—combined with the uncertainty of Abuela's future, the uncertainty of her own future, balled into an avalanche of anger. Heat replaced the numbness. Evie stomped toward Oskar. His face betrayed no emotion. He just stared at her as she approached, unmoving. She stopped a foot from him, pushing all of that fury into a bullseye on his forehead, and waited. She understood now how someone could want to hit him.

"You have nothing to say to me?" she asked when the silence had stretched on too long. All the things she'd said to him all summer... she'd told him her deepest, darkest feelings and desires. She'd given herself to him in every possible way. He owed her a sentence, at the very least.

But Oskar just tensed his jaw and swallowed, Adam's apple bobbing in his throat. Emotion snuck onto his face then and he grimaced beneath the weight of what looked like humiliation. He said nothing.

Evie reared back and slapped him across his beautiful, deceitful face. His head jerked to the side, absorbing the impact. She instantly wished she'd hit him harder. It wasn't as satisfying as she'd hoped it would be.

"You can't just use people!" Her voice erupted panicked, screaming, and unfamiliar to her own ears. "Pushing away the people who care about you won't bring your family back." A sob rattled around in her chest. He stared at the ground, refusing to look up. This was it—the cold hard truth. He didn't feel the same thing she did. He'd fooled her with his silent charm. She could hit him and scream at him all day, but nothing would change that fact.

She took the locket out of her back pocket and hurled it at him. It smacked him in the chest and fell to the ground at his feet.

"I found that in the pond. You can add it to your shrine." She turned and stomped past the paintings on the ground, leaving them behind. He didn't stop her. Agnes stood helpless, watching her go.

SIXTY-EIGHT
Oskar's Journal

I am a fuck up.
This is what people get for believing in me.
This is what I get
for trying to be anything
but a fuck up.

SIXTY-NINE
Evie

T he next forty-eight hours were a blur of near-intolerable emotion for Evie.

When Iceland disappeared beneath her feet, covered quickly by wispy clouds, she stared out the freezing window of the plane and let hot tears warm her face.

If she'd learned nothing else this summer, it was that she couldn't trust her instincts about anything. Not about Abuela's condition, and not about the intentions of others. Even Agnes! Agnes had willfully lied, covered for him. That betrayal hurt almost as much as Oskar's.

She catalogued every moment of her summer on the five-hour flight to Boston. Was there a sign at any point? An explanation that should've tipped her off? She couldn't think of any. She only remembered the things he did to reinforce her feelings for him. That first night by the fire. The days in the orchard. The fact that he'd bought every single one of her paintings. The look in his eyes in the lighthouse—if that wasn't love, she'd never be able to identify it. She had *felt* it, so clearly. But maybe what she'd been feeling was the love he had for his family. Perhaps he'd misplaced it on her because of the paintings.

Every attempt she made to sleep was thwarted by the raw churning beneath every inch of her skin. So she remained awake and endured it. Her ears popped so violently on descent that it shook her from her melancholy for a few moments, almost welcome compared to the pain of simply breathing.

To make matters worse, the connecting flight to Miami didn't leave until 4:55 the following morning. They had a six-hour layover. She couldn't sleep in the cold, hard airport chair, either, while people banged luggage against her legs.

Papá only spoke to her in snappy, incomplete sentences. He snored intermittently beside her as the clock ticked by like a torture device. Precious seconds and minutes and hours. Now that they were back in the States, she could feel every mile between herself and Abuela, every moment that she wasn't by her side.

After another plane, and another five hours in the air, they were finally on the way to the hospital. A new worry rose to the surface: she would see Abuela, but how would she look? Would she even look the same? Would her injuries have destroyed the warmth around her eyes? The delicate skin of her hands?

As they drove to the hospital in the late morning sunshine—which looked worlds apart from the sunshine in Iceland—Papá told her for the fifth time how disappointed he was in her, and how they'd deal with her actions as soon as Abuela got better.

If Abuela got better.

When they entered Miami-Dade General, Evie took shallow breaths, trying unsuccessfully to avoid the antiseptic stench that burned the inside of her nose. Breathing through her mouth didn't help either. Her stomach dropped more dramatically than usual in the elevator. She was an exposed nerve, susceptible to every tactile sensation, despite her sleep-starved brain. When the automatic doors opened, she hurtled down the hall alongside Papá into the unit. Toward the door with *Perez* on the whiteboard.

This was it.

A young doctor met them at the doorway and offered his hand as he introduced himself to Papá. He opened the door, and their quiet, polite conversation drowned in the chorus of beeps from the various machines surrounding Abuela.

Evie went straight to her bedside, and her eyes filled for the hundredth time in a day. A soul-deep wrenching nearly made her collapse. Beneath a mound of white sheets and blankets was Abuela, with lines and needles connected to her as if she were an alien experiment. The swelling around her face made her virtually unrecognizable. Her normally smooth brown skin was covered in splotches, like someone had flung pink paint on her while she slept. Which seemed much less violent and intrusive than what had actually happened.

A large plastic tube was taped to the outside of her mouth. Evie couldn't imagine how badly it hurt, or how Abuela could breathe with that thing going down her throat. She listened to the whoosh of the machine next to her as she realized that Abuela *wasn't* breathing. The machine was breathing for her.

I did this.

Evie wanted to fall on the ground and sob. To beg God to forgive her for every stupid thing she'd done this summer. For her selfishness, her recklessness. But it wouldn't change anything now.

"She's improving," the young doctor said to them. "The swelling has diminished substantially."

If this was substantial improvement… Her stomach clenched and rolled.

"If she continues to improve at this rate," the doctor continued, "we'll go ahead and try to extubate her this evening. By the end of the week, depending on how she does, we'll start thinking about discharge goals."

Looking at her now, Evie wasn't so sure. Because despite what the doctor was saying, she'd never seen Abuela like this. So sick and defenseless and old. Her hair hadn't been that gray a couple of months ago, she was sure of it. Instead of a few gray sprigs at her forehead and around her ears, the gray had crept all the way up the crown of her head. The black was sparse and hidden underneath all the silver.

Maybe life moved faster as a person got closer to the end. Everything blurred. The background noise sunk further into the abyss. Evie had to cross her arms tightly across her chest to keep from flinging herself into the bed with Abuela and begging her to be okay.

"I don't know where we'll put her after recovery," Papá grumbled, hunched in a defeated posture. "I can't believe the incompetence of a health care team that'd give a candle to someone with dementia as progressive as hers."

A lump formed in Evie's throat. She hadn't told him that it was all her fault. How could she? If he didn't hate her already, he would once he learned that little nugget of truth.

"I'm definitely going to speak to a lawyer about it." *A lawyer?* Evie's heart skipped a beat. "Someone has to pay for all of this." He motioned to the machines and the hospital bed and circled the room with his finger in a 360-motion.

The young doctor stared down at his clipboard, seeming uncomfortable.

She glanced over at him as he ran his hands through his greasy black hair, anxiety etched into the lines of his face like they were drawn with permanent marker. It hit Evie then. This was an inconvenience to her Papá. It interrupted his work, his life, his bank account. Despite the fact that his mother was suffering in a hospital bed in front of him, he was worrying about how he was going to pay for it all. Maybe those tears he shed before they left were for his wallet.

Anger elbowed the sorrow out of the way, and Evie sniffed. Stood up a little straighter. She'd wait until the doctor left, and then she'd tell him the truth. He'd already planned to dump her off on a woman who wanted her dead before she was ever born. She didn't care if he hated her now.

The door clicked open behind them. They both turned to see the new person, and the bottom dropped out of Evie's stomach when she saw the familiar white-blond hair, the newly happy made-up face.

Evie whirled on her Papá with a hiss. "What's she doing here?"

"Could you recommend a list of facilities we could look into post discharge?" Papá asked the doctor, ignoring Evie.

"Certainly." The doctor clutched his clipboard to his chest. "I'll make sure the nurse gets it to you as soon as possible. Try and get some rest and I'll see you all tomorrow."

Evie could feel her standing behind her, her presence a negative force that might suck her up like a vacuum. She refused to turn around. Why would he call her and have her come here? She couldn't begin to understand.

When the door clicked behind the doctor, Rhona spoke. "She looks terrible."

Evie's anger boiled over then. She twisted around, wishing she could hit her the way she'd hit Oskar. Her father watched her, wide-eyed. She wished she could hit him, too.

"You can go," she said to her mother. "You're not part of this family anymore."

Rhona might look surprised if she were capable of feeling anything. Instead, she just stared at Evie, face unmoving.

"Evelyn!" Papá's anger didn't affect her now. They'd been mad at each other all summer, and part of her was glad he was as frustrated in this moment as she was. Of course everything was more intense and dramatic now that Rhona was here. Evie couldn't, for the life of her, figure out what he'd ever seen in this woman.

"It's okay," Rhona said, holding a perfectly manicured hand up to hush his impending lecture. "She has a right to feel that way."

Evie narrowed her eyes. What manipulation was this? She wasn't falling for it.

"Please *just go*. Abuela needs her family, and you are not family."

"Evelyn," her papá said again, more stern than before. "School starts soon. I have to take care of this situation with Abuela. Your mother is here to take you back with her."

Evie stared at both of them in horror. They both towered over her, threatening. If they thought she'd leave again, before she knew if Abuela was okay, and after she just got here, they had another thing coming.

"You can both go to hell." She grabbed her purse and stormed out of the hospital room, ignoring them as they called after her.

SEVENTY
Oskar's Journal

Pain swims hot
like the magma beneath my feet.
I would welcome emptiness at this point.
I'd invite it in, let it engulf me
with its freezing cold flames.
Whatever shred of hope she made me feel,
it left when she did.
The axe dangles,
trembling
afraid of what it's about to do.
I grip it tighter
hold it with both hands.
To prevent it from getting away.
Regret, rage, humiliation—
they all swirl at odds with one another.
I swing the axe.
Make contact with the bark.
It makes a gash,
a tiny wound in comparison
to the ones I wear inside.
I swing again.
Cherries fall around me.

They hit me in the head
as the tree shakes
under the weight of my axe.
I'm d-d-doing you a fffavor!
I scream.
The past should be the past.
We never use these cherries, anyway.
It's as useless as dreams
and only invites more pain.
I swing
and swing
and swing and swing
and scream and scream and scream.
Until
something thick and heavy hits me,
pins me to the ground.
I flail around, pinned beneath the weight.
When I look up,
I meet Agnes's watery green eyes.
My own tears sear hot trenches in my face.
Guh-guh-go away!
I scream at her.
My voice cracks.
Agnes pins my arms to the ground,
speaks with unprecedented sternness.
Stop this. You have to stop this.
It's this tuh-tuh-tree!
It's torturing mmme!
It's the reason she spent the summer here!
My own voice is foreign to me.
They all loved you, Oskar.
But you have to let them go.
Didn't you understand the message you were supposed to
   get?

Go look at those pictures the lass painted.
Really look at them!
There's a message in every single one.
There's a lot of life out there for you, Oskar!
My throat burns
as I choke on the sobs.
She squeezes my arms.
Shakes me.
We survived, Oskar!
The accident didn't take us.
The tears roll off her face and drip down to my neck.
We are meant to go on.
We must keep living!
She gathers me up in her arms
and hugs me,
a desperate embrace.
And for the first time since she arrived in Iceland,
five years ago,
I give up and hug her back.

SEVENTY-ONE
Evie

*H*er skin stuck to the vinyl cushion beneath her.

Though the sun had retreated a few minutes ago, behind the safety of the horizon, the remnant heat hung thick in the air, so hot she couldn't breathe. Her hair stuck to her temples, and tears cut paths down the side of her face into her ears. Sweat pooled at her throat, between her breasts, behind her knees. She missed the cold.

Every three seconds, the swing squeaked.

Evie used to lie on her back in this swing when she was younger—eyes closed—trying to imagine the squeak noise was something besides a swing, that she was somewhere else, in some other place. She was on the back of a safari truck while a baby elephant called for its mother in the distance. A flock of low-flying seabirds squawked overhead as she sunbathed on the beach. A sailboat pole creaked under the pressure of a sea wind. That last one was her favorite. Paired with the rhythm of the rocking motion, she could imagine herself lying in the bottom of a boat, somewhere at sea, totally adrift.

All those times when she was younger, she had fantasized about being somewhere else. Now, she just wanted to be here. She wished Abuela was inside, baking pastelitos, or mopping the floor and screaming for her to come pick up her Barbies before she threw them in the trash—interrupting her daydream. She'd only wanted to be on that boat.

She was adrift now, to be sure. In a sea of unwelcome change.

When she left Miami less than two months ago, she had a best friend. A quasi-boyfriend. A father she'd propped on a pedestal he didn't deserve. A mother who was too far away to cause further damage. Most importantly, she had Abuela. With less gray hair and more mental capacity.

The summer, or time in general, was a cruel bully.

She knew it was them when she heard the engine approach and felt the warmth of the headlights on her face. Still, she kept her eyes closed. Even as they slammed the car doors and climbed up the creaky wooden steps. Evie kept her foot firmly planted on the porch railing, using it to keep the swing moving.

"We thought you'd be here," her papá said, voice much gentler than it had been hours earlier in the hospital room.

She didn't respond. She'd stormed from the hospital, got a cab, and came straight to Abuela's. She didn't know what she'd hoped to find here. The old version of Abuela, maybe. A parallel universe she could step back into and leave the current one behind.

Instead, she found a locked door and an empty house. Story of her life.

"Evie," her mother spoke up. "Abuela is awake."

Her eyes snapped open then. She hated that Rhona had been the one to deliver the good news. She didn't want to hear anything from her stupid, candy-pink mouth.

"They extubated her," she continued. She sunk into a rocker next to the swing. "The swelling has gone down more. She's going to be okay."

Evie sat up, her feet catching on the wooden boards and slowing the swing to a stop. "So you left her there alone?" She glared between her parents. "She wakes up, and your first order of business is to leave her again?" If she was being honest, she was just as angry with herself for not being there the minute she'd opened her eyes.

"The nurses and respiratory therapists are with her now, doing an assessment. They asked us to step out," her papá said, almost defensive.

Good. He should be defensive.

"She's going to be okay, *mija*. The doctor thinks she may be able to leave the hospital by the week's end." His optimism gave her no comfort. Go where? To some other hellhole nursing facility? All alone?

"If you want me in New York," Evie said, "then fine." She'd been thinking about it all afternoon, and she'd made a decision. "But only if you transfer Abuela there, too. Some place where I can visit her every day and remind her of who she is. Maybe if she gets well enough, she can move in with me once I graduate and move out on my own."

"Evie, the dementia… that part isn't going to get better. We have to be realistic—"

"I won't go without her. That's my condition. Take or leave it."

"You are hardly in any position to be making demands, young lady." Papá's forehead crinkled and his nostrils flared. "I haven't forgotten about your tryst in Iceland."

A bubble of angry laughter climbed out of Evie's throat. "My tryst? Well, Papá, it could be worse. I could've abandoned my family entirely, like the two of you."

His face morphed into an expression she'd never seen before, not even in the lighthouse. Evie had never tested his limits. She'd never talked back to him. She'd never disrespected him. This new development carved new depths of anger into his face. His mouth opened to say something, and Evie braced herself for whatever it was.

"Stop," Rhona said to him before he could respond. He clamped his mouth closed. Evie hated the way he always listened to her. No matter what she did to him, no matter what kind of person she was, he was still so hopelessly in love with her that he'd position himself at her feet and be her doormat as long as she had dirt to wipe on him.

She would always have dirt to wipe, Evie was sure.

"She has a point, Alberto. You'll be in Iceland, and then who knows where your next assignment will take you? It might be good for Isolina to be near family."

"I don't know anything about the facilities there." He grumbled.

"There are lots of great facilities in the city. Places we could easily take public transit to every day."

Evie's mouth hung open. Rhona was actually taking her side on this. It was one for the record books.

The car ride back to the hospital was silent.

At least the truth was out in the open now. They both know how she felt, where her priorities were. Abuela had been the reason she'd given Rhona her respect. It wasn't something she'd earned in any way. Giving birth to someone doesn't automatically make a parent deserving of respect. Especially when, if not for her Papá, Rhona would've discarded her before she took a breath. Forget what the Bible or the priests or the nuns said. What Abuela said. Evie was nearing adulthood, and she'd never expect anyone to respect her if she hadn't given it to them first. Only respect begets respect. Rhona taking her side about moving Abuela to New York was the closest thing she'd ever done to earn it.

They waited outside the hospital room door until the nurse had finished assessing Abuela and giving her a bath. When she exited the room and waved them inside, Evie's heart beat wildly. She didn't even care that Abuela might tell them about the whole candle thing and wreck every bit of progress she made with her negotiations. Suddenly, all that mattered was telling Abuela she loved her.

She rushed into the room where Abuela sat propped against her pillows. Their eyes met. Wrinkles creased around her dark brown eyes and she stared at Evie in confusion.

Now she'd give anything for Abuela to tell on her. To yell at her. Any sense of recognition at all. Evie's breaths came faster and tears spilled over her bottom lashes.

Something changed on Abuela's face then. A slight head tilt, then her eyes widened, ever so slightly. A smile pulled the wrinkled corners of Abuela's mouth into a shaky grin, then an all-out, open-mouthed smile.

"*Nieta.*"

Evie collapsed on her shoulder, sobs shaking the entire bed.

SEVENTY-TWO
Oskar's Journal

I listen to them
Just out of sight from below.
I don't know how he'll react,
Agnes says to Edvin.
To which news?
Edvin asks,
and I hear the smile in his words.
He already knows about us,
Agnes says with a giggle.
A giggle!
It's a side of her I can't reconcile.
We have to tell him everything else though.
This shoves my curiosity
into ravenous mode.
Tuh-tuh-tell me what?
    I ask
from the top of the stairs.
They both look up
from where they sit at a table in the shop,
huddled together like lovers.
They exchange a look.
Edvin stands.

Adjusts his tie and grins.
It seems the Westminster Conservatory
at Rider University in New Jersey
wants you to audition for them.
The director called me today.
They're very impressed with the new video audition we sent.
After Boston and Philadelphia turned me down,
I retreated into solitude.
I moved back into my bedroom
after what happened at the tree.
Left the paintings in the lighthouse
because I couldn't keep looking at them
knowing I might never see her again, either.
But this news about school—it gives me new life.
I try not to let it show.
I shrug.
Okay.
I jog down the steps,
head for the orchard side door.
I've been playing music nonstop,
and my favorite place
is by the fire.
Even though
I have nothing to burn
except wood,
since I've been cut off
from my *gras* man.
Wait, Oskar, Agnes says.
There's one more thing, lad.
I take a few steps toward them
and pause by a display of jams.
The lass's father is back.
I saw him at the petrol station this morning.
My mouth goes dry as bone.

Was ssshe—
But I can't finish
before Agnes shakes her head.
She wasn't with him. But that doesn't mean...
I nod,
do an about-face,
and take the stairs to my room
two at a time.
I grab my coat and hat from my room.
The weather has taken a wintry decline
since she left.
Even the earth gets cold without her warmth.
As I bound out the door,
Agnes calls behind me.
Where—
But I'm already gone.

It's a suicide mission.
I'm well aware.
I'll kill you,
that's what he said to me
that day in the lighthouse.
I looked it up.
And if that's what happens,
it's more than I deserve.
After they all died,
I laid awake at night,
thinking of all the things I'd say to them
if I still could.
But they're dead.
This girl,
the one with the big brown eyes
that see right through me,
she's still alive.

And if I don't tell her
in my own words
that I'm sorry,
I'll never forgive myself.
I'll never be able to move on.
My fist shakes
as it hovers over the door.
I'm a coward,
afraid to knock.
I stand there,
trying to psych myself up.
Reminding myself I'd give anything
to be slapped by you again,
because that would mean
you're touching me
and there's still a chance
to fix everything I ruined.
He opens the door before I can knock.
It doesn't take long to see
he's still pretty pissed.
I grimace
waiting for the blow
that doesn't come.
What do you want?
Isn't it obvious? I want to say.
But since he hasn't punched me yet
I don't push it.
Is sh-sh-she…
Of course I can't even get the words out.
The humiliation isn't even as potent
as the fear
of not knowing
if I'll be able to see you.
He crosses his arms over his chest.

Grins.

It's pretty fucking alarming.

He grabs the door to slam it in my face,

but I stop it

with my hand.

His eyebrows arch in surprise.

I'm sorry.

I can hardly believe

it came out smoothly.

You're sorry?

Of course he wants me to say it again.

I nod.

Well, I'm not the one you should be apologizing to.

She's in New York, with her mother.

Disappointment crushes me.

I nod again.

C-c-c-could I have her address?

He didn't want to give it to me.

He called me a *pendejo.*

Asshole.

I looked that up, too.

I deserved it.

I am an asshole.

He made me beg.

I begged.

But finally,

he gave it to me.

SEVENTY-THREE
Oskar's Journal

Agnes told me
I should listen to the message
the *Aisling* tree
had for me
when I tried to cut it down.
It wasn't my finest moment, I know.
So I have spent the past couple of weeks
staring at your paintings,
trying to decipher
what they were trying to say.
At first I thought they were literal:
Ivan sitting bored in the shade.
My mother planting a tree, begging it to grow.
The northern lights swirling above the lighthouse.
My family in the pond, together and alive,
just days before the accident.
My mother walking away.
A hand holding a locket.
But then I got really baked (haha)
on my remaining stash
and looked at them again.
Ivan wasn't bored;

he was waiting for me to live.
My mother wasn't waiting for a tree to grow;
she was waiting for *me* to grow.
The northern lights weren't just putting on a show
the autumn when I was ten,
they are *still* putting on shows,
as you and I both well know.
My family wasn't just together
in the pond a few days before they died,
my family is still together.
In my heart.
Always.
My mother wasn't walking away;
she was telling me to walk away.
To chase dreams
and maybe love,
the same way she did.
And finally,
the hand holding the heart-shaped locket
should be you.
And I
should
live.

SEVENTY-FOUR
Evie

*E*vie felt like a lab rat in a New York City–shaped maze.

It had taken her until the end of her second week of school to figure out the subway schedule. From her mother's apartment (she still refused to call it home) in Queens, she took the bus nine blocks to Public High School 87. Magnet Arts had rejected her on the basis of a late submission.

Though she hadn't made any friends yet, people were strangely accepting. It was a completely different experience than Saint Bart's had been. It was nice to be in a sea of diversity, rather than stuck with a bunch of entitled rich people. Maybe her father had known this all along when he'd planned to send her here.

Then again, maybe she gave him too much credit.

After school, she took a twenty-minute train ride, then walked a quarter mile east to the Waterside Retirement Community in Flushing. It was a sprawling brick building that took up three city blocks in the combined residential and commercial area. They had an aquatics program, a culinary program, a billiards room, and a twenty-four-hour on-call memory program staff.

Rhona had found it.

Evie didn't believe that a handful of good deeds would erase a lifetime of their fractured mother/daughter relationship. But it was a good start. Ever since she'd been living with Rhona, she'd started to see things in a different light. She'd begun to get to know the woman that was hidden inside a shell of depression all those years before.

Evie waved to Mr. Peterson, the kind old doorman, as she entered through the automatic doors into the lobby and signed in. After an elevator ride to Abuela's third story apartment and a knock on the door, a young nurse she hadn't seen before let her in.

"You must be Evie." She smiled. This staff was a far cry from the grumpy women that worked at the old one. The ones who couldn't be bothered to set up a damn video call. "She's waiting for you. I was just leaving."

Abuela was perched on her recliner, crossword puzzle open on her lap desk. Her pen hovered over the boxes, face contorted into a frown. Evie braced herself for whichever Abuela she'd meet today.

She wasn't always coherent. Some days the confusion was mild—she'd call Evie Rhona, or forget they were in Queens instead of Little Havana. Other days, she'd cry until she fell asleep. Evie would stay with her on those days, hoping and praying for better days to come.

"Hola, my Evie." She smiled. Thankfully, this wasn't one of those sad days.

Well, it was still sad. Things would never go back to the way they used to be. She'd stopped longing for things she couldn't change. She wasn't a little girl anymore. She had to accept that sometimes, shit is grim.

"What's on your mind, *nieta*?"

So much. But it wasn't about her anymore. It was about Abuela.

"Not much. How was your day? Did you go swimming again with that cute memory care therapist?"

Abuela dropped her pen next to the crossword puzzle and pulled her glasses off. She pinned Evie in place with an irritated expression. "I don't want to talk about me, *nieta*. I want to talk about you."

Evie shrugged. "Nothing much to talk about."

"Have you spoken with your papá?"

Evie avoided her eyes. No, she hadn't. He'd made it clear he was busy with work, which was the reason he'd been trying to ship her here for months now. He hadn't called her, so she hadn't bothered, either.

"He's only trying to do what's best for you, *nieta*. All that working is for you."

Yeah, well. She wasn't going to trash talk her papá to Abuela. That would be a losing battle. She'd discuss it with her priest, if she ever made it back to Mass. Rhona wasn't exactly the religious type, so Evie would have go on her own time.

"They're both only trying to do what's best for you."

At this, Evie laughed. This level of lucid was almost inconvenient, but she wasn't sorry for it.

"You have to forgive them both. If you don't, you'll spend years and years in pain."

Evie looked up at her then.

"Were you mad at your parents? After they sent you to Miami?"

Abuela's eyes shone with something—tears or impending laughter, Evie wasn't sure—and she smiled. "Mad doesn't even begin to explain it, *nieta*. I didn't understand why they would send me away. How could I be safe anywhere they weren't? With nuns who didn't know me? Every week at Mass, I had to confess my unwillingness to forgive them for abandoning me."

Evie swallowed a lump in her throat. That was scarily familiar.

"It wasn't until you were born, *nieta*, that I realized they did me a favor. If I hadn't come here, I would've never had your father. He would've never met your mother. We would've never had you. Everything is a result of something else. Sometimes bad things can yield very good things."

Evie thought about that for a moment. She'd resented where she came from for so long. She'd clung to Abuela's legacy because it was something she could be proud of. It was a story of triumph, of overcoming adversity, of making a new life.

"Your mother didn't love you the way you deserved to be loved, Evie, I do not deny that. But it's taken her until now to learn to love herself. Only now is she capable of giving you what you've always deserved. Give her a chance."

Just being here was a huge step, so right now that would have to be enough. She didn't say as much to Abuela because she didn't want to disappoint her. She just nodded.

"And your father," she said. "He calls me every day. To check on you."

Evie swallowed. This surprised her more than anything. She always had to pester him to call Abuela before. Now he did it without having to be reminded?

"He doesn't know I sent you that candle," she whispered. "I never told him."

Abuela smiled. "He already knows, *nieta*."

Evie's mouth fell open. She didn't want to cry, but the pressure of it tickled the back of her lids. Her eyes swam hot and hazy. "But he talked about suing Sunny Acres…"

"They were supposed to be screening my mail. He knew all along that the candle came from Iceland."

"But why didn't he say something?" Anger took over now. He let her lie to him, outright. She felt incredibly stupid and small. Of all the things she'd done to disappoint him, that was the worst, and he'd let her get away with it.

"Evie," Abuela said, reaching over and taking her hand. "Promise me something."

She couldn't really deny her anything in this rare moment of crystal-clear conversation.

"Promise me you'll learn to forgive. Forgive them. Forgive yourself. Everyone makes mistakes."

Evie swallowed a shaky breath. "I promise."

She thought about that promise all the way home. Could she forgive her papá for being so focused on his work he forgot her all the time? Could she forgive her mother for checking out for her entire childhood?

Maybe.

But then she thought of Oskar. She'd spilled her guts to him all summer, she'd shared every secret part of herself with him, only to overhear him call it nothing. She tensed her jaw and focused on a piece of gum on the floor of the train.

She pulled out her phone and noticed an unread message on her messenger app.

Loretta Devereaux: I heard about your Abuela and I'm so sorry. I'm glad she's okay. Also, I just thought you should know that Ben dumped me. After we did stuff. Be glad it wasn't you. I probably deserved it. I'm really sorry.

Evie was surprised that it didn't give her any comfort. It made her sad for Loretta, the girl who sat down beside her at lunch one day because she couldn't stand to see her looking so lonely. *You look lost,* she'd said. *Want to sit with us?* After that moment, she was never alone again at Saint Bart's. That was worth something.

Evie clicked reply as she stepped off the train at her stop.

Evie Perez: I forgive you. And no—you didn't deserve it. Nobody deserves that. Also, I know friendships aren't perfect. Thank you for being kind to me when I was all alone. Good luck with your senior year.

She knew that she and Loretta would probably never cross paths again. And that was okay. Maybe some people were meant to come into your life, but maybe they weren't meant to stay.

Her stomach twisted when she thought about Oskar. She didn't want to group him into that category too. But could she forgive him?

No, she didn't think she could. Not that it mattered, since she'd probably never see him again, anyway. She just hoped she haunted his dreams the way he haunted hers.

She typed the code into the keypad of her mother's apartment and the door buzzed open. Her flip-flops took the steps two at a time, slapping against the bottoms of her feet. She hoped Rhona was still working. She didn't want to spend the evening with her mother after Abuela's lecture. She wasn't ready to be all forgive-and-forget with everybody. Not yet.

Evie opened the door to the tiny one-bedroom apartment and found it in a mess, as usual. Rhona had left the futon unmade with blankets scattered everywhere. Evie didn't let that annoy her, though it took some concentration. Rhona had taken the couch as her bed and let Evie have her bedroom. Evie was grateful for that.

She tossed her keys on the table, next to a brown UPS box addressed to her. She glanced at it briefly and turned away. She wasn't in the mood to see anything from her papá, either.

But the return address made her do a double take.

Oskar Eriksson
Ránarbraut 1, 870
Elská, Iceland

It wasn't until that moment that it occurred to her she didn't even know his last name. Eriksson. Maybe words weren't all that important after all.

She ripped the box open with a rabid urgency that gave her a paper cut. Heart beating a mile a minute in her chest, she parted the box flaps and peered down inside.

A glass bottle with red liquid was wrapped in bubble wrap and wedged perfectly between the top and bottom of the box. Next to it, a red leather journal cushioned it in—the one he'd ripped from her hands that morning in the lighthouse. She lifted it from the box, cold against her trembling fingers, revealing the small plastic container full of fresh cherries underneath.

And in the corner of the box, at the very bottom, was a tarnished silver locket.

How could he know where she was? Unless...

She opened the front cover of the journal, and a letter fell out, her name scrawled on the envelope in his neat, all-caps handwriting.

Dear Evie,

I'm a selfish asshole.
There are no excuses for what I did,
so I won't make any.
If you throw this away,
without reading any of it,
it'd be exactly what I deserve.
But this is for you,
not me.
I owe you the truth.
About everything.
I always understood you,
maybe better than anyone else,
because you held nothing back with me.
I wanted to be near you,
but not just because of the paintings.
You're the most magnetic person
I've ever met.
You introduced yourself to me as Evelyn.
But when you thought I didn't understand,

you showed me Evie.
The real you.
I want to return the favor,
introduce you to the person who fell for you
all summer long.
I've never let anyone
read any of my journals.
Before now, I always threw them away
the minute I filled them up.
They're embarrassing.
Full of bad poetry,
unfinished songs,
and scattered thoughts of a sad guy
who lost everyone he ever loved.
Including you.
They say that time heals all wounds,
but I disagree with that.
I think the wounds are always there,
no matter how much time passes.
Sometimes, someone comes along
and becomes a balm,
a distracting anesthetic.
I write words, songs, music
for the same reason you paint.
Our bodies and souls inhabit this earth
a short time in the grand scheme of forever,
but our art is as immortal
as our wounds.
For the first time,
I want to be heard.
You are the reason.
This journal starts a week before I met you.

I just want you to see yourself
as I see you.
I want you to know the truth.

-Oskar

SEVENTY-FIVE
Oskar's New Journal

Agnes digs through the top drawer
of my bureau
and peeks over her shoulder at me.
What about socks? Do ye have enough socks?
Edvin steps over and shuts the drawer.
Oh, for God's sake, Agnes!
Get out of the boy's sock cubby.
He has plenty.
I stare down
at the full suitcase
on my bed.
I haven't left Iceland
since I visited Scotland
as a small boy.
Before Ivan was even born.
Are ye nervous about the flight?
The flight is the least of my worries.
Edvin answers for me.
He's going to be fine, mín. I'll be with him,
Edvin says.
We'll be back before you know it.
Well, I will,

he adds.
They might love this guy so much,
they decide to keep him early.
Panic sets in around her eyes.
They can't do that, can they?
You're auditioning for the winter term!
Relax, Edvin laughs.
We'll be in America for four days.
Then he's all yours until January.
Agnes nods and throws her hands in the air.
Och, what a silly wench I am!
All these years of pushing you out the door
and now I'm upset about it!
I step into her space
and give her a hug
now that the seal has been broken.
Thank you, Agnes,
I whisper.

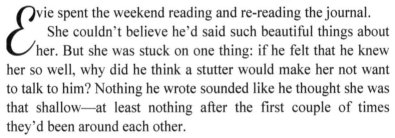

SEVENTY-SIX
Evie

*E*vie spent the weekend reading and re-reading the journal.
She couldn't believe he'd said such beautiful things about her. But she was stuck on one thing: if he felt that he knew her so well, why did he think a stutter would make her not want to talk to him? Nothing he wrote sounded like he thought she was that shallow—at least nothing after the first couple of times they'd been around each other.

She read each of the entries where he'd psych himself up to tell her the truth, holding her breath, as if she was going to read a story that was different from the one she had already lived. She got to the last page, and read the very last entry one more time.

"If she's amazing, she won't be easy. If she's easy, she won't be amazing. If she's worth it, you won't give up. If you give up, you're not worthy. Truth is, everybody is going to hurt you; you just gotta find the ones worth suffering for."
-Bob Marley

Evie,

I hope this has given you
some peace about what happened between us.

There isn't a day that passes that I don't think of you.
I'm going to be in New Jersey on Monday, September 12th.
I have an audition at the Westminster Conservatory at Rider
  University,
for admission in the upcoming winter semester.
If you can find it in your heart to forgive me
for being a coward, an asshole, a complete idiot
who should have told you the truth
a long time before now,
I'd love it if you could be there,
in the main theater,
at six o'clock p.m.
If not, I'll understand.
You are worth suffering for.

-Oskar

Evie had less than twenty-four hours to decide if she was go-ing to go.

As she stashed the note and journal on the top shelf of her closet, she noticed something familiar in one of the unpacked boxes on the floor. Opening the flaps, she pulled out the canvas of her self-portrait—the one she'd done in class.

The colors were over-blended and unnatural, the brushstrokes painstakingly hidden.

She didn't have any of her paintings from Iceland, only the sketchbook where they'd all started—but she knew they were nothing like this. Those paintings she'd done in Iceland were created with reckless abandon, without a worry in the world about who would see them or what they would think. She hadn't tried to cover her brushstrokes.

But this self-portrait, she thought as she ran her fingers over the smoothness of the paint, had been created with fear. Her father was right—it did look like Abuela when she was younger. Evie had painted a lie.

She shoved the self-portrait back in the box and reached further into the back of her closet. When her fingers found the blank canvases and the leather messenger bag, abandoned for nearly a month, she pulled them out and took them to a spot by the window. She set up her workspace, facing the mirror.

This time, she would tell the truth.

Beneath her paintbrush, a girl emerged. But not just any girl; not a carbon copy of Abuela, nor an intentional opposite of Rhona. Not Alberto's daughter or Loretta's ex-best-friend or Ben's one-time kissing target or Oskar's summer love. This girl was all of those things, but she was also so much more. She was Evie: a girl scared to fail, but willing to try. A girl who loved art, but on her own terms. Hours passed, and as her paint soaked the canvas, her tears soaked her shirt.

With every brutally honest flick of her wrist, she captured the flaws and let the brushstrokes show.

A knock interrupted her as she put finishing touches on the painting. Rhona peeked her head inside the door.

"You doing okay?"

Evie wiped at her eyes. "I'm fine."

Rhona stood in the doorway, teetering—seemingly unsure of whether to come in or leave. She finally decided on coming in. She wore pajama pants and a sweatshirt, fuzzy socks on her feet. It was as casual as Evie had seen her since she'd come to New York.

Rhona stopped beside her, staring at the painting, mouth agape. Evie took a deep breath, but she didn't attempt to hide her work. She tried to remember what Abuela said about forgiveness instead of being irritated by the interruption.

"It's really you," Rhona said, awe in her voice.

"It's me," Evie repeated. A long moment of silence passed between them until she looked up and met her mother's gaze in the mirror in front of them.

"I'm so sorry," Rhona said. It surprised Evie more than if her mother had handed her a bag full of hundred-dollar bills. "I know I've been a terrible mother. I was real sick for a long time. I can't change all the mistakes I've made, but I can do my best to be here for you now."

Evie didn't know what to say, so she just nodded.

"I want you to be happy. To make better choices than I did. I didn't have anyone to guide me when I was your age. But you… Evie, you have so many people who love you. You'll never be alone."

Evie racked her brain for a few moments, trying to think of a way to respond.

"Thank you for helping me talk Papá into bringing Abuela here. It makes me happy to see her every day."

Rhona reached down and patted Evie's shoulder awkwardly. "Your abuela needs you, just as much as you need her."

"I agree." Evie thought for a moment. "You know, I miss Miami, but I think I'd miss it even if I still lived there. Does that make sense?" What she missed couldn't be recovered with geography alone. Things changed, and she couldn't stop it from happening.

Rhona nodded. "I think so."

The two of them stilled in the silence of each other's company. Not all change was bad, Evie realized.

"Well." Rhona headed for the door. "If there's anything you need, I'm here. Okay?"

Evie looked up at her. "There is one thing."

SEVENTY-SEVEN
Oskar's Journal

The heat of the lights prickle
against the back of my neck
as I set up.
Eight pairs of eyes bore into me
from the judge's table.
My hands tremble.
I've never played on a stage before.
Never in front of a team of foreign professionals
or in a sparsely populated dark theater.
The velvet seats of the audience are red.
The curtains at the edge of the stage are red.
Everything is red
and it reminds me of her.
I clutch my dad's old guitar against my chest
and step up to the microphone.
Give me strength, Pabbi, I think.
I look past the lights as I speak,
searching the seats with bodies in them.
When I speak into the mic,
my broken strings echo through the auditorium.
This is an original co-co-comp-composition,
called M-m-m-magnetic M-m-midnight.

My head isn't in the game.
I'm still looking for her.
Begin when you're ready,
the judge in the middle says.
I nod.
She isn't going to show.
I draw a breath and play for her anyway.
With every chord I strum,
every lyric I sing,
I imagine she's there,
offering me forgiveness.
I saturate every part of the song
with the longing I've felt for her
since that day in the orchard.
I didn't mean to cause trouble, she said to me.
But she upturned my whole life.
She made me feel alive again.
At the end, I open my eyes,
look up,
and there she is
in the back of the auditorium.
Everything stops.
The air between us becomes a live wire.
I'm suddenly glad
I didn't see her before I began.
I would've fucked the whole thing up.
She's the most beautiful thing I've ever seen.
Long dark hair curtains her shoulders,
and I remember the precise way it smells.
Like some perfect combination of flowers and fruit
that'd make a perfumier a fortune.
A cherry red shirt clings to her body.
Red.
Always red.

Like the orchard.
The color of passion.
The color of the blood surging
through my veins now
at warp speed.
It throbs and vibrates
at my lips, my fingertips, my throat
and especially in my chest.
Her dark eyes shine with so much light
that the current between us
is unmistakable.
Even from here.
Even in the dark.
A smile
that could redefine *smile,*
because it tells me she sees me.
She has always *seen* me.
She came because she wanted to,
and she doesn't hate me, after all.
My heart is a timpani.
This trip
was worth it,
even if her face in the crowd
is my only reward.
My feet tingle with the need to run.
But in her direction this time.
Suddenly, I know
it doesn't matter where I am
as long as she's there.

SEVENTY-EIGHT
Evie

*E*vie recognized the lyrics the moment he'd started singing.

That's because she had read them in his journal over and over since Friday. The fact that he'd turned the most romantic moment of her life into a song, that he'd use it as an audition to get into a prestigious music college, rendered her completely speechless.

From her dark seat in the back of the theater, her knees shook. If the judges had felt even a fraction of the intensity from him that she did, he'd get in, no problem.

"Thank you, Mr. Eriksson," the judges said to him when he finished. But he wasn't looking at them, he was looking at her.

Evie stood and walked down the velvety carpet toward the right-side stairs leading up to the stage. Everything that happened between them, everything she felt as she listened to his voice, *his beautiful voice*, made her stop a few feet short of him. What if she'd built it all up in her head? What if things weren't the same now that they both knew the truth about each other?

Maybe he wouldn't even get in to school here, and he'd go back to Iceland and she'd never see him again. The doubts piled up in her head as he descended the stairs.

He stopped in front of her. She'd never seen him dressed so nicely. He wore dark dress pants, a white button-up, and a red skinny tie. She glanced down at his shiny black shoes. New, for sure. Much different than the rugged brown boots she'd always seen him wear.

She glanced up. He was smiling. Dimples showing, left deeper than the right. Crooked teeth on display. Stormy eyes stormier than ever. Messy hair somewhat tame, with the help of some hair gel. For once, she was the one who couldn't speak.

He stuck out his hand.

"Huh-Hi," he said. "I'm Oskar."

Hearing his voice, the depth of the baritone, the way the cadence vibrated across his lips, shook some emotion loose. Her eyes watered—God, just great, she was going to cry.

"Evie." She smiled, taking his callused hand.

An awkward silence followed. She had to say something. "I loved your song."

I loved you, she wanted to say. *Maybe still do.* But that would be going too far. Not yet. Not today. One thing at a time.

His smile grew wider. "I loved your p-p-paintings."

She swallowed the clump of nervousness threatening to choke her up. "I'm painting again. Those cherries you sent me, and the wine…"

"They inspire, d-d-don't they?" Hearing his voice like this, in regular conversation, was surreal. She nodded.

"How long are you here?"

"Until Wwwwednesday."

She could work with that.

She realized she was still shaking his hand. That whole time, they hadn't let go of each other. They both glanced down at their joined hands at the same time and dropped them, laughing.

"You wwwant to—" Oskar pointed at the door at the top of the auditorium.

"Yes," Evie answered without letting him finish.

They walked side by side toward the exit, and Oskar waved to Edvin, who was sitting in the audience, grin plastered on his face.

When they opened the theater doors and stepped into the fading afternoon sunshine, she turned to him. There were a million things she wanted to say to him, but she blurted the first thing that came to her mind.

"I'm sorry I hit you."

He laughed then, a hearty, full-bodied laugh. It was music to her ears, the same way it had been every other time she'd heard it. He stepped closer to her, too close, and before she could finish saying *I'm serious*, he lifted the words right off her lips with his mouth. Right there on the busy sidewalk outside the theater, with college students passing all around, he kissed her.

She was certain that meant he forgave her, the way she knew she was going to forgive him. The way she had already forgiven him. When he pulled away, she asked him, "Have you ever been on a subway before?"

He grinned and shook his head.

"My mother gave me some money to come here and show you around. I mean, if you don't mind getting lost. I still don't know my way very well."

He took her hand. "We'll find our wwwway."

Those were the only words she ever needed to hear.

ACKNOWLEDGEMENTS

I’ve always believed in magic. It's the people who believed alongside me, though, that made my debut novel a reality.

My sincerest gratitude to the magic makers of Owl Hollow Press: to Hannah Smith for seeing the potential in *The Language of Cherries* and for making it possible to share with the masses; to Olivia Swenson, for waving an editing wand over my blunders and sparing me from Ben Benson levels of shame; and to Emma Nelson, for going above and beyond on all fronts. A huge thanks for my beautiful cover—it's a spellbinding work of art that captures the heart of the story. It has been a pleasure and an honor to work with each of you.

To my literary agent dynamic duo, Kate Testerman and Hilary Harwell: thank you for championing my work, helping me improve it, and steadfastly pursuing a path for it. Your unfaltering enthusiasm made it impossible to give up. I cherish our partnership more than you'll ever know.

Sonia Hartl, my goddess-level original critique partner: without you, I'd still be introducing coyote people at the 11th hour. Your critiques have been priceless, both for what they've taught me about writing and for your comment bubble comic relief. I owe you my most heartfelt thanks and foouuuurrrr wwwaaaaatttteeerrrrss for reading this book in every single one of its iterations over the past few years. DEP! I love you big.

Kes Trester, the most glamourous mentor a girl could hope for: thank you for your belief in me long before this work was fully formed, and for always being there to walk me through conflict, whether in inconsistent plot beats or real-life social anxiety. You're a Hollywood Starlet of a friend.

Kristin Reynolds, enchantress poet and human totem: In the words of Murakami – *'There's something about you. Say there's an hourglass: the sand's about to run out. Someone like you can always be counted on to turn the thing over.''* Thank you for turning over my hourglass each time it ran out. I will always do the same for you.

My beloved writing den—Kristin Wright, Elly Blake, Mary Ann Marlowe, Summer Spence, Ron Walters, and Kelly Siskind: thank you for being the angels on my shoulder (or the devils, as the situation sometimes warrants). You are a vital part of my writing process and my every day life. You each inspire me with your master class writing talent and your capacity for kindness. The love and acceptance you've shown have helped me power through many hard days. I've learned so many crucial elements of craft from you. This book would not be the same if you hadn't been there from its inception. I adore every single one of you. I'd list all the ways in which you've made me better, but *it's too risky!*

To Rachel Lynn Solomon: I am so grateful I've had the opportunity to learn from you. Your debut novel is still one of the most beautiful, bittersweet books I've ever read. Thank you for being such a lovely and generous fellow writer and friend.

Roselle Lim, thank you for being my go-to on all things art related. You helped me shape Evie into someone almost as cool as you. You are a brilliant writer and a human cupcake.

Janet Wren, I'm so glad we met all those years ago. Thank you for being there for me, from honest critiques to late night laughs to kid birthday parties. We are long overdue for a pool-plotting sesh.

Anna Birch, Tracie Martin, Carlee Karanovic, and Margarita Montimore: thank you for your early reads and brainstorming huddles. I'm so fortunate to have each of you in my life!

Thank you to Brenda Drake for creating the Pitch Wars community, because without it, I would've never met any of the amazing people listed above.

The Writing Barn in Austin, Texas holds a significant place in the journey of this book, as well. In 2015, I workshopped a very rough, incomplete draft of The Language of Cherries there. That 4-day intensive workshop was a game changer, because it made me believe I might actually be a writer. Much love to Bethany Hegedus, Matt de la Peña, Cristina Adams, Rebecca Maziel Sullivan, Gail Shepherd, Shelli Corneilson, Varsha Bajaj, Shellie Fault, Lindsey Lane, and Heather Harwood for outstanding notes that helped shape this book from a wee little scribble to a more complete body of work. And to Carrie Brown-Wolf and Claire Campbell, fellow wine shamans: out of all the amazing things that came from the workshop, my favorite is still getting you two as critique partners.

This book would not be possible without the generosity and expertise of Cristina Adams, Evie Knight, and J.R. Yates, who provided thoughtfully critical sensitivity reads. Thank you to Mara Rutherford for sharing your inside knowledge of Iceland. You each taught me something important and expanded my understanding of experiences beyond my own.

To April Simmons, my soul sister, without you I'd never have written any book. It was you, in 2011, while we were confined to desk duty in that awful clinic who said, "You want to be a writer, so what are you waiting for?" You gave me the courage. And free therapy ever since. Please hereby accept my undying love and pumpkin spice flavored kisses.

To my brother, B.J. Prince, who is far more talented than I am in almost every way, NEENER NEENER I WROTE A BOOK AND YOU DIDN'T! Just kidding. Mostly. I love you.

To my nieces, Gracie Schildmeier and Caitlyn Gordon: I hope my main characters are always as strong, smart, and beautiful as you two are. You make excellent muses!

I truly believe that behind every successful woman is a squad of successful women who have her back, and these are mine: Rima Joffrion, Angie Holliday, Julie Walsh, Shawna Parker, Kim Collins, Jennifer Schildmeier, Crystal Morris, Becky Blanton, Gwen Blanton, Rebecca Yates, Amanda Wick, Melissa Speary, Hailey Moore, Jamie Gordon, Julie Machin, Kristy Wyatt, LeAnn Carver, Annette Bassett, Tamara McGuire-Hall, Amy Redd, Robyn Bivens, Ashly Harris Coggins, Julie Carter, Joy Stringfield, Summer Carter, Jess O'Neal Bayne, Joanna Diamond, Melissa Rhodes, Shelly Walker, Rachel Cernogorsky, Jessica Watson, Dawn Mahaffey Gramling, Katrina Russell, Sereen Aiken, Courtnie White, Jamie Durham, Kim Authement, Sarah Gross, Tamara Small, and Jenn Bussell. Thank you all for your enduring friendships and your professional and emotional support. You have kept me sane and encouraged me in every aspect of my life for many years. I will love every single one of you forever.

Speaking of forever love—to my boys, Jonathan and Jackson: I am enchanted as I watch you grow up. The two of you are living, breathing proof that magic exists. I'm so lucky I get to be your mom. There is no job title in the world that will ever be more important to me than that, but I am so grateful you don't mind sharing me with my characters. You both inspire me with your compassion, wit, and excellent taste in music. You keep me young. I love you so very much, and I'm so proud of you both.

And to my husband, Jeremy: you are the love of my life, a super dad to our boys, and an absolute ace at everything you do. If I hadn't already given you my heart, I'd rip it right out and slap it in your hands, comic-book-style. You're the Joker to my Harley. The passion between my characters will always be a direct reflection of the passion I feel for you. Thank you for supporting my dream and never once questioning its viability, even as we pay student loans for a nursing degree I no longer use. You believed in me first and best. I look forward to these seventeen years becoming seventy.

JEN MARIE
Hawkins

Jen Marie Hawkins is a nurse-turned-writer. She writes books for young adults and the young at heart. She is a creative writing coach for Author Accelerator, and her short works can be found in literary magazines including the *Decameron Journal.* Two of her novel-length manuscripts have been finalists for the YARWA Rosemary Award and the RWA Maggie Award.

Originally from South Carolina, she now resides in the Houston, Texas area with her husband, two sons, and enough animals to qualify her home as a wildlife center. When she isn't reading or writing stories sprinkled with magic, you can find her cuddling her boys and daydreaming about traveling the world.

Jen is represented by Kate Testerman of KT Literary Agency.

Find Jen online at jenmariehawkins.com
#TheLanguageofCherries

CPSIA information can be obtained
at www.ICGtesting.com
Printed in the USA
LVHW032056080720
660120LV00005B/772

9 781945 654459